The PENDRAGON™ fiction line presents the best of modern Arthurian literature, from reprints of long-unavailable classics of the early twentieth century to new works by today's most exciting and inventive fantasists. The titles in the series are selected for their value to both the casual reader and the devoted scholar of the rich, varied story cycle known as the Matter of Britain.

PENDRAGON™ Fiction

The Follies of
SIR HARALD

PHYLLIS ANN KARR

GREEN KNIGHT PUBLISHING

Please address questions and comments concerning this book, as well as requests for notices of new publications, by mail to Green Knight Publishing, 900 Murmansk Street, Suite 5, Oakland, CA 94607.

Green Knight Publishing
Publisher: Peter Corless
Executive Editor: James Lowder
Consulting Editor: Raymond H. Thompson

Visit our web page at: http://www.greenknight.com

FIRST PAPERBACK EDITION

10 9 8 7 6 5 4 3 2 1

Green Knight publication GK6212, December 2001.

ISBN 1-928999-21-2

Printed in the United States

Acknowledgments

To Ruth Berman, a.k.a. "Ruth of the Far North,"
for valuable advice on matters kosher.

To Cherith Baldry,
whose breathtaking account of the Loholt episode
(alluded to by Felicitatus of Beaumarches),
and whose question whether Sir Harald
would ever find a bride,
materially affected the shape of Part the Fourth.

AUTHOR'S NOTE

The present story has occasional historical accuracies, such as married priests, snail shells used for winding embroidery silks, and—sadly—the medieval Christian attitude toward both left-handed and Jewish people; but it should not be mistaken for historical fiction. In seeking to emulate Chrétien de Troyes, I've just let myself have fun.

PART THE FIRST:

The Storming of Quillerstone

A month after Pentecost in the year of the marriage of Erec, son of Lac, King Arthur and his court partook in a great tournament in the plain below the proud city of Tenebroc.

Pennons flew there aplenty, in red and blue and white. Lances gleamed beneath coats of crimson and silver, azure and gold, applied here in dapples and there in broad, bold bands. Helmets caught the sun in glints of vermilion and green, yellow and rich, bright gold. And many were the brilliant new sleeves, scarves, and wimples that fluttered merrily from the bright mail of those upon whom they had been bestowed as tokens of love.

Knights and nobles had gathered there from all parts of the world, to bewilder the eye with a sea of brilliant arms and shields freshly painted in every color known to brush and every device that mind or fancy could invent, all their bearers perched mightily atop great chargers of every description—white and dark, sorrel and tawny, spotted and bay. There any glance that was quick enough might espy the Valiant Prince of the shield with the red horse's head, the brave young Knight of the Burning Pestle, the gallant Disinherited Knight, the peerless Knight d'Eon, and even the famous Knight of the Woeful Countenance.

And as the colors dazzled and bewildered one's gaze, so did the dins, when all these champions came clashing together, dazzle and deafen one's ears, as brave warriors toppled one another smashing and crashing to the ground, drew their swords—or sometimes not—took, rescued, and recaptured prisoners for two entire days of glory and renown. And, if hopes were disappointed, of both the gallant knights and the fair ladies who cheered them on, and if a few hearts were broken during those two days, nobody much noticed, for praising and lauding the glorious victors.

Winner of that tournament was Prince Erec himself,

which all agreed to be the most satisfactory outcome possible. Second only to the noble bridegroom was Sir Gawen, the first and greatest knight of all the Table Round and cosponsor of this particular tournament, whom many or most suspected of having held himself back a little in order to ensure that this time the primary honors would go to young Erec. Among all the others who acquitted themselves satisfactorily, I must mention three in particular, not so much for the measure of their success—since several of their fellows did as well and better—as for the part these three are to play in the pages that follow.

First and second of these three were Sir Labigodés the Courtly and Sir Letron of the Polished Manners, both of them notable Knights of the Table Round. Both were blond, Sir Letron tall and clean-shaven, Sir Labigodés shortish and bearded; but otherwise as indistinguishable as Cinderella's two stepsisters, although with manners as gentle as those ladies' were ungentle. Which of these two should be mentioned first and which second, we must leave to themselves to decide . . . and that they never will, because each will always insist upon deferring to the other. As last of my three, I name Sir Kay the Seneschal, who would never willingly defer to anyone: I name him here because for once he took a prisoner—only a single prisoner—but that was more than he had accomplished in any other tournament for many years.

Sir Kay's single prisoner was a black-bearded, unruly-haired knight called, for his rash and reckless deeds, Harald de Folgeste. This knight had the peculiarity of preferring his left side, which lent him sometimes an advantage and sometimes not. Wielding sword or mace left-handed against right-handed men, accustomed as they were to fighting other right-handed men in a right-handed world, he took them by surprise and forced them to fight awkwardly, while he himself was of course accustomed to his own way of combat. In the joust, however, he must perforce couch his lance with his clumsier right hand and arm; and it was this, perhaps, that allowed Sir Kay to unhorse him in the initial onslaught.

Sir Harald scrambled at once to his feet—this was still in the days of chain mail, when a knight fully armed was expected to be able to leap into the saddle without the aid of so much as his stirrup—and drew his sword. His black charger Goblin moving out of the way in a manner born of experience, Sir Harald shouted up to King Arthur's seneschal, "Now fight me afoot!"

"Why should I defeat you twice?" Sir Kay returned. "Go to my tent and wait for my other prisoners to join you. You may have the honor of being first to make your surrender formal."

So boasting, Sir Kay turned his horse Feuillemorte, who was the color of an oak leaf deep in autumn, back toward the thickest of the fighting.

With an oath, and flushing furiously beneath his helmet—for there was one among the onlookers whom he had desired with all his heart to impress, even though he did not yet wear her favor—Sir Harald thrust his sword back into its scabbard and sprang again into Goblin's saddle without setting foot to stirrup, thus proving that nothing save his pride had suffered in his fall.

For a moment, then, he hesitated, tempted to re-enter the battle as though some comrade had hurried to his rescue. But none had, this time; and the eyes of the Aloof Fair One, as well as others, might be upon him. So, before any squire or herald came close enough to seize Goblin by the bridle and scold Sir Harald for remounting at all, he rode from the field of his own accord, head still held stubbornly high.

❖   ❖   ❖

At that tournament, there could be only one choice for Queen of Love and Beauty: Prince Erec's own bride, the beautiful Enide. Dame Guenevere herself had graciously acceded to her with a kiss on her blushing cheek. But, had it not been for the presence of both Erec's fair bride and Arthur's peerless queen, a certain other lady must have been named to bestow the victor's crown.

This maiden was known only as the Aloof Fair One, for she chose of her free will to follow the ancient custom of revealing her true name to the world only upon her marriage . . . and that, she proclaimed, would be to a man of her own choosing, into whose ear she would breathe her name first, before announcing it to any other. Every knight and fighting squire who did not already have a lady, and a few who did, or who had been disappointed in some earlier expectation, had pressed around on the eve of the tournament, hoping against hope to wear the favor of the Aloof Fair One; and she had caused her waiting-maid (a local girl) to admit them one by one into her tent (borrowed for the occasion), where she granted each an interview, but gave her favor to none.

When Sir Harald's turn had come at last, he found her seated gracefully upright in her backless chair, facing the entrance. She had looked him down and up slowly, at her elegant leisure, all the while drawing the fine veil she would grant—or not—as her favor back and forth between the fingers of her left and right hands alternately. At length she had said, with a kind of sigh, "All these bearded gallants look so much alike! Do you wear your sword on the wrong side, sir, to set yourself a little apart from all the other bearded knights?"

Sir Harald, who had trimmed his beard with especial care just before coming to her tent, went down on one knee and said, "My damsel, I will shave it off! As for my sword, I wear it on the right because it comes easier for me to wield it with my left arm."

"A left-handed knight?" she answered with light, clear, and mocking laughter. "I could never grant my favor to any knight who fights on the wrong side! Perhaps you do well to hide your true face beneath a beard." But she briefly allowed him her hand to kiss—her left hand, with the veil still drifting down from between her fingertips—and, as he finished laying his kiss tenderly upon those delicate white knuckles, she flicked the fine silk fabric up to tease his face for one soft instant.

In the end, she might have lent her favor to either Sir Labigodés or Sir Letron, who had courteously waited until every other wishful warrior had had his turn; but each of these final two deferred to the other until the lady told her maid to admit them both at once, and then each insisted his friend to be the more deserving of the honor of wearing the maiden's favor, until she wearied of laughing and bade them both begone empty-handed.

Since they, alone of all that throng, had come less in hopes of wearing her favor than in pure mannerliness and desire to compliment a fair stranger, they left in some relief, each happily commiserating the other on his failure.

Of that last interview Harald de Folgeste knew nothing. He knew only that, ardently though many desired it, nobody at all wore the Aloof Fair One's favor; that she had brushed his face with it as he kissed her fingers; that she had mocked his left-handedness but given him her own left hand to kiss; and that for her favor he had promised to shave off his beard. He did not guess that she had treated every other man much the same, according to whatever flaws and failings she could quickly spy in each. Some she had even mocked for their lack of beards, whether due to youth or the razor.

However, he had no great length of time, there at the door of Sir Kay's tent, to mull over yet again every word and gesture of yesterday's interview with the Aloof Fair One. Nor was the first man to join him any fellow prisoner, but the seneschal himself, in an even more surly mood than usual, because his very next encounter after that with Harald de Folgeste had seen him toppled from Feuillemorte.

"What are you doing here?" he demanded of Sir Harald. "Come to have your laugh at the poor old seneschal, have you?"

"Not half an hour ago," Sir Harald answered stiffly, "you bested me, my lord. I have come, as you required me, to make formal my surrender. Unless you deign to grant me now the swordplay you denied me then."

"Oh," said Sir Kay. "It's you, is it? You ought to thank me for refusing to fight you on foot. The man who unhorsed me—by purest luck—was less generous, and now I am doubly bruised. Well, come in and drink a cup of ale while you pledge me your horse and gear." This, for Sir Kay, was courtesy. Perhaps his latest bruising had softened him for the hour, despite his heightened surliness.

Sir Harald followed him into the tent, where, at Kay's nod, the waiting attendant poured two beakers of ale. Pulling off his left gauntlet, Sir Harald accepted one of the beakers but, before touching it to that of his conqueror and drinking, he said, "I hope, my lord, you will at least show the generosity that befits a Knight of the Round Table, and let me keep my horse."

"Sir . . . Whatever-Your-Name-Is," Sir Kay replied (for

Harald de Folgeste was not yet a household name, except in his own household—and even that was not truly his own), "you may keep your shield, but, in case you failed to understand my words just now, I have losses of my own to pay. I will accept your horse and other equipment, or their ransom, any time within the year."

This was no generosity on Sir Kay's part, but simply the standard terms. For answer, Sir Harald turned his beaker upside down, cast it to the ground after the spilled ale, and quitted the tent without another word to his conqueror, but with rage storming across his otherwise rather handsome features.

"I may keep my shield," he muttered, striking it hard with his own left fist and scarcely stopping to grimace at the pain this caused his bare knuckles. Sir Harald understood the seneschal's offer, not as a small scrap of generosity, but as an implied statement that his shield with its identifying blazon—a broad sable bend dividing an ermine-spotted background diagonally from dexter base to sinister chief canton; his name, so to speak, on the field of battle and honor—was not worth demanding, and he himself by the same token scarcely worth conquering.

Curious as it seems, since the greater any knight's prowess, the greater any other knight's glory in defeating him, in his own present disappointment and perpetual sarcasm Sir Kay may indeed have intended his words exactly the way they were interpreted. Whatever the case, the seneschal did not trouble himself to call out after his one ransomee, but simply drank his own ale whilst instructing his attendant to clean up the mess and help him get his armor off, in no particular order, and then see that the gauntlet Sir Harald had accidentally left behind was returned for the nonce; though that could certainly wait until the servant had drunk some ale himself. Strange to record, churl though King Arthur's sensechal was invariably styled amongst his fellow knights, he had exceptionally loyal servants.

As for Sir Harald, he stormed the whole way back to his own tent, never noticing a dark-robed palmer, fresh from the Holy Land, who almost stepped into his way, thought better of it on overhearing the knight's angry mutterings, and stepped back again, tucking his head more deeply yet into his dark hood. No one else even thought about crossing the path of the black-bearded Knight of the Bend Sinister.

Sir Harald had brought as his attendant a serf, a sturdy man called Garth, of middle years and grizzled head. Attending his surrogate master at this tournament was a great pleasure for Garth, who had never before in his entire life been farther than three miles from his master's castle, and then only on errands. Garth had watched his current master's fall, taken charge of the black warhorse Goblin while Sir Harald betook himself to Sir Kay's tent, and now waited at the entrance to Harald's own pavilion, gazing with all his might at the bright colors and merry crowds around about, his mind pleasantly wrangling with his stomach as to whether he might spend one of his carefully hoarded farthings for a sausage.

Seeing Sir Harald come striding up, Garth stepped respectfully aside and asked, "How went it then, my lord?"

"He will graciously permit me to retain my shield!" the knight flung back, storming into the tent and throwing himself with clash and clatter into a fortunately sturdy camp-chair. "Devil take me if my lord seneschal ever touches Goblin or any piece of my gear!"

"It's that Aloof Fair One," Garth commented mildly, following Sir Harald in and letting the door flap shut. "Though why any man would want to worship such a cold ladyship. . . . Aye, well, I guess it's something only knights and noble folk understand. Still, if I might make so bold, Your Worship's head will feel clearer once Her Aloof Ladyship is out of your heart. Now," he went on, helping Sir Harald out of his armor, "which do you want first, ale to drink or water to wash in?"

"I want . . ." Sir Harald replied, rubbing his beard reflectively, ". . . a razor. And a few moments to myself, for thinking. Go buy me a razor," he added, jerking his head toward the small coffer that held his own store of coins. "And something for yourself—sausage, pasty, it makes no difference to me, provided you eat it slowly and take your time getting back with the razor."

Garth left with a grin of pleasure for himself and a frown of worry for his master.

❖   ❖   ❖

When the great tournament was done, Sirs Letron and Labigodés, the two most courtly and courteous knights of all King Arthur's court (not even excluding Sir Gawen!), made up their minds to go adventuring a little while, just the two of them together, accompanied only by their field attendants: each had two squires, two servants, and a single cook. In addition, in case they should rescue any lady who might then need her own attendants, Sir Letron had two pages and Sir Labigodés one. This last imbalance at first troubled our two heroes greatly, until at length they decided to share Sir Letron's extra page, having him henceforth serve them—until and unless they succoured some stray lady—on alternate days.

Left to themselves, they might never have decided this, for Sir Letron persisted in offering his friend the additional page, and Sir Labigodés in politely refusing so unselfish an offer; but the page himself finally suggested the solution. He was a bright, sturdy boy of about thirty, by his own choice a page for life, named Tamba. The other two pages were young men on the very verge of squirehood.

As for the cooks, they squabbled as enthusiastically as their masters deferred, until, to keep the peace, Tamba helped arrange that they should do the cooking on alternate days. All the other members of the company got along with one another like meat and salt, as the saying goes; and, with so many cheerful attendants on hand, Tamba had little enough to do except the occasional peacemaking, which suited him very well indeed.

They had journeyed thus, from Tenebroc, for half the long morning, when the younger of Sir Letron's pages shot an arrow and killed a rabbit for that day's stewpot. But before they could reach the prize, a great gray wolf bounded across the trail, snatched the rabbit up in his jaws, and kept to his stride with scarcely a pause. The entire company, except for Tamba and the two cooks, gave chase, pursuing the beast deeper and deeper into the forest.

As they ran, they began to hear someone singing. At first it was only the sound of a distant voice, like that of a young woman, but soon they came close enough to catch the words:

"Oh, Everywhere, Who gives us all,
Pray hear all creatures when they call."

About this time, one of the squires cast his javelin and wounded the wolf in its left haunch. The beast gave a terrific skriel of pain—but without dropping the rabbit—and ran on, furiously limping, in the direction of the voice, though it had suddenly fallen silent.

The party redoubled its efforts, Sirs Labigodés and Letron by now in the rear, despite being the masters and leaders, because they alone had not dismounted, and their light riding hackneys were having some difficulty with the undergrowth. When at last they charged into a clearing, a strange sight met their eyes.

A young woman who looked thirteen—at oldest, fifteen—with brown hair and freckled skin, sat in the midst of a gathering of every kind of bird that flies in the air and beast that walks on the ground. Her garment was the simplest robe of tattered blue, her feet were bare, and her features seemed more those of a mischievous boy than a demure damsel; but what color her eyes might be, none of the men could ever say, though she was never slow to look any of them in the face.

Wrens and sparrows, robins and bluebirds, larks, nightingales, and swallows, partridges and bustling grouse, ducks and stately wild geese, and also a pair of snow white swans; hawks, too, and shrikes, vultures and wise old ravens, and even an owl blinking sleepily in the daylight; roe deer and black bears, wild boars and wily foxes, martens and badgers, stoats and weasels and even a few otters away from their pond; shrews, and squirrels both red and gray, rabbits and hares, lynxes and hedgehogs, moles and voles and scurrying mice; turtles and lizards, toads and frogs, snails and slugs and sleek, shining snakes; and myriads even of the tiniest things—spiders and butterflies, beetles and bees and curling caterpillars—all humming around in peace with her and one another, and, strangest of all to say, accepting the sudden arrival of so many armed men and boys with neither alarm nor tokens of menace.

The wolf whom the knights' party had been chasing crouched at her feet, whining and gazing up at her as if for protection; and she, even as they watched, fondled his head and knelt to rub his wounded flank. With a long sigh, he laid his head on his front paws, let the rabbit roll from his jaws, and shut his eyes to sleep. The girl picked the rabbit up by the arrow that still skewered it, rose, and held it out to the onlookers.

"This must be yours," she said quietly.

Sir Labigodés the Courtly, reading the situation, got down from his horse and came forward, squires and pages and servants stepping aside for him. "My damsel," he said, "it would provide scarcely a mouthful apiece for each of us, but for your pet, a full and nourishing meal."

"We pray you, therefore, accept it for your poor beast," added Sir Letron of the Polished Manners, coming forward afoot in his turn.

"My lords, we thank you!" she answered with a grin, and half a dozen small birds, which had briefly fluttered away, settled once again on her head and shoulders, while two dozen squirrels, rabbits, mice, voles, shrews, lizards, snakes, and other assorted small creatures bustled closer around her feet. "But let me give back your arrow, at least," she went on, working it smoothly free while neither breaking it nor doing any further harm that they could see to the small, broken corpse.

The page whose arrow it was stepped forward and held his hand out in silent wonder. Nobody else moved. The girl gave him the arrow, turned and laid the broken rabbit gently near the head of the sleeping wolf, knelt a few moments longer to wipe her hands clean of blood on the long grasses, and then turned back to the awestruck men.

"My lady," Sir Letron brought himself to ask, "was it you who were singing so sweetly just now?"

"Was I?" She blinked and, looking round at them, laughed suddenly and merrily. "Oh, how solemn you all look, standing there like saints' statues!"

The spell was broken—all the creatures flew, scampered, or otherwise betook themselves away, according to their kinds, leaving only the dead rabbit, sleeping wolf, riding hackneys, and human beings in the clearing. The knights' people glanced around at one another and rubbed their noses. What, after all, had they witnessed here that was so greatly out of the ordinary? Could not any saint— and saints were plentiful enough in those days—gather a peaceable kingdom of animals around him or her simply by sitting still for a little while? Could not any competent cook, in the mysteries of the kitchen, remove an arrow equally neatly from a carcass? As for the costly color of her garment, did not its very fraying tell them it must have been the charitable gift of someone both rich and generous? Why, the girl was not even especially pretty! No, she was only some poor young hermitess of the wood or foolish tomboy trying to imitate these new wandering friars one heard tell of, nothing more. Certainly nobody to cause any grown man a moment's awe.

And yet, curiously, for all their punctilious observance of every courteous nicety, our two knights found themselves—when they were not calling her "child" with various complimentary adjectives—addressing her as "my lady," though "maid" or "damsel" would have been more technically correct.

"Fair child," Sir Labigodés inquired, "where do you live?"

"Wherever I can," she answered with another laugh.

"In that case," said Sir Letron, "if it please you, my lady, travel along with us. With all our hearts, you will be more than welcome."

There were some glances amongst the squires and servants at this, for would any saint or apprentice saint who sat at ease amid so many animals, predator and prey alike, approve of anyone else eating meat in her company? And perhaps these followers' glances were not as carefully veiled as their masters would have wished, because the Maid of the Wood responded, "Suppose your way is different from mine?"

"Our way lies nowhere in particular," Sir Labigodés replied. "Wherever my lady wishes, that way we will follow for a while."

"Let me see," she argued, smiling. "Pray correct me if I am mistaken, but it seems to me that in this time and country, a maiden is free to wander anywhere alone, and no knight may offer her any violence without disgracing himself forever in all the courts of Christendom."

"That is our good King Arthur's law," Sir Letron affirmed, bowing.

"But if a maiden travels with a knight, all that any other

knight need do is defeat her escort, and then he may have his way with her and never be blamed for it?"

"That is the custom," Sir Labigodés replied, "long established through venerable age and usage." And he bowed again in his turn.

"Why then, it appears to me that a maiden would be safer to travel alone!"

"But see, my lady," Sir Letron protested, "you will have in us not one knight protector, but two!"

"And two dear friends," added Sir Labigodés, "who would never fight each other for the favor of any lady, no matter how fair. . . ."

"But would instead leave her the choice," Sir Letron finished for him.

"Moreover," Sir Labigodés appended, "I grieve to point it out, but even in this country there remain a few rogues and ruffians who care nothing for King Arthur's law and the disgrace attendant upon attacking any lady who travels alone."

Now, much of this was spoken in pure polite compliment, since neither knight stood in the slightest danger of losing his heart to the girl that way. Nor, indeed, did any of their followers, for even when the glamour of her first appearance had dissipated like mist, there remained something about her that quietly prevented such thoughts from rising, any more than they would have risen in the presence of some fey elf or puckish woodland sprite. Nevertheless, it was true enough that both knights, with their reasoning minds, felt true concern for the dear child's safety on the road. And, since she was obviously a saint— at least in training—no one found it inappropriate that she should be treated like a gentle-born lady, despite her rags.

"Well," she said at last, "since it seems that our roads lie together, my lords, at least for the present, I will welcome your company with all my heart!" So saying, she smiled in such a way that it took in not only both the knights, but the squires, pages, and servants as well, so that all of them felt amply compensated.

"Gramercy, fair child," said Sir Labigodés. "And now, if it please you, permit me to bear you on my horse."

"Or, my lady, should it please you, allow me to offer my mount for that honor," Sir Letron put in.

"Indeed," Labigodés acknowledged. "I spoke in haste. Your Ladyship might indeed find my friend's saddlebow the more comfortable."

"But that of my friend Sir Labigodés is no whit inferior," Sir Letron insisted.

By now, both of the horses in question were nudging and nickering as eagerly as the knights, although with no hint of deferring to each other. Tamba not being present to offer a compromise, the Maid of the Wood resolved the problem by suggesting, as she rubbed the muzzle of Sir Letron's horse with one hand and that of Sir Labigodés with the other, "Suppose we were all to walk as far as the footpath?"

This solution they readily adopted, the Maid of the Wood walking between the two horses with one hand resting on either glossy neck.

Only the page who had shot the rabbit, long ago as it seemed by now, although in fact it was not half an hour, looked back as they left the clearing, and saw—or thought he saw, for he told no one else at the time and in later years came to believe that he had dreamed it—the wolf licking its flank, which appeared quite healed, while the rabbit hopped quietly away, with just the smallest trace of blood still visible on its brown fur.

Whether this sight had been an actual glimpse or merely a dream, the lad never shot that particular arrow again, but saved it carefully all the rest of his life, as page, squire, knight, and, eventually, lord of his own manor . . . for he regarded it, in either case, as a relic of sorts.

The Aloof Fair One left Tenebroc completely alone save for her horse, a biddable white palfrey whose back was broad enough for both her and the bundle of spare clothes which was all she called her own. Many a knight, not only those who had begged her favor at the tournament's beginning, but also others, offered to serve as her escort to wherever she was going; but she preferred to trust in the law and custom of the land concerning maidens who traveled alone.

Hardly was she out of sight of the city, however, when a palmer came up behind her, riding his mule not over-hastily, but at a pleasantly brisk amble . . . which he slowed to the pace of her palfrey as they drew abreast on the road.

Looking down on the hooded man, for her mount was the taller, she said: "I ride alone."

"As do I," answered the palmer.

"For the sake of safety and my honor."

"I have no designs on either. We simply happen by chance to be traveling along the same road."

"In that case," the damsel said, a little less haughtily, "as long as it is clearly understood that you are not my escort, you may travel at any pace you choose."

So they traveled along, separately yet side by side, for the better part of two hours; and during that time—since traveling in silence is such tedious work that people who try it often talk to themselves or their mounts or even the road from time to time—the lady and the palmer traded comments with each other, progressing from occasional observations, through pleasantries and witticisms, to longer tales, she drawing upon old romances and he upon his late experiences in the Holy Land.

Who knows but that they might have gone on from tales to deeper revelations, if a knight in full armor, riding a great black warhorse and bearing on his ermine shield a black bend sinister, had not suddenly charged out of a side road straight into their path, where he reined to a stop facing them.

"Sir," the new arrival said, addressing the palmer and politely assuming him to enjoy the rank of knighthood, "you are unarmed. Will you surrender her at once, or would you rather wait for me to unarm and fight on foot?"

"Sir," the damsel put in, cold and calm as a statue of Minerva, "you are mistaken. I ride alone. This palmer simply happens to ride in the same direction, by purest chance."

"Moreover," growled the palmer, his voice grating huskily from the depths of the hood that, despite the clear warmth of the weather, he had never once shaken back upon his shoulders, "I have sworn an oath never again to wield any weapon of war in my own native land. But whatever you do, Sir Knight of the Bend Sinister, will not lack a witness!"

So saying, he turned his mule and rode a few lengths

back, far enough to emphasize that the maiden was traveling alone, but still near enough to see and hear what transpired next.

Sir Harald frowned after him in perplexity. Having been among those knights whose escort the Aloof Fair One had refused, he had expected to find her traveling alone, and, even though finding the palmer with her was not, after all, the stroke of good fortune it had looked at first, the left-handed knight felt that he had already come farther than he cared to retreat. "Well!" said he. "Then my damsel should not mind riding along in the same direction with me, instead."

"I should and do mind, my lord. Very much." She made to turn her palfrey and ride back the way she had come.

He lunged over—at some peril to his balance, but his good mount Goblin adjusted in time—and seized her palfrey's bridle. "My maiden, I regret having to insist, but you are no longer traveling alone!"

"And what, may I ask, is the name of my new knight escort?" she inquired coolly, eyeing his shield. "I fail to recognize either your voice or your device." This was a barbed and pointed insult, since she had given him audience only the day before.

"My name," he bargained, "in return for yours, fair maid."

"That would be a very poor exchange for me, seeing that your name is so soon to be held in disgrace throughout every court of the world."

This was much what Garth had already warned him, on being sent home to have the castle's best apartment and most biddable serving-maids prepared to receive the Aloof Fair One; and Sir Harald was ready with his reply. "Then I will spend my life snug in my own court." (Only it was not truly his, though he was treating it as such.) "It will be pleasant enough, once you have come to love me."

She raised one fine brow. "Pray, Sir Knight of the Bend Sinister, do not make yourself a fool as well as a villain."

"They call every lover a fool," he answered with a rueful laugh. After a few moments, he succeeded in working her palfrey's reins up over its head, the better to lead her mount along beside his.

Both Sir Labigodés and Sir Letron always carried amongst their pack goods a change or two of fine garments for any ladies whom they might encounter in need of rescue or a change of clothing or both. Because Sir Labigodés was, for a knight, almost small, ladies seemed to him reasonably large, and he provided accordingly; while Sir Letron, being big and tall, saw most women as petite and packed as if for elfin dames. The diplomatic page Tamba had thus no need to decide which knight should present the Maid of the Wood a new gown: all that Sir Labigodés could offer were considerably too large for her, but Sir Letron's green saddlebag with the silver tooling offered a kirtle and bliaud that fit her nicely. So as not to slight the other knight, she accepted from him the loan of a silk wimple and veil. Since these were scarlet shot with gold, and the kirtle and bliaud green, many an elegant lady would have kept to her curtained bed rather than be seen in such motley attire; but the Maid of the Wood simply borrowed from Tamba a spare crimson cloak, along with a silver brooch to hold it in place, and for footwear a pair of saffron-colored shoes from Sir Letron's younger page, and deemed herself presentable.

So, indeed, she was—just as, in some curious, tatterdemalion manner, she had been even when they first found her: It was akin to the difference between a ragged dandelion of the forest and a jester-faced pansy of the garden.

To the party's great, if secret, relief, she made no difficulty about anyone's diet. For herself, she ate sparingly, but of whatever was offered her. When the page who had shot the arrow ventured to ask her, timidly, if she would not rather have eaten only pulse and greens, she replied, "Do the plants not give up their lives, too, for feeding us?"

"The tree did not give up its life to feed me this apple," Tamba pointed out.

"That's true," she agreed at once. "And if you drop the core cleverly, its seeds may even grow into a new tree, after all."

At about this point their midday meal was interrupted by the arrival of a strange knight in black armor. He rode a white warhorse, a white plume trailed from the crest of his helmet, and his shield was of vair in black and silver with a black chevron cutting up and down across its center. Behind him came two squires mounted on hackneys, one leading a pack donkey and the other the knight's palfrey, which he must have abandoned for his charger just moments ago.

"Scoundrels!" he accosted them rudely. "Which of you dares joust with me?"

The whole party, except for the Maid of the Wood, got to their feet.

"Shall you answer him," Sir Letron asked his friend, "or shall I?"

"By all means, dear friend," Sir Labigodés replied, "pray speak for both of us, but only if it should be to your taste to do so."

"I would be honored, friend, but are you quite sure that you would not prefer that pleasurable task yourself?"

"If you truly think it will prove a task, good Letron, I will eagerly undertake it on behalf of us both. But if you, in fact, regard it as a pleasure and an honor—"

"Joust or not," the Knight of the Black Chevron demanded, "who will *answer* me?"

"It is unmannerly to leave our guest so long unanswered," Sir Labigodés murmured to his friend; and Sir Letron, nodding, replied to the Black Chevron Knight:

"Either of us will gladly joust with you, good sir, at your choice, or both of us in turn, should you so prefer. Only, let it be for mere, pure love of the exercise, with no other prizes claimed or taken." These terms were both permissible and courteous, if agreed upon in advance.

"It's a cowardly offer," the Knight of the Black Chevron said in a voice of scorn, "but I shall accept it, if either of you should succeed by any mischance or foul accident in unhorsing me. But, as for myself, when I defeat you, I shall claim my due: horse, arms, and—" He scanned the company until his gaze lighted on the Maid of the Wood. "Call her your lady, do you? Well, she's not much, but no knight is any the worse for some woman to ride at his horse's tail. I will claim her, along with the rest of my prize."

The Maid of the Wood laughed, but as she did so she covered her mouth with one hand as if not wishing to remind Sirs Letron and Labigodés of her words in the glade.

Nevertheless, as one, both knights were already turning to her.

"My lady . . ." Sir Labigodés began.

"Do such terms please you?" Sir Letron finished.

"When has it ever been a question of pleasing the woman?" replied the Maid of the Wood.

"I believe," Sir Letron told his friend, "that we have our answer."

Sir Labigodés nodded, turned back to the Knight of the Black Chevron, and told him: "Sir, we will not joust with you for love and honor nor, willingly, for prizes and prisoners."

"But know," Sir Letron added, "that we be two of King Arthur's Knights of the Table Round, and, should you insist upon fighting, we stand ready to defend this lady who honors us with her company."

"We both of us stand ready," Sir Labigodés emphasized, laying his hand on Sir Letron's shoulder.

The Knight of the Black Chevron sat in his saddle studying them for a moment or two. But he was one knight with two squires, while they were two knights with four squires and nine additional attendants, of whom even the cooks and churls looked ready, at need, to defend their maiden and be damned to the Code of Chivalry. So at last, saying, "Keep your pride and your scrawny little lady, then. I will find myself a better elsewhere," he motioned the appropriate squire to bring up his palfrey, sprang into its saddle from that of the warhorse, in plain sight of them all, and off he and his party rode.

Sir Harald had the Aloof Fair One halfway back to the castle that belonged by right of inheritance to his trueborn half-brother . . . who had been away so long on crusade that Harald had fallen into the habit of treating the place as his own.

He felt less sure of the Aloof Fair One, and had therefore kept tight hold on her palfrey's bridle the entire way, which put some strain upon his left arm. His right ached from carrying his cumbersome lance all this way for himself. He regretted the absence of both his attendant and his own traveling hackney; but Garth had grumbled so much on hearing the plan, Sir Harald felt that ordering him to help carry it out would have given them both considerable grief. Therefore, the knight had sent the extra horse back with the serf rather than risk its encumbering his own freedom of movement. This had seemed a good idea, at the time. Now, it seemed annoyance piled on annoyance. Sir Harald was not in the best of tempers. But then, we have not yet seen him in a good mood, nor are likely to for a while.

Nevertheless, from time to time, he tried making courtly speeches to the Aloof One, addressing her as "my fairest maiden," "matchless mistress," and "the peerless Pearl of my heart." Not once, since she had told him not to make himself fool as well as villain, had she deigned to give him a single word—no, not so much as a nod or a shake of her shining head, not even when they passed a crystal stream and he offered to fetch her a draught of its pure water in a small silver cup he had carried along for such a purpose, if only she would promise not to ride away. She had simply sat on her palfrey, gazing neither at nor away from him, but at something—he could not guess what, unless it were a bird or a leaf—beyond his shoulder.

This failed to improve his mood. He fretted as much at the lost opportunity to dismount and fill the cup for her, which variety of action would have eased his muscles a little, as he fretted at her continued refusal to speak to him, even to benefit herself. Still, to have given up so soon would have been out of keeping with Courtly Love, and also proved him laggard in sense of purpose. Therefore, he held fast to hope, his road, and her horse's reins.

They were within another half-hour's ride of the castle when a knight in black armor, with a shield bearing a black chevron on a field of black and silver vair, rode suddenly up to block their way.

"Villain!" cried he. "Prepare to lose that lady!"

"If I am a villain," Sir Harald responded, "you are another. Try to take her!"

The Aloof Fair One broke her long silence at last, to complain to the world at large: "Has any maiden before me ever been blessed with two such gallants?"

"Probably not," the world at large answered her, in the form of one of the Black Knight's two squires, who, apparently sensing her reluctance to remain with either champion, rode up quickly to hold her horse's bridle pending the outcome.

The Knight of the Black Chevron rode back along the roadway until the foes were about as far apart as they would have been in the lists at a formal tournament. Then both men couched their lances, and the charge commenced.

Just as they met, the Aloof Fair One unexpectedly shrilled, "Oh, bravo! Bravo!"

Goblin, being a steed who understood his duty, paid no attention to the sudden sound; but the Black Knight's white steed shied a little. Perhaps this threw the Black Knight off balance, or perhaps his prowess lay largely in his tongue, or it may simply have been that pure outrage lent some extra force and skill to his left-handed opponent. In any case, this time both champions—or villains, if you will—tumbled from their horses, to the mocking laughter of the Aloof Fair One.

Scrambling at once to his feet, Sir Harald drew his sword from the scabbard that hung at his right side. The Knight of the Black Chevron rose more meditatively, but drew his sword with equal vigor and dealt his opponent a blow that might have taken off his head—but, ducking a little, Sir Harald lost only his helmet, and meanwhile whipped his own blade round and low from behind to smack his antagonist square on the back of the thighs.

Had that blow been struck with the edge of the blade, it might have sheared through mail and all. Being smitten with the flat, it merely caused the Black Knight to sit down with an abrupt and very hard, shuddery noise.

"Your horse and arms," Sir Harald said, "are mine. You may keep your shield."

For answer, the Knight of the Black Chevron moved his head as though studying the situation as best his helmet-vision allowed. More meditatively and gingerly than before, he climbed to his feet and stood for a moment, swaying slightly, as though waiting for his head to clear. Then, all at once, he turned to his white charger—who had come up beside him, looking as embarrassed and apologetic as it is possible for a warhorse to look—sprang into its saddle, and spurred away as fast as he could go.

"Coward!" Sir Harald bawled after him. "Miser! Come back and finish the fight, then! Two falls in three!" As these words had no effect on the Knight of the Black Chevron, who may already have been out of earshot, with one squire close on his heels, Sir Harald turned to the remaining squire and began, "Tell your coward master—"

"Here," the remaining squire replied, passing the reins of the Aloof Fair One's mount into Sir Harald's mailed hand; and then, doffing his cap in brief salute, he added, "Good day, my lord," and galloped off after the other two.

"His horse and arms are mine!" Sir Harald shouted up at the one person who remained to hear him. "By right of conquest! You saw it—you witnessed it—I won them. . . ." He broke off and frowned in a baffled way, like a philosopher gazing into a mirror.

The Aloof Fair One deigned to address him at last. "I think I remember you now," she said. "The beard suited you better. Grow it back."

"What?" said Sir Harald. "Oh. As soon as I can." His frown traveled almost abstractedly to his lance and helmet, where they had fallen along the roadway.

"I mean to take this opportunity," the Aloof One announced, "to go apart by myself into the woods for a moment or two." As he turned to look at her, she laughed, not at all kindly. "You need have no fear! Were I to attempt flying on foot, I should make of myself an even greater fool than you."

"Just a moment then, my damsel," he answered, looking around again. After a short consideration, he sheathed his sword and led her palfrey forward to where his helmet lay—a good, sturdy casque of strong iron, designed to withstand heavy blows. Still holding the rein, he set the helmet upright and ground it a little into the road, so as to create as a rough-and-ready stepping block for the lady.

Disdaining its assistance, she hopped down and disappeared among the trees. Sir Harald smacked left fist into right palm in pure frustration; but since both hands were gauntleted in mail mittens, he needed a few seconds to shake out the worst of the stinging. Next, after taking hasty advantage of her absence, he retrieved his lance, which was fortunately still whole.

As he turned back to the horses, the Aloof Fair One, moving more quickly than anyone had ever seen her do before, darted out of the woods again and leaped into her saddle, in the process kicking the knight's helmet so that it rolled to the side of the road.

Sir Harald sprang to Goblin's back and gave chase at once, catching her up within a few paces. When he recaptured her mount's head, she gave him a cold stare and a colder shrug before resuming her frostbitten silence.

He had contrived to keep hold of his recovered lance, but his helmet now lay forlorn on the edge of the roadway. He looked back at it flashing like wanhope in the sun. The loss of a good helmet was no mean expense, but to attempt recovering it right now would entail the even greater loss of his lady fair, so, for the nonce, Sir Harald abandoned it.

The mysterious Knight of the Black Chevron, having played his part in this episode of the Aloof Fair One, has ridden out of it.

Not so Sir Labigodés and Sir Letron with their party, including the Maid of the Wood, who sat that evening at a simple supper of venison pies and roast partridge, dates and nutmeg cakes, plovers' eggs and small fishes baked in rolls of white bread, and such other poor dishes as the two cooks (having forgotten their alternate-days arrangement) could set before them after only two hours at the camp-fires. They were enlivening this plain fare with conversation as witty as it was courteous, when who should walk up to them, leading his mule, but that same palmer who had ridden for part of the morning—not with, but along-side the Aloof Fair One, as they traveled by purest chance in the same direction down the same road.

"Be welcome, good pilgrim!" Sir Letron greeted him, standing.

"Come, dear stranger," Sir Labigodés added, standing at the same time. "Join us in our humble repast."

The entire party, even including the Maid of the Wood, who could have been exempt by reason of her gender, had followed the knights' lead in rising politely to their feet; and one of the serving-men was already fetching out an extra trencher. But, without doffing his hood, the palmer shook his head.

"I may eat with you," said he, "but only on condition that immediately thereafter you follow me to the assistance of a fair maiden in the greatest of distress."

"By my beard!" cried Sir Labigodés, who never used any stronger oath than that. "We will follow you at once!"

"And finish our repast on the way," added tall Sir Letron.

The new plan was not greatly to the liking of their followers, who had looked forward to a night's rest and now must pack up again without it. Yet they set to work with only a very little grumbling, and that only to one another and in lowered voices. Indeed, Sir Letron's suggestion was not entirely necessary, for only the squires, pages, cooks, and serving-men would need to finish their supper along the way, the knights being able to finish theirs, along with the palmer, while the others unpitched the pavilions, restowed all the gear, and resaddled or reloaded the animals. The Maid of the Wood had long since finished her meal, save to nibble a sweetmeat now and then for the sake of mannerliness.

It became more mannerly, now, as well as more urgent, to hear the palmer's story as he delivered it between bites, each successive morsel of food vanishing like a mark of punctuation into the cavern of his hood right after a phrase had issued out of it.

"She who was known at the recent tournament as the Aloof Fair One—" he told them, and delicately thrust a bite of venison into his hood with the tips of three fingers "—fairer, some believed and even said aloud, than Prince Erec's beautiful bride, or even than Dame Guenevere herself—" another bite "—has been waylaid and abducted by a false traitor knight—" another bite, and so on "—one Harald, rightly surnamed Folgeste for his mad deeds, who keeps a castle not far from here.

"It is not Harald's castle," the palmer went on, after taking a long drink of ale. "It is the keep of his half-brother, who took the cross some years ago and followed the call of the Crusades. Harald is a bastard. Though raised up and trained in arms side by side with his trueborn brother, he could never sit on the Quiller Couch."

"I think," Sir Labigodés remarked, as the palmer paused to drink again, "that I have heard tell of this perilous couch."

"The fairy Morgan fashioned it—did she not?—for the fair castle of Quillerstone," Sir Letron added.

"She did," the palmer affirmed, "at the earnest request of the present holder's grandfather, who was very wealthy.

That deadly couch, which I have seen with my own eyes—and all that you have heard doubtless falls short of the truth—rests in a small hall of its own, built for no other purpose, between the great hall and the chapel. It looks like a most welcome resting place, with a long cushion covered in rich, tawny-golden velvet, and silken pillows stuffed with fine goosedown. And trueborn heir or rightful owner—they and they alone—can sit or even sleep upon it in perfect safety and comfort. But let anyone else, whatever or whoever, attempt the same, and the Quiller Couch turns into the ferocious Quiller Lion, with a back more sharply spiny than that of any hedgehog, and devours the usurper at once, unless he be very fast indeed on his feet."

The Maid of the Wood asked, "Is there anything to warn away the unwary?"

"The little hall has a strong and sturdy door," the palmer told her, "which can be locked and bolted from the outside, both to keep the unwary out and, should occasion demand, to keep the lion in until it changes back into the couch. This happens after it has digested its meal, or after about an hour if it has not fed, or instantly upon being touched by the true owner or heir."

Sir Labigodés returned to the subject of the distressed damsel. "How long ago was it that this false knight waylaid the Fair One?"

"This morning at about the hour of Nones. I witnessed it myself."

Sir Letron raised his knuckle to his mouth as if to chew it in perplexity, but remembered his manners in time and lowered it again, asking only, and with the utmost respect, "Were you traveling with her, good sir?"

"I was not," the palmer explained yet again. "By pure chance, I merely happened to be traveling in the same direction, along the same road. But even if I had been accompanying that fair maid, I could hardly have counted as her knight escort, unarmed, unarmored, and unhorsed as I am, and having sworn the solemnest of vows never again to wield any weapon of warfare in mine own native land, nor to bare my head by daylight or firelight until . . . the time is come."

"Then she was indeed traveling alone," Sir Letron clarified.

"Completely alone," said the palmer. "Without so much as a page to attend her."

Tamba, who had kept himself close enough to overhear most of their council, murmured under his breath, "I wish that I had been there as her page!" No one heard him except, perhaps, the Maid of the Wood.

"I fear," Sir Labigodés was lamenting, "that by this time he has already had his evil will of her."

"And nothing remains for it," Sir Letron agreed mournfully, "but to blacken his name throughout all the courts of Christendom and beyond."

"Perhaps he has," mused the Maid of the Wood, "and perhaps not. But even if he has, is that any reason to abandon the poor woman?"

"*No*, by my oath!" cried the palmer. "It is all the more reason to save and comfort her!"

"By my friend's beard," remarked Sir Letron, who had none of his own to swear by, "they have the right of it! I am ashamed of my last words. . . . They were true enough in themselves, but they included only half of the task before us."

"Come, then," Sir Labigodés seconded him. "Onward, as soon as we may. Although in any case, he will surely have her in the castle by now."

"If so," Sir Letron observed, "we will simply have to lay it under siege."

Let all readers set their minds at ease on one point, at least: Sir Harald has not yet had his will of the Aloof Fair One. Perhaps the Knight of the Black Chevron would have, but there was some limit to even the rashness of Harald de Folgeste. Having his prize secure in the castle he was treating as his own, he had given her over into the care of the three waiting-women whom the chaplain, on Garth's instructions, had chosen for her, and watched them lead her away with the greatest deference . . . but also with no little pride, seeing that not one of these three was truly of gentle birth, although all were respectable and the chief of them was the chaplain's own wife. (In those days, a simple priest might marry and raise a family, so long as he was not a monk.)

Sir Harald had then ordered dinner to be served in two

hours, so the damsel should have sufficient time to rest and recover from the rigors of the road.

He himself oversaw the stabling, both of his steed Goblin and of the Aloof Fair One's palfrey. Then, after letting Garth disarm and reclothe him into more comfortable garments—in this case, soft chainse and silky bliaud—he settled at last in his own apartment. Here, two hours later, Garth found him sitting on the bed and frowning fixedly at a rose.

"Sir," said Garth, "dinner is prepared."

"Thank God for that!" Sir Harald exclaimed, casting the rose down onto the coverlet.

"But Her Aloofness refuses to come down for it. She wants food sent up to her rooms instead."

"*What?*" Sir Harald exclaimed. "I have spent this last hour and more meditating on her perfections, and she will not so much as take her meal with us in the hall?"

"Meditating on her perfections, sir?" Garth repeated, respectfully enough, but privately wondering how any man could meditate a whole hour on that particular subject.

"It is the duty of every knight in love to spend all his free moments meditating on his mistress' perfections, is it not?" Sir Harald demanded.

"If I might make so bold, sir," Garth replied, "you have seized the lady and brought her here against her will, when she was traveling alone. And before that, you made up your mind never to turn your horse and arms over to Sir Kay, who won them in fair fight. And both those things are dead against the Code of Knighthood, as well as I understand it, even if I am just a simple serf. I don't see how you can pick and choose which parts of it you're going to follow, and which parts you aren't."

Sir Harald snorted. "Name me one knight who does not do just that!"

"Sir Gawen," Garth suggested at once.

"I said a knight, not an archangel! Very well, have them take a tray of the best to her—four trays, if her women are to eat there, too. And a tray of the leavings here to me. . . . No, wait." He changed his mind, or perhaps let his stomach change it for him, being growlingly empty after the morning's exertions. "If the boards are already raised, I'll come down to the hall to eat, even if Her Perfection won't."

Sir Harald was not the only person in Quillerstone to feel disappointment that the Fair One remained Aloof and would not come down into the great hall to dine. The castle had been without a mistress ever since the passing of the rightful lord's mother. That was why it housed no gently born ladies just now, and therefore no young pages, either. As for the older pages, the squires, and the two vassal knights, they had all departed with the trueborn brother for the Holy Land; and, with half a dozen men-at-arms and yeoman archers remaining to help him ward Quillerstone and its people against attack, which was unlikely in any case during the reign of the great King Arthur, Sir Harald had hesitated to seek any more knights or squires until such time as he found that he could safely sit upon the Quiller Couch.

When dinner was finished, he sent Garth back along the road to find his helmet, while he himself went down to the small hall for yet one more try at that perilous piece of furniture. Unlocking the door with the key, which he wore always at his belt when at home and carried with him whenever he went abroad, he shot back the bolt and entered.

After shutting the door behind him (for he disliked observation when making these attempts) but leaving it ajar (for he might well have to beat another hasty retreat) he crossed the neatly tiled floor, mounted the low dais, and stood frowning down for several heartbeats at the couch. Finely and luxuriously cushioned though it was, with deep, down-stuffed, silk-encased pillows, it seemed somehow to return his gaze with a baleful stare. A less stubborn man might have lost courage, but at length Sir Harald turned and lowered his posterior, though without relaxing the muscles of thigh and calf, down onto those invitingly menacing cushions.

At the first touch of the angry bristles, he was up again, sprinting back across the chamber and out the door, to slam it shut behind him and drop the bolt even as the roaring monster's sharp claws raked its other side. The inside of that door was more heavily scored and shredded than any cat's favorite scratching post, yet so thick was the lumber that it would hold up to twenty years of monthly attacks.

Two ostlers were passing when Sir Harald burst through the door and slammed it shut, but they politely pretended not to notice and went on about their errands. He stood watching and listening until the door ceased to vibrate, signifying that the terrible lion with its spineful back had probably returned to the dais and lain watchfully down while it waited to turn back into the couch . . . although several hours must pass before Sir Harald undid the door again to peer cautiously in. Meanwhile, turning the key in the lock, he panted, "Can Godfrey still be alive?" Then, his face darkening, "Or does this mean that anyone else—anyone else at all in the land—could be rightful lord before the bastard son?"

So saying, he smashed his fist against the door with such force that the beast on the other side roared again, and did not settle back into the couch for ten minutes longer than it would otherwise have taken.

In my quest for the best dramatic transitions, I have gone a little out of strict chronological sequence: The above events, from Sir Harald's arrival at Quillerstone with the Aloof Fair One to his latest trial of the Quiller Couch, actually took place before the finding of Sirs Letron and Labigodés by the palmer, which happened that same evening, about the time that, back in the castle, the Aloof Fair One was refusing to come down to supper, exactly as she had refused to come down to dinner.

As most of the knights' party, from the cooks to the experienced page Tamba, could have predicted had they been consulted, it was really a bit silly to pack up and set out at once, since after barely an hour it grew too dark to proceed farther, and they had all the work of setting their camp up again, this time by lanternlight. Courteous as ever, the two champions apologized to their menials for the extra work, though less profusely than they apologized to the palmer for the enforced delay.

Because they had been later and wearier into their cots that night than they otherwise would have been, most of them slept longer the following morning. Not so, however, the youngest member of the group—Sir Letron's junior page—who rose in pure excitement before the sun, groped into his clothes, and, finding no one else astir, went a little way into the woods alone as soon as the earliest dawnlight made it possible.

I would drop the modest veil of privacy over what he did there in a tiny clearing, but that its results bear somewhat upon our tale; for, relieving himself at a small shadow, he made it stand up, shake itself dry, and resolve before his eyes into a dark bear cub, clumsy, curious, and unlearned as yet in the proper relations between its own kind and the human. It padded over to sniff at the boy; and when he bent and rubbed its fur, it reacted much like some over-grown puppy or huge kitten, rolling over and snapping upward in a friendly, playful manner.

Charmed, Sir Letron's page hunkered down and played on with the cub in innocent happiness, never remembering how close the mother bear must be, nor noticing when she hove up behind him on her two hind legs, poising her forepaws over his head. Not until she began her roar did he look up—when he froze, the cub forgotten at his knee.

But in that moment, a voice sang from the far edge of the clearing:

> "Good lady, calm, remember Who is here,
> Whose Presence gives and takes away all fear!"

Stepping forward in the gently growing light, the Maid of the Wood picked up the cub and held it out to its mother. The great bear seemed to hesitate just half a heartbeat longer, then dropped down softly on all fours, missing the page with that grown-up bearish grace that masks itself as lumbersomeness, and lovingly licked the back of the girl's hand.

The Maid of the Wood set the cub back down at its mother's feet, and rubbed both their heads. Nodding to her with contented little sounds, the bears turned and padded away through the undergrowth together.

"Now," the Maid of the Wood murmured with a wink to the page, "let's keep this our own secret, just between us two."

He nodded breathlessly, then at last bethought himself to thank her in words before scrambling to his feet and running back to the tents.

In his dash from the clearing, he half bumped into the palmer, who had appeared as unobserved, in his turn, as the Maid of the Wood had before she started to sing. Pausing just long enough for a nod, a bow, and a hastily mumbled apology, the boy ran on to safety, leaving the palmer eyeing the Maid of the Wood.

"Good lady, be calm," the palmer said quietly, and, it must be confessed, rather needlessly, since she had never been otherwise. "I, too, will keep this secret, since that seems to be your wish."

"Thank you kindly, sir," she answered, winking at him much as she had at the page. "I think he's learned this particular lesson well enough, don't you? And he will remember, without anyone reminding him again."

Later that same morning, as the palmer led them toward Quillerstone, the Maid of the Wood interrupted her own song with a sudden cry of joy, jumped from the jennet they had given her to ride, and ran to the roadway's edge to pick up something she had glimpsed glinting in the bright sunlight.

"It is Sir Harald's helmet," said the palmer. "I know it by its black plume."

"Which looks rather the worse for wear," Sir Labigodés observed.

"No matter," Sir Letron replied, "so long as the helmet itself still be whole."

"A little dent here and there," said the Maid of the Wood.

"I have seen far worse," said Tamba, who happened to be closest to where she stood turning it back and forth delightedly in her hands.

"Why would any knight have abandoned a perfectly good helmet, wanting only a touch of straightening and a fresh plume?" Sir Letron wondered aloud, meanwhile dismounting so as to be ready to help the Maid of the Wood back into her saddle.

"Perhaps he regards it as no longer his," Sir Labigodés suggested, dismounting at the same time and for the same purpose. "His horse and arms are forfeit to Sir Kay, are they not?"

"All the more reason to take care of them," Tamba argued. "Otherwise, he will have to pay the ransom for something he no longer possesses, and so lose it twice!"

"He does not intend to fulfill the obligations of a fairly vanquished knight," said the palmer. "Not even when the victor is a champion of our good King Arthur's Table Round. I overheard him mutter as much on quitting Sir Kay's tent."

"He is doubly a traitor, then," Sir Letron opined.

"Trebly," Sir Labigodés amended with the utmost courtesy, "since the castle itself is no more his own than either the fair damsel or his horse and arms."

"But perhaps not," the Maid of the Wood put in, still turning the helmet round and round. "Don't we all sometimes say things in anger that we don't really mean?"

"Sir Kay surely does!" the irrepressible Tamba cried with a laugh. "Let us confess that our kind seneschal's tongue might try the patience of a saintlier knight than this Sir Harald!"

"Hush, page!" Sir Letron reproved, and Sir Labigodés explained, "Never speak an ill word of thy superiors." But, for all their inborn politesse, the one knight's eyes twinkled and the other's lips twitched in amused agreement with Tamba's words.

Seeing both champions equally ready to help her remount—which polite assistance she might not have needed at all, strictly speaking—the Maid of the Wood resolved a dilemma that might have used up half an hour by handing the helmet to the taller one, saying, "Good Sir Letron, won't you please be so kind as to keep my prize safe for me till I want it again?" and adding to the shorter one, "Good Sir Labigodés, thank you so much for holding the stirrup for me!"

They had not progressed more than a quarter of an hour when whom should they meet, mounted on a little donkey and peering anxiously this way and that along and to each side of the road, but Garth. Several of them dimly recognized his face from glimpsing it at the tournament of Tenebroc, but only one could call him by name. "Garth, is it not?" said Tamba. "Sir Harald de Folgeste's own servant!"

"Rather," the palmer corrected the page, "the serf of Quillerstone's true master."

Ever courteous to all, whether highborn or lowly, albeit to each in his or her degree, Sir Labigodés addressed the serf. "Good fellow, thou seem'st to search for something."

"My master's lost helmet, good Your Worships," Garth

replied, tugging his forelock as he pulled his donkey aside out of the roadway.

"He calls Harald his 'master,'" the palmer muttered loudly enough to be overheard.

"My master for the nonce," Garth explained, lifting his eyes to look at the palmer as shrewdly as a serf might dare. "In place of my true master, who left us years ago to go on crusade. My first loyalty is always to Sir Godfrey le Blond, if so be he's still alive."

The palmer nodded, as could be seen by the movement of his enshrouding hood.

"Good fellow," said Sir Letron, "thy master for the nonce is a scoundrel and a traitor, who hath both usurped the property of his trueborn brother and falsely abducted a lone maiden against her will and the law of our good King Arthur." He did not mention the horse and arms Sir Kay had won, since, with a year's grace, it was not yet proven that Sir Harald would wrongfully withhold them.

"He was wrong about that Aloof Fair One," Garth confessed, still staring at the palmer. "I tried to warn him— with all respect, Your Worships. But he hasn't dishonored her yet. As for the castle, whether he's 'usurped' it, rightly speaking, we'll have to see if Sir Godfrey ever comes home. But he's kept it well enough, anyway; and he's still the only master I've got just now, good Your Worships."

"Thy loyalty does thee proud," Sir Labigodés said with approval. "As for thy master's helmet. . . ." Both he and Sir Letron glanced at the Maid of the Wood. When she smiled and nodded slightly, Sir Letron finished for his friend: "We ourselves hold thy master's helmet, and will continue to hold it, as hostage."

"He'll be sorry to hear that, Your Worships. He was in a rare temper when I couldn't find it yesterday."

"He did not beat thee, I hope?" cried the palmer.

Garth looked surprised. "No, sir," he answered, squinting at the palmer again. "He never strikes people, sir. Only other knights. In combat."

This time there was something suggesting reassurement in the nod of the palmer's deep hood.

Garth went on, "But he threw a chessboard, worshipful sirs, so far it hit the wall. The chessmen scattered like slops of milk when cow kicks the pail."

Tamba, the Maid of the Wood, both of the younger pages, three of the squires, the four serving-men, one of the cooks, and—some said later—several of the horses and other mounts, all laughed heartily at the homely image. The rest of the party, except perhaps the palmer, at least grinned or smiled.

"It's a fine helmet," the Maid of the Wood said when she finished laughing. "Losing it would upset any knight."

"No doubt it was also a fine chessboard," said the palmer.

"Well, sir, they're repairing it, and most of the chessmen will be all right again with just a little paint. But it wasn't only the helmet, you see, Your Worships. The Aloof Fair One wouldn't come down to supper last night, any more than she had come to dinner before that. And then he'd almost got gobbled up again by the couch—"

The palmer interrupted, causing both Sir Letron and Sir Labigodés to wince a little, even if the speaker he interrupted was a serf. "So he has been trying to sit on the Quiller Couch, has he?"

"Aye, sir," Garth answered, gazing harder than ever at the hooded figure. "And it won't let him. So it seems our good Sir Godfrey must still be alive. But what with this and that and the other, it wasn't a very good day for my present master."

"Garth," the Maid of the Wood asked reflectively, "suppose we were to take you hostage?"

He looked up at her with hope. "It might work, Your Ladyship. So please Your Worships, it might just work. Maybe not today, nor tomorrow, nor even the next day . . . but after a week or two, when he's had a little more time to get tired of that Aloof Fair One and her tricks—if you'll forgive my tongue. Maybe even sooner, if he thought you were ill-using me."

Sir Letron shook his head with finality. "It would be discourteous even to pretend to such a falsehood, no matter how estimable the goal."

"And equally lacking in courtesy," opined Sir Labigodés, "to hold any lady—maid or matron—at no greater exchange value than that of a helmet and a serf."

"And then, too," Sir Letron mused, "there would still remain the question of the usurped castle."

"That there would, my good friend," Sir Labigodés agreed. "Once again, you have encompassed a most difficult problem within a few well-chosen words."

"Good Sir Labigodés, you are, as ever, too kind."

"Not at all, my best of comrades. I merely give you your due."

After thanking his friend with a courtly nod, Sir Letron turned back to Garth and concluded regretfully, "And so, good fellow, with all due thanks for thy well-meant if ill-considered offer, we must bid thee return for the present to thy present churlish master."

"In the hope," Sir Labigodés added as a grace note, "of fair deliverance, in the fullness of time, into the hands of a better."

Garth shrugged, gave his forelock another tug, and glanced up at the sun. "So please Your Worships, then, if I go now, so I can be back there in good time for dinner."

I wonder what Sirs Letron and Labigodés would have thought could they have seen the Aloof Fair One and Sir Harald at that very moment, she standing precariously on a merlon of the high battlements, he framed in the doorway to her apartment, looking less across at her than up toward Heaven.

To begin with, he had had some little difficulty locating her at all, for she had insisted on changing her quarters thrice since being installed in what the castle at large had fondly considered the finest apartment, and neither the three women assigned to wait on her nor the lads they occasionally enlisted to assist in trundling such chests and chairs as she might elect to take with her from place to place had managed to keep Sir Harald fully apprised of the various moves.

He had finally run her to earth near the top of the tall North Tower overlooking the water—for the castle of Quillerstone was built on a small island near the shore of a large lake and joined to the mainland by a causeway long and wide enough for one pair of mounted knights to ride a joust.

The Aloof Fair One had caused her door to be bolted from within. Sir Harald rapped on it with his fist. When the face of the chaplain's wife—or, rather, her hazel eyes, for she was a short woman—appeared at the little, barred peep-window, Sir Harald delivered his carefully rehearsed speech in carefully modulated tones:

"I pray you, tell your mistress that her worshipping slave most humbly begs an audience."

"You must let him in," the Aloof Fair One answered in a cold, clear voice before the chaplain's wife could speak. "He is lord and master here, and he will enter perforce, to have his way upon a poor, weak captive woman, will-she, nil-she."

"Sir," murmured the chaplain's wife, "pray, be easy! She's that much of a lady, that there's no pleasing her in anything!"

Sir Harald shut his eyes, tried to remind himself that she might have some cause, from her own vantage point, to consider herself aggrieved, and waited for the chaplain's wife, with the help of the falconer's sister, who was taller, to draw back the bolt and open the door.

"And now," the Aloof Fair One went on, clasping her hands to her breast in a gesture that might have looked piteous had it been less graceful, "he will certainly order you, my women, to leave us alone, and, since he is lord and master in this place, you must obey his least command."

"No need for that," Sir Harald said stiffly. "I have come but to beg whether my damsel will be so kind as to favor her humble servants with her attendance today at dinner."

"What?" cried the Aloof Fair One. "Sir, will you force these unfortunate women to remain, thus making them, perforce, partakers and accomplices in your infamy?"

At that, the chaplain's wife and her companions, the falconer's sister and the fletcher's daughter, who had been almost a full day learning the humors of their new mistress, all bustled past Sir Harald and out the door.

"You might as well go with them," he told the Aloof Fair One, standing farther out of line with the doorway. "It seems you've already been making free with my castle."

That was when she had opened the opposite door and stepped out onto the battlements. That was when he, following to find her perched as though ready to jump, had rolled his eyes upward to Heaven.

"But, thank God," said the Aloof Fair One, "there yet remains to the poor, captive maiden one final way to hold her fate in her own hands, one last and desperate means of escape from tyranny and dishonor."

"Spare me this!" he exclaimed. "We both know I am not going to offer you any violence! Or I'd have done it already, out there in the woods."

"I know no such thing, sir. Out there, you might simply have feared discovery by some chance passerby."

"The Knight of the Black Chevron, for example? I suppose you think he would have rescued you? Handled you gently?"

"I should have met, at least, no worse treatment at his hands than at yours."

Sir Harald almost laughed. "If you truly believe that, you're even more of a maiden than we took you for! Now come down before you fall off by accident," he added, taking one step backward into the room.

She sprang featly down to the battlement floor, but remained near an open crenel as she went on: "And he might have respected the law and custom of King Arthur's land, leaving me alone entirely, had I been truly alone, without knightly escort."

"Possibly," he conceded with skeptical sarcasm. "I'm sure it takes a true lover to throw away his knightly reputation for his lady's sake and then put up with her humors while waiting for her change of heart."

She answered Sir Harald's tone rather than his words: "If you truly believe that you saved me from cruel danger at his hands—some cruel danger that I should have faced with or without your presence—why have you not boasted to your people here of your great and glorious victory over the Black Chevron Knight?"

Sir Harald had spoken of it to no one, not even Garth (who knew only that the Aloof Fair One had kicked away his helmet when using it for a mounting-step), both because he was a little ashamed of failing to collect the horse and arms he had won, and because he was, secretly, a little more ashamed of his firm resolution to cheat Sir Kay exactly as the Knight of the Black Chevron had cheated him, and so had no wish to risk the subject being brought up. But he said, bluffing, "How would you know whether I've boasted about it or not, shunning our company at dinner and supper and every hour between?"

"The women whom you have assigned to serve as my guards—or 'ladies in waiting' if you will—have not shunned all contact with the rest of your castle. If you had spoken of that combat, they should have heard, and repeated it to me."

"My sweet damsel," he said, swallowing hard, "will you please come down for once to take your dinner with us in the hall?"

"Suppose," she replied coyly, "only suppose that I were to tell them myself all about the Knight of the Black Chevron and that singular victory you won over him, covering yourself with such signal honor?"

He counted slowly to ten and then repeated, "Will you kindly come down to dinner?"

"Will you kindly allow me to ride away again afterward, as freely as before you outraged both me and the law of our kind king?"

"How big a fool do you think I am?" he demanded. "I have already destroyed my honor for love of you! Would letting you go bring it back?"

"Sir," she replied, very coldly, "did I ever ask for your love?"

To that, there could be no reply. Sir Harald turned and strode from the apartment, leaving her to tell her borrowed serving-women whatever she would about the interview.

"My dear good friend," said Sir Labigodés to Sir Letron as they sat in their saddles watching Garth until he and his donkey were well out of sight, "might I make so bold as to offer you the poor opinion of one weak and fallible mortal?"

"So that the opinion be your own, my dear friend and companion, it will be most welcome to my ears, as the thought of one whom I must ever regard as wise and learned beyond measure in all the ways of true courtesy."

"It is this, then," said Sir Labigodés. "In my humble opinion, which, despite those sincere kind words, for which I shall ever thank you, remains but weak and fallible, it seems somewhat . . . less than mannerly . . . to have applied the term 'churlish'—however well deserved—to any knight in words addressed to the loyal and worthy vassal whose misfortune it is to serve such a master."

Sir Letron looked thunderstruck. "My very wise friend! You are right—nay, your words are too kind, and fall far too short of the truth! It was unbearably, unpardonably rude!"

"Be comforted, master," said Tamba. "Remember, the man Garth is but a serf, and for that reason if no other a churl himself."

"All the worse!" cried Sir Letron, whose intense courtesy set him somewhat apart from most of his age in such matters as these. "For in insulting his master, I inadvertently insulted his own condition, and he, as serf, could not so much as give me back such answer as I deserved! Oh, I am—I, myself—the worst of all unmannerly churls!"

And so it might have gone on for the better part of the day and night, with the poor knight refusing all comfort, if the Maid of the Wood had not remarked with a wink to Tamba, "Yes, indeed, it was surely just as bad as any sin Sir Harald himself has ever committed!"

Sir Letron paused, considered the matter, wiped his eyes, and said slowly, "Well, I would not, perhaps, go quite so far as that. No, good my lady, with the deepest and utmost respect for your opinion, I think that I would not go quite so far as to say that of my own unfortunate offense."

"Nor would I," Sir Labigodés agreed, "weak and fallible though my poor opinion has ever been."

They then commenced to reassure the Maid of the Wood that, although their joint opinion differed from hers, her judgment was not in any way or whit inferior—nay, no doubt, hers surely exceeded theirs as the sun's light exceeded that of the crescent moon, even though they must still and nevertheless, with all due and worshipful deference, in honest honor disagree. Since she wisely offered no further opinions, but kept silent throughout all this, it required a mere half hour, after which most of the party had forgotten what it was all about in the first place, and the two leaders decided that, if they progressed at a leisurely pace, they ran little risk of overtaking Garth and rudely reaching the castle ahead of him.

"They are *what*?" cried Sir Harald.

"Holding it for ransom, sir," Garth repeated dutifully.

Sir Harald looked around for something to throw and,

there being no more chessboards ready to hand, made do with his half-drunk flagon of ale. As it sluiced its remaining contents across his chamber, struck a tapestry so hard that it thudded against the wall behind, and fell badly dented to the floor, Garth went on:

"And they called you a scoundrel and a traitor, sir. Oh, and a churl, too."

"A helmet as ransom for a gentlemaiden, and they call *me* scoundrel and churl?"

"Well, they didn't say it was her they'd try to ransom with it. In fact, they themselves admitted that trying that would insult Her Ladyship," Garth explained, omitting that there had been some brief talk about including him along with the helmet in the proposed trade. "Ransom, maybe, to get you out to fight them."

Sir Harald smashed his fist down so hard on the sideboard that the ale-jug toppled over and the knight himself winced.

Garth caught the jug before too much of its contents spilled, set it upright again, and said, "I tried to warn you how it would be, sir."

"You did," Sir Harald agreed wearily, flexing and unflexing his hand to make sure he had done it no serious damage. "You've been a better servant than I probably deserve. But—God's Blood, if they'd suggest I would need any such bribe to come out and fight them, when I stand ready to fight any man in fair combat or foul! Bareheaded, if need be!"

"Need won't be," Garth answered comfortably. "Not for that, anyway. We'll set to hammering the dents out of one of your old helmets right away."

"Eat your dinner first." Dismissing the serf with a wave of his stunned but otherwise still sound left hand, the knight added, "Tell them I'll be down in the space of an *Ave* or two. The Fair One will not."

Garth hesitated briefly, but decided not to say anything more about the strange palmer whose face had been completely hidden and voice somewhat muffled by the heavy dark hood. Instead, he glanced at the dented flagon, ale-stained tapestry, and wet floor, said, "I'll send someone to clean that up right after dinner," and left the apartment.

Sir Harald lingered long enough to stare ruefully at the

damage he had just done, swallow some ale directly from the jug, and transfer his gaze to his shield, which he was keeping in his room to brood on whenever his head ached too badly from trying to meditate like a good knightly lover on the perfections of his mistress.

The tales had it that a villain should enjoy the upper hand for a little while at least. And yet, not only had his evil reputation already begun, not only was his brother Godfrey's couch lying in wait to gobble him up, not only had his best helmet been lost to fall into the hands of his insulting new enemies, not only did the Aloof Fair One still refuse to so much as take a meal in his company, but his face itched with the new beard he had begun growing for her—even though he suspected that when it was grown, she would scornfully bid him shave it off again.

He was midway through his midday meal when one of the baker's sons, who helped stand sentry two days a week, brought him word that more than a dozen people were pitching their pavilions on the mainland side of the causeway.

"God's Blood!" said Sir Harald, recognizing at once who the party must be. "Could they not even let me eat my dinner in peace?" And, motioning the chaplain's son, who was the closest thing to a page that Quillerstone Castle had just now, to refill his drinking beaker, he carried that and the leg of a roasted swan up to the watchtower battlements with him, to let his enemies see that they had come at an inconvenient hour.

This was not entirely fair, since, Garth having reassured them as to the safety of the Aloof Fair One's person and honor, they had had not the least intention of hailing the castle until after they had all finished their own dinner, which their cooks were even now preparing.

"Look there!" Sir Letron exclaimed, glancing up at the walls above the gate. "Can that be the traitor himself?"

"It can," the palmer affirmed dryly.

"Rude of the fellow to keep us from our dinner," Sir Labigodés remarked, as if this were the blackest yet of Sir Harald's criminal activities.

"Although," said Sir Letron, still feeling tender himself over his own late horrendous lapse of courtesy, "if he were to bid them raise the portcullis and offer us hospitality, that would go far to mitigate the apparent unmannerliness."

"That is true enough, in its way," Sir Labigodés agreed. "But it would make matters very awkward for us. How could we rescue his prisoner, if he were our host?"

The palmer put in, "The demands of chivalry must surely outweigh those of hospitality."

Sir Letron shook his head. "With all deferential respect, good friend, I feel far from confident on that point. The demands of chivalry bind only knights, squires, and pages, whilst those of hospitality bind all hosts and all guests, of whatever degree, and must therefore be considered the more universal and sweeping."

"We must simply avoid the problem," Sir Labigodés said, answering his own riddle, "by refusing to accept the villain's hospitality, should he offer it, which I expect he will not. As you see, the portcullis remains lowered."

"Well," Sir Letron concluded with a sigh, "if he is to act rudely, all the more reason for us to act politely. Let us go at once and exchange our challenges with the courtesy that best beseems true knights."

Sir Harald, meanwhile, was chewing his roast swan; drumming his fingertips impatiently on his wooden beaker; and wondering how long, after interrupting (as he interpreted it) his midday meal, they now intended to keep him waiting. He was about to hail them first—and neither his words nor his tone would have made the situation any better than it already was—when at last he saw the two good knights mount their chargers and start across the causeway, riding exactly side by side.

That they approached on their warhorses rather than their palfreys was in itself a declaration of hostility—as if Sir Harald had needed any such declaration. Swallowing a bite half chewed, he cleared his throat with a hard gulp of ale and shouted down, "If you want a fight, I want my helmet back first!"

King Arthur's champions halted their horses a few yards from the gate and gazed up.

"Forgive us if we err, Sir Harald," the smaller one with the fine golden beard called back up, "but is not that helmet part of the armor forfeited to our seneschal, Sir Kay, in this tournament just past?"

"What if it is? I still have the use of it for a year, don't I?"

"True, by the best terms of chivalry," the tall, clean-shaven knight conceded; and it may have been only Sir Harald's own guilty conscience that colored the words with suspicion. "We shall most gladly give you the loan of it," Sir Letron went on, "if you will come out and fight one of us."

"Both of you, if you like! Friendly fight, or to the utterance?"

"Honor demands that we warn you," Sir Labigodés explained, "there can be no such thing as friendly combat between us until you have released the gentlemaid whom you hold unlawfully, treacherously, and outrageously as your prisoner."

"I thought so. In other words, you won't go away until and unless I've killed both of you."

"We must respectfully advise you, sir," said Sir Letron, "that we will not go away until the damsel is free; and, if you should kill us twain, other and better of our good King Arthur's noble champions will take our place, until our righteous purpose is achieved."

Sir Harald hurled the swan's legbone down so hard that it hit the water with a greater splash than the swan herself had ever made while alive.

"Or, should you choose to refuse honorable combat," Sir Labigodés added cheerfully, "as is certainly thy prerogative as wrongdoer, we must needs besiege thee in thy brother's rightful castle."

"God's Blood, I stand here ready to fight your whole damn Round Table!" Sir Harald shouted, flinging the beaker of ale after the swan's legbone. "Which one wants to try me first?"

"We both of us burn to break lances with thee, recreant knight, in the cause of the excellent fair maiden," Sir Labigodés answered politely. "But courtesy demands that I defer to my good friend."

"And I," Sir Letron responded, "must equally yield the honor of first trial to my dear comrade, as the worthier and courtlier man."

Sir Harald stared at them open-mouthed. "I'll fight you both at once, bareheaded and unarmored as I stand!"

"No! Oh, no!" cried they both at once.

"That would be the grossest of sins against courtesy," Sir Letron explained in shock, and Sir Labigodés expanded:

"It would be unforgivably, unpardonably rude! No, thou must even make the choice, recreant knight," he added, seeming to regard "recreant knight" and "thou" as the polite and proper terms of address for such as Harald de Folgeste.

"Yes," agreed Sir Letron, "in courtesy, Sir Traitor, we leave the choice to thee."

"Ihesu, Mary, Joseph!" Sir Harald exclaimed, regretting that he had already thrown everything handy. "You won't slough *that* off on me, too! Besiege away, then! Or decide it between yourselves. I am going to finish my dinner!"

With that, he stamped back down to the courtyard, where he found all the people of the castle, except of course those in attendance on the Aloof Fair One, quite naturally gathered to await the outcome. Those in front were squinting out anxiously between the bars of the portcullis.

"But why would you not pick one out and fight him, sir?" the chaplain's son spoke for them all.

"And have him complaining in a thousand words that I ought to have picked his comrade as the better man—or whatever else their courtly little game might be? God's Blood, no! They won't catch me that way!"

Sir Harald looked around and moderated his tones. "I am flattered that all of you felt compelled to interrupt your dinner over this foolishness, but food remains to be eaten. We have no need to worry about siege conditions for a while, anyway."

❖　❖　❖

Meanwhile, shaking their heads sadly, Sir Labigodés and Sir Letron turned their chargers—with some care, seeing that the causeway was just wide enough for them to ride two abreast—and returned to their camp.

"Not only traitor, scoundrel, and churl," Sir Labigodés mourned,

"But, as appears by his refusal to come out and fight, a coward as well," Sir Letron finished.

"And a boastful one at that," Sir Labigodés added, "considering all his bold words before the actual refusal."

Deep within his enshrouding hood, the palmer shook his head. "Whatever else he may have become, and even though his bravery may lie more in rash recklessness and stubborn defiance than true valor, Harald de Folgeste was never a coward."

Although Sir Harald made it clear—by not so much as ordering the heavy outer gates closed, but trusting all to the stout wooden portcullis—that he rather scorned his challengers, it was not quite so ridiculous as might at first glance appear for two knights, four squires, three pages, and a handful of servants to lay siege to an entire castle. If the causeway could be held by a few men against attack, it could equally well be held by one or two against any attempt to leave the island by land. True, the castle could be resupplied by water, and the village of Quillerstone lay barely a quarter of a mile on the mainland beyond the besiegers' camp. But once King Arthur's knights and the palmer had explained the situation to its headmen, the village agreed to keep to itself and provide the castle no succor save what the besiegers might, in extremity, courteously allow by way of food and medicines. Our heroes counted mainly on boredom and bad conscience to work upon those within; and, anyway, they would never have wanted starvation to pinch the very maiden they had come to rescue. Anyone else who happened along would be far likelier to enlist their services on the side of King Arthur's champions than on that of Sir Harald; or, if they chanced to be villains themselves, take their falls from our heroes without even thinking whether they might offer assistance to an unrelated fellow villain.

In the event, however, no passers-by at all having come along that first day, next morning the palmer crossed the causeway an hour after breakfast, to try his own luck.

"Who goes there?" called the blacksmith's son, a lad of twelve, who was serving as sentry that watch.

"Tell Sir Harald de Folgeste," the palmer replied, "that one is here who desires a boon of him."

"But you belong to them over there, don't you?" the boy asked, peering over at the knights' tidy camp.

"I am *with* their party, but not *of* it."

Unwilling to leave his post when anything so exciting as a siege was going on, the boy called his message down to those of his comrades who happened to be about their day's business in the courtyard, some of whom had already noticed the palmer; and shortly Sir Harald himself appeared once again on the battlements above the gate. Today, in polite deference to being under siege, he wore his surcoat, embroidered with the same identifying device as that on his shield, directly over his chainse or undertunic, but no other armor in between.

"Well?" he began. "What boon can I give you that your heroic friends cannot?"

"The boon of bringing words of comfort and good cheer to keep up the spirits of that hapless maiden whom you hold here as prisoner."

Sir Harald laughed.

It was a laugh neither of scorn nor rancor nor malice, but of pure and simple amusement, like a child laughing at the antics of a clever fool. Slumping behind the battlements, he laughed until tears ran down his cheeks, prickly as they were with a three-days' growth. At last, gasping beneath his breath, "He'd do better to keep up the gaoler's spirits for holding such a prisoner," he wiped his eyes, hauled himself back to his feet, turned outward to face the palmer again, and told him: "Sooner than you could comfort her, your friends over there might be able to win her freedom, if they could ever settle who should fight me first."

"They think thee a great coward for refusing to fight yesterday."

Half an hour ago, this pronouncement would have thrown Sir Harald into another fury; but now, still refreshed by his long, cleansing laugh, he answered almost mildly, "And I think them a pair of great fools."

"Would you have me tell them so?"

"I would courteously shout it across to them myself, if . . ." Sir Harald's words trailed away as he leaned farther through the crenel, staring down at the hooded palmer. "Let me see your face, and I may let you in, after all."

"I have taken a vow to let no man see my face until . . ."

"Until?"

"Until the hour is come!"

"What if I were to knock that hood off your head in fair fight?"

"I have taken a further and even holier vow never again to wield any weapon of war in my own native land."

"That's a great pity! Otherwise, you might comfort the Aloof Fair One by fighting me yourself for her freedom."

Commencing to grow angry again, Sir Harald quit the battlements with curt instructions to his people that they should leave the portcullis firmly in its place and not summon him again until somebody on the besiegers' side showed a grain of sense.

"He thinks us fools?" Sir Letron passed it off with a smile. "Well, let him think so, and take what comfort he can in the thought when he lies in dusty and well-deserved defeat."

"Yes," Sir Labigodés agreed, "for what harm can the opinion of a rogue traitor do us? And when you begged admittance for the purpose of offering the poor maiden words of comfort and good cheer?"

"He laughed," the palmer replied without embellishment.

The champions of the Round Table and all their people—with the possible exception of Tamba, who allowed himself a soft chuckle—found this far more serious than Sir Harald's expressed opinion of their own characters.

"Ah! The cruel and cowardly dog!" cried Sir Labigodés.

"Thus callously and unchivalrously to deny his poor captive even the smallest scrap of human comfort in her durance!" added Sir Letron.

"He laughed," the palmer repeated. Although he might have sensed the nature of that laugh while actually overhearing it, he had already had time to forget everything but the bare fact, coupled with his own lack of fully adequate response.

"Am I not a fair soothsayer?" said Tamba. "But, in all fairness to even the worst of villains, we do not truly know that he is denying her all human comfort, only that he refuses her the same from us outside."

The Maid of the Wood spoke up. "We do not even know that he would refuse each and every one of us. Tomorrow, let me try!"

"You, dear child?" Sir Labigodés promptly protested. "Surely, he would roast you whole!"

"And gnaw your sweet bones like an ogre," Sir Letron added.

"To do any of that," she pointed out, "he would first

need to let me in. But Garth told us that Sir Harald has spared the Fair One's honor and never strikes anyone, except other knights. And we all agreed that Garth is honest."

"Honest, surely, but a mere serf nonetheless," argued Sir Labigodés, whose outlook on such matters was not quite as all-encompassing as that of his friend.

"Moreover," added Sir Letron, "though all that the poor, honest fellow told us of his undeserved master may have been true enough when he spoke it, as he himself in his most commendable loyalty understood it to be, in the interim much may have changed."

"I think that we should allow her to try," the palmer said, although without revealing what he had witnessed in the clearing with the page, the cub, and the mother bear.

"Yes! Masters," cried Tamba, "did I not predict truly his response to our friend palmer here? Yet now I foresee and prognosticate that not even a Harald de Folgeste could offer harm to this Maid of the Wood, who will no doubt do as she wishes in any case, with our blessing or without."

So they argued for most of that day and into the evening, the knights fretting over the dangers they imagined to the Maid of the Wood; the palmer and the eldest page stoutly maintaining her cause; and she herself saying relatively little, but that little always quietly, calmly, and to her own point. Emboldened by Tamba's example, the squires, younger pages, and servants also debated the question among themselves, some *pro* and some *contra*; and even the cooks spoke a word or three about it between basting meat and cutting pastry dough.

Sir Labigodés and Sir Letron went to their pallets late that night, fondly imagining that they had carried their case. But in the first light of dawn, while the two champions still dozed, the Maid of the Wood had Tamba bring her the helmet, which, after all, she herself had found.

While the page was fetching it, she asked the palmer, "Can you say how heavy the portcullis of Quillerstone might be?"

"The nails are iron indeed," he answered, "but the bars are of hard wood, and the wheel in the gate-room, which I have seen, is large. The Aloof Fair One might use that wheel to raise the grating with her own white hands, if she were at liberty to do so, and if the key still hangs on its hook outside the gate-room, ready to the watchman's hand."

"Good. I'll try to get it raised for you—early tomorrow morning, most likely. But you must promise me this," she told both palmer and page, for Tamba had come with the helmet in time to hear her words about the portcullis. "Your masters must not wear their armor when they come inside, because Sir Harald will not be wearing his."

"Easy enough to arrange," Tamba answered with a grin. "Their own courtesy will convince them."

Then, before King Arthur's knights were awake to stop her, the Maid of the Wood took Sir Harald's helmet and skipped forth along the causeway.

So disdainful was he of his enemies' might, and at the same time so confident of their courtesy, that Sir Harald had dispensed with a night watch—after all, any belated wayfarers who might otherwise have needed midnight hospitality would meet it from the besiegers—and posted his watchers only during the day. He himself, however, not having passed the best of nights, rose very early to stroll the battlements while waiting for Mass . . . which he usually attended, not out of anything resembling the special piety required to attend a simple, everyday Mass in this our own degenerate age, but merely because in those times it was the custom of all Christendom—even villains—to attend daily Mass whenever one was convenient. It was, perhaps, like their morning news broadcast from Heaven.

He had more than half expected the besiegers to try some new trick today, but he had not expected it to come so early. Nor had he expected it in the form of a rather small maiden who carried a burden the size of a large pumpkin and wore a green kirtle and bliaud with a scarlet wimple and veil, their colors only just discernible in the dawnlight. In wonderment, he bent his steps to the gate-tower. Reaching that vantage point in almost the same moment that she paused before the gate, he leaned over and called bemusedly down to her:

"Do those great fools know you're daring the dragon alone, my damsel?"

"Not yet," she called back. "Is that you, Sir Harald?"

"Coward and recreant knight? The very same."

"Good! I have your helmet for you." She held her burden up so that he could see it as clearly as the light allowed.

He almost chuckled. "That might throw even them into a rare rage."

"Then hadn't you better let me in before they find out?"

"What ransom do you ask—to fight me or to comfort my 'prisoner' with words of cheer?"

"Oh, I certainly wouldn't ask to fight you! A few moments with the Aloof Fair One might be welcome, woman to woman."

"Woman to woman, the sovereign liege lady of my heart's undivided adoration might just be bearable." Saluting the newcomer with a wave, Sir Harald took the key from its hook beside the door, let himself into the gateroom, and quickly raised the portcullis just high enough to admit her. It rose almost soundlessly, being well oiled for ease in operating the mechanism; and he lowered it again as soon as, watching through the courtside window, he saw her safely within.

"Why, you aren't even wearing your sword!" she observed, holding his helmet out to him as he came down to join her.

"Why should I, safe within my own castle walls? Because a pair of courteous buffoons camp at my threshold and please to call it a siege?"

She chuckled. "And to think they called you—no, not a dragon—but an ogre."

"Did they?" Feeling that recreancy had at least freed him from some of the courtly niceties, he went on, "And you, my lady? Is there any name you prefer to be called by?"

"Whatever name anyone may choose to lend me," she answered merrily, "or no name at all, if that is what you please."

"At least it is not 'Aloof.'"

"Nor 'Fair,' neither!" she added, laughing. "Where are you keeping her, sir?"

"From hour to hour, I can never be sure. The day before yesterday, at dinnertime, she was at the top of the North Tower. She may have changed her apartments several score of times since."

"Ah! You have given her the freedom of the castle, then?"

"It pleases Her Aloofness to pretend otherwise, whenever she is settled in one apartment or another or back to the first for half an hour. No one ever sets eyes on her outside those various 'prison' chambers or on her way between them. Our priest and his son, and a few others, keep up with her whereabouts through her serving-women; we can find out from one of them where my Lady Butterfly may have lighted for the moment, whenever you wish. She might even come down to Mass today," he added, neither very hopefully nor particularly wistfully. "How soon will you want to return to the besiegers' camp?"

"No hurry," she assured him. "Certainly not until after Mass."

The Aloof Fair One did not appear in the chapel for Mass, but her three serving-women did, bearing the message: "The poor captive most humbly begs that her stern captor generously permit his priest to bring the Sacrament to her cell whenever his leisure might afford." Again rolling his eyes Heavenward, Sir Harald told the chaplain to go to her immediately after the service or whenever else he liked.

Meanwhile, Sirs Letron and Labigodés, clad in full armor and followed by their squires, likewise armed, rode their warhorses over the causeway and up to the gate, where at the moment Garth was on watch duty, standing in for the fletcher's daughter.

"Hail, good Garth, thou best and most loyal of servitors!" Sir Letron cried, recognizing him and still eager to make what amends he could for his terrible *faux pas* of two days past. "Be'est thy master within?"

"Are Your Worships showing a grain of sense today?" Garth replied, anxious and respectful both at once. "He said not to bother him again until you were."

"If it be sensible," Sir Labigodés responded, "to fear for the safety of a young maiden, our most tender and dearly beloved companion, now within the hold of a recreant who hath already most notoriously seized and made prisoner another fair maid—if such be the case, yes, I should say that we show great sense indeed."

Garth, who had not yet seen the Maid of the Wood since meeting their party on the road, scratched his head. "The lady who was with you? I didn't know. . . ."

But by now, Mass being over, Sir Harald and the Maid of the Wood had come out of the chapel and, hearing the clamor at the gate, crossed from the inner courtyard to the outer and thence up to the portcullis, through which they observed the champions' party.

"I may be a recreant ogre," Sir Harald growled for their information, "but this damsel came here freely, and freely she shall return to you whenever she wishes. Come back when you can show me more sense than this!" So saying, he turned on his heel and stepped several paces away, where he paused, signifying that he had no more to say to King Arthur's men but would wait for his new guest.

"Didn't they give you my message?" she asked the heroes through the portcullis.

"They did," admitted Sir Letron, "but—"

"Why, then, please go back, take off your armor, and wait. Don't worry about me. I'm perfectly safe."

With that, she rejoined her host, leaving the armed men outside to return to their camp and obey her, wriggling out of their armor, but spending most of that day speaking of this development in tones of wonder and apprehension.

Like other well-regulated castles, Quillerstone had a small, lovely enclosed garden of herbs and flowers, which ought to have belonged strictly to the mistress of the fortalice, her chosen ladies in waiting, and her gardeners. Since Quillerstone had had no mistress for many years, this garden had come to be used by the priest's family and any others who cared to help maintain or enjoy it. Two days ago Sir Harald had hoped that the Aloof Fair One would claim it for herself, but so far it was virtually the only place the castle had to offer suitable for a gentlemaiden's privacy that she had *not* tried, nor seemed likely to try within the foreseeable future. Thither, then, he led the Maid of the Wood to wait until the good priest should finish his errand of mercy.

"What is that key you wear at your belt?" she asked as they walked, the castle's various dogs and cats running about her legs as enthusiastically as ever they had fawned on him.

"The key to this place," he replied, with a tap to the wall of the little building they chanced just then to be passing. "The Hall of the Quiller Couch."

"The famous couch that devours anyone who sits on it?"

Sir Harald nodded ruefully. "Anyone and everyone, save the castle's rightful lord and his heir. That is why I keep it locked and the key safe upon my own person. In my grandfather's time, and even my father's, the castle lost several of its young boys and a cook's daughter, who crept in mischievously and could not resist trying it out."

She observed, "You treat this key with greater care than the one to the gate-room."

"That one's safe enough. The watchman must be able to raise or lower the portcullis at need, and anyone who dared leave unauthorized at night would wake somebody up while trying to get the horse and supplies needed for any such escapade."

Of course, now that King Arthur's champions had set up their camp just on the other side of the causeway, a refugee would need only such a small lamp or candle as anyone might find ready to hand. Perhaps Sir Harald half hoped, behind some secret door in his mind, that his lovely, disdainful prize would take the trouble to avail herself of the opportunity. But in his stubbornness he might well refuse to open that small door in his own mind, and the Maid of the Wood refrained from opening it for him, falling instead to chitchat of other matters.

Although along with the Sacrament, the priest took up the message that the Aloof Fair One had a newcomer of her own sex waiting to see her, she kept the poor cleric with her for the entire morning, complaining to him of her captor. What she said, the good chaplain never repeated and largely forgot, quietly letting it be believed that she had spent all those hours under the Seal of Confession—although, in fact, she had not.

As for Sir Harald, he passed the forepart of the day in the garden conversing with his guest, which he found far more congenial than sitting alone with himself while striving to meditate upon the manifold perfections of his reluctant liege lady; and, when midday arrived, he escorted the Maid of the Wood to table without remembering to send anyone to ask whether or not the Aloof Fair One might deign to take her dinner in the great hall.

After dinner—the best meal that the castle folk had enjoyed in several days, since for the first time since his return their castellan was in easy good humor, despite his prisoner somewhere above and the besiegers outside—he and his new guest returned to the garden.

He had never before noticed what a great number of living creatures it contained. Truly, it was a Noah's Ark in miniature! Birds of at least a dozen kinds seemed to redouble their song as the Maid of the Wood sat in their midst, and sometimes they even fluttered down to perch a few moments lightly upon her head or shoulder, paying no heed to the castle's tawniest tabby, who lay purring in her lap and graciously returned the feathered ones' indifference. Butterflies, too, alighted from time to time in her veil or gown, there to fold and unfold their wings as if glad to serve her as jewels. Once a great, glowing green beetle briefly played the same part. Another time, Sir Harald plucked a brilliant orange caterpillar from her sleeve and watched it inch up his own left hand, amusing himself to fancy that it seemed discontent at the change, until it reached his wrist, when he shook it away to the ground . . . where, strangely enough, an earthworm seemed almost to be caressing her shoe. Toads and frogs, lizards and snails, he saw as if for the first time since his boyhood, in their own whimsical beauty. Once a shining emerald-green snake with red eyes—that would have made another maiden scream—slid, gentle as the earthworm, over her toe, without disturbing either her, the tabby's kittens playing round her ankles, or even the mouse that he could almost have sworn he glimpsed hiding in her hem. Now and then a bee or wasp would buzz close, never threatening to sting, as though offering homage; and a fat spider spun a web between two leaves of a flower so near to where she sat that, when it had finished and for some reason crawled away to the blossom, he carefully picked the silken lace with its supporting leaves and presented it to her, joking that the little creature had given her a gift.

Before long, he was to wonder if those few hours had been, at least in part, a dream. Certainly it seemed a rude awakening when the fletcher's daughter brought word down at last that the Aloof Fair One had somewhat recovered from the fit of fainting despair she had fallen into after dinner in her own rooms, and thought she might be strong enough, now, to face a visitor from that blessed world outside her prison walls, which she herself might never, as she feared, enjoy the freedom of again.

The Maid of the Wood found the Aloof Fair One industriously winding colored embroidery silks upon snail shells, which Sir Harald's grandmother had long ago laid by in a small coffer for such a purpose, and looking no more pallid and indisposed than a juggler in the middle of his performance. At her visitor's appearance, she clapped her hands and briskly bade her attendants go into the next room and begin packing for another move, since she had decided the light was best in the apartment where they had first put her, after all.

"I was sorry to hear of your illness," the Maid of the Wood said as the priest's wife, fletcher's daughter, and falconer's sister left them alone.

"Was *he*?"

"More annoyed than sorry, I think."

"Good!" declared the Aloof Fair One.

"I don't think he believed for a minute that you were truly fainting and weak."

"No more was I! But, of course, he cannot be sure. No annoyance I can cause that man is sufficient repayment for what he has done in seizing and imprisoning me."

"It was very wrong of him," the Maid of the Wood agreed. "Did you know that he leaves the key to the gate-room on a hook beside the door, that he has not bothered to set any night watchman now that King Arthur's knights are camped at the far end of the causeway courteously besieging the castle, and that—this is on the authority of the palmer who was traveling, entirely by chance, alongside you when Sir Harald seized you, and who seems to be fairly well acquainted with Quillerstone—you could raise the portcullis yourself, with your own white hands?"

"These unfortunate serving-women have told me as

much," the Aloof One replied. "But if I were to make good my own escape into my champions' camp, what might become of Sir Harald then?"

"I'm not sure," the Maid of the Wood admitted. "But in any case, his name is going to be disgraced in every court throughout Christendom as soon as word of all this gets out."

"That much, he knows. He has all but boasted of it as a reason why I should accept his love!"

"Oh, dear!" said the Maid of the Wood. "Well, they may want to send him to King Arthur for judgment anyway."

"Would even that be enough?" The Aloof Fair One shook her head. "I mean to cause him as much pain as he has caused me grief. For this reason, and perhaps others, I might do well to be rescued by better knights than he, rather than escape through my own efforts. Still, I will consider the matter."

"If you should decide to escape tonight," the Maid of the Wood begged her, "could you please send me word? I'll arrange to sleep here in this apartment. Having left it just now, you won't want it back again very soon, will you?"

"My dear," the Aloof Fair One assured her, "I *want* no apartment at all beneath Sir Harald's roof. But, no, I can make shift with my other half-dozen lighting places for as long as you might require this one, which is not my favorite in any case."

The Maid of the Wood stayed to supper in the great hall, and nothing that the Aloof Fair One had said to her in any way altered her former attitude toward her host. There was much laughter and jollity over supper that night, even more than there had been at the midday meal; and when at length the last merry tale had been told and sentimental song sung, and the guest announced that they had kept her too late and now she must spend the night in the castle, something much akin to a cheer echoed around the vasty chamber.

Following her request, Garth showed her to the apartment that the Aloof Fair One had vacated that afternoon. At the door, she hesitated. She had left instructions that Sir Labigodés and Sir Letron must come unarmored, but not unarmed—else how could they arrest their malefactor or wreak any righteous work at all? "Garth," she said, "good Garth, please tell no one, but tomorrow something may happen. It will be safest if your master finds no sword or other weapon at all close to his hand."

"Safest for whom, my lady?"

"Safest for Sir Harald. These two courteous Knights of the Round Table will never strike nor allow injury to any unarmed foe."

Garth nodded soberly. But after her door was shut, he muttered to himself, "Safer for his body, maybe. Not for his proud spirit."

All the other folk of the castle, except perhaps those dancing attendance upon the Aloof Fair One, went to their beds well contented, with little remembrance that they lay under siege by two of their sovereign King Arthur's noble champions. As for Sir Harald himself, he kept no diary— few people, if any, in those days of precious parchment and laborious letters had ever even imagined such a thing as a personal diary—but if he had, he might have written in it that night: *She is like the sister we should have had.* She had even made him forget the tedious itch of his fledgling new beard.

The Aloof Fair One sent no message that night, and an hour before dawn the Maid of the Wood rose from her bed and went quietly, by waning moonlight, to the battlements above the gate. Here, sure enough, she found the key unguarded on its hook beside the gate-room door. Smoothly entering, she relocked the door from the inside and settled down to wait, singing as if unaware that she sang, though as softly as a feather laid on spun wool.

At about the same degree of dawn twilight as on the morning before, but today because for the first time in several nights he had slept soon and soundly, and awakened refreshed, Sir Harald crossed the still-drowsy courtyard and mounted to the battlements. He seemed to hear, faintly and as though muffled by distance, some soft measures of song; but, fancying it the lingering remnants of a pleasant dream, he never looked toward the gate-room door, nor noticed its missing key. Instead, humming in time with the imaginary—as he supposed—music, he briefly rubbed the stubbly shadow that covered his cheeks and chin (he had made up his mind not to see the Aloof Fair One again until it was a full-grown beard once more), then rested both hands on the stoneworks and amused himself with gazing at his enemies' encampment. Seeing it abuzz with more early activity than he would have expected—considerably more than at this time yesterday morning—he never looked around and down to observe Garth, whose day customarily began at about this hour, who today had watched him cross the courtyard, and who now was carrying his sword half furtively to the foot of the battlements.

So well-oiled was the mechanism, so loud Sir Harald's own humming and so dreamy his musings, that it hardly penetrated his awareness how the portcullis was rising until he beheld men pelting from the camp to the causeway.

Waking to danger, he leaned far enough over to confirm the fact, then whirled to the door and grabbed for the key. His hand met bare stone and wooden doorframe. A few heartbeats of staring; of venting his anger in a hard if futile tug on the empty keyhook; of kicking the door, hammering it with both fists and loud shouts, then kicking it again until it shook . . . but no one answered, no one emerged, and the portcullis continued to rise. He directed another glare at the causeway—they were almost over, the lot of them, and if in the sinking fury of the moment he wondered that they came without horse or armor, he set it down to intended stealth. One more fierce kick to the door, and, shouting the alarm, he began his dash down the stairs.

At their foot, Garth wordlessly handed Sir Harald his sword. Seizing it, he sprang into position directly in front of the opening.

Tall, long-legged Sir Letron—this was to prove relevant—had reached the gateway first, but there waited for Sir Labigodés to take the lead. For once, this was not entirely pure and unmitigated courtesy: The portcullis had risen just high enough to admit the shorter knight readily, but the taller one had to duck his head a little. At their heels came their squires, pages, and servants—all their company except the cooks, and even they were not completely unrepresented, for the palmer, in deference to his vow never again to wield any weapon of war, waved a cook's ladle instead.

All these had followed, however, only in case of need. Even as they crowded inside, Sir Labigodés commanded, "Stand ready, good men," and Sir Letron explained, "Attack no one without provocation."

Hearing this, Sir Harald shouted to the castle people, who were naturally thronging to the outer court behind him: "Stand back! They want me alone," and waited, mending his stance and holding his sword at the ready.

"My dear good friend," Sir Labigodés said to Sir Letron, stepping a little aside, "having myself enjoyed the honor of being first through the gates, thanks entirely to your kind courtesy, I must beg to return you the honor of being first to fight him."

"No, no, my best of comrades!" Sir Letron replied. "Along with the entry, I proffered you the first attack, being myself unworthy of that privilege for reasons that you in your generosity seem already to have forgotten."

Sir Harald rested the tip of his sword on the ground and stared at them.

"Dearest Sir Letron," Sir Labigodés urged his friend, "believe me, in your finely tempered soul you blame yourself overmuch for the tiniest of faults! I pray you, make amends by serving as the first to teach this dog his lesson."

"My most amiable Sir Labigodés, you offer me this in the purest generosity of a noble heart, knowing that once you have taught him his lesson, there will be naught remaining for me to chastise."

"*Someone* attack me!" Sir Harald shouted, lifting his sword again.

Sir Labigodés glanced at him as if he were more annoyance than threat, and then went on to Sir Letron: "But, my dear good friend, again you do yourself too little justice! In what way will there be any more of him remaining for my gentle correction after you have fought him first, than the other way around?"

"If that were true, my best of companions, it would be all the more reason why I should not chance robbing you of your opportunity."

"God's Blood!" bawled Sir Harald. "I'll fight you both at once!" And he charged.

No one doubted these champions' courage and prowess. Separately, they had done and were yet to do countless great deeds and right many wrongs. And, if their united approach fell a little short in some ways, they nevertheless displayed precision teamwork in stepping so far apart that Sir Harald could not easily reach either one, but had to stand baffled between them, staring back and forth at first one and then the other.

"Sir!" Labigodés cried, sounding more shocked than at any of Sir Harald's previous peccadilloes. "Would you force us to the height of all bad manners?"

"Two against one!" added Sir Letron. "'Twould be unforgivably rude. For shame, sir, for shame!"

At about this moment, the Maid of the Wood appeared on the scene, having descended from the battlements with the gate-room key still in her hand. Taking in the scene, she shook her head at Sir Harald's sword and exclaimed sorrowfully, "Oh, Garth!"

Sir Harald had assumed—as well as he could assume anything in the rush of things—that his fair prisoner had chosen to take her revenge this way, rather than make a decent midnight escape of it. Now, his guest's "Oh, Garth!", her place on the bottom stair, and the key that she carried quite openly, combined to give him a fairly accurate idea of the true state of affairs. To understand what he did next, we must remember two things: his temper, and the fact that wiser heads than his would have judged his guest—this maiden whom he had already begun to love like a sister—guilty of betraying him to his enemies.

Seizing the Maid of the Wood by one wrist, he hauled her at a run through the outer to the inner courtyard, fiercely waving a *"Keep back!"* at the castle folk with his sword. Confused and alarmed, they parted for him and then milled about, unsure whether to follow him or his command. Only Garth attempted the former course, and this put him among the invaders, whose pursuit the rest of Quillerstone's people, insofar as they were doing anything, were managing to baffle and befuddle.

Meanwhile, Sir Harald reached the Hall of the Quiller Couch, where he held the maiden caged between his arms as, dropping his sword at his feet, he shot back the bolt and unlocked the door. Shouting, "Don't sit on it," he thrust her inside, slammed the door, and dropped the bolt into place.

And stood there for a heartbeat or two, quivering, staring horrified at his own hands where they still rested on the bolt.

The command he had just given her was exactly the kind that invites its hearer to disobey. . . .

Inside the small hall, the Quiller Beast gave a great roar.

"Oh, God!" Sir Harald cried, shooting the bolt free again, snatching his sword up from the ground, and kicking the door open, all in so near the same motion as made no difference.

His guest had indeed sat on the couch, was sitting on it still, and it had indeed turned into the Quiller Lion. But it stood still at its ease on the dais. The spines on its back lay down flat and smooth as fur, and it was bending its huge, tawny head beneath her hand, fawning like a dog and purring like a cat as she petted and caressed it.

Staggering forward, Sir Harald let his sword fall again, this time at her feet, and knelt. The lion growled at him, but he paid it little heed. "Lady," he said, "this can only mean that you should be mistress here! To you, I surrender."

"For once, Folgeste, you have made a shrewd move," a voice said from the doorway. The palmer had been first to break through the confusion and reach them. "You chose well in proffering your surrender to the Lady of the Animals."

Sir Harald stood, turned, and frowned a moment at the man in the hood. At length he said, deliberately: "I did not do it to escape due punishment."

"Prove your proud words," the palmer replied, punctuating his sentence by flinging the cook's ladle he had been carrying into a corner of the chamber. "My vow does not forbid me the free use of these fists God Himself put at the ends of my wrists for a fair exchange of buffets, man to man!"

The left-handed knight stepped forward at once, suddenly remembered that he no longer enjoyed the freedom of his own actions, and looked back at the Lady of the Animals.

By now Garth and the other castle people, as well as our two Round Table champions and their men, had all— or most of them—arrived as close to the Hall of the Quiller

Couch as they could fit. As long as the palmer stood in the doorway, no one else could actually get inside the building; but Sirs Labigodés and Letron, with nobody to dispute their precedence except—inversely—each other, took their places looking over his shoulders, while Garth and the ebullient Tamba squeezed in closer than they ought properly to have dared, peeping over the champions' shoulders.

"For now," the palmer told them, "stand a little back. The traitor and I are about to play a game of Trade the Buffet, provided that she who has just accepted his surrender grants him her permission."

Looking from the palmer back to Sir Harald, the Maid of the Wood smiled and nodded.

Sir Harald stepped forward again and presented his black-stubbled chin. "Strike," he said. "Do your worst."

The palmer shook his head. "For the badness of thy conscience, I grant thee the first blow," he answered, striding farther into the room.

For a moment, Sir Harald hesitated. Then, half growling, "Oh, no! Oh, no! You won't catch me into playing this damn Courtesy Game, too!" he drew back his left fist and dealt so fierce a buffet that the palmer staggered backward against Sir Letron. That knight helped keep him upright, but in his near fall the hood tumbled down to his shoulders, revealing a blond-bearded face with keen blue eyes and fine, handsome features, crowned by a head of golden hair.

After one nod of confirmed suspicion, Sir Harald resumed his stance, head a little back and chin a little forward. Next minute, with a tooth-jarring blow, the palmer sent him reeling backward to fall and lie stunned at the haunch of the lion, which moved out of the way just in time.

The Maid of the Wood had jumped to her feet. "Oh, dear!" she said, eyeing the fallen knight. "I hope you haven't damaged my prisoner too much, Sir Godfrey!"

"Sir Godfrey?" cried Sir Labigodés. "Sir Godfrey le Blond?"

"The trueborn lord of Quillerstone?" echoed Sir Letron.

By now, of course, the revelation of the palmer's identity could have come as a surprise to nobody else; and it may well be that Sirs Letron and Labigodés merely feigned their astonishment for the sake of good manners.

"The same," Sir Godfrey acknowledged, mounting the dais and seating himself on the Quiller Lion. Strange to say, although it accepted his backside without growl, protest, or ruffled spine, it did not turn into the couch again. This rather disappointed him, but he went on: "My bastard half-brother had recognized me long before he struck his blow."

The Maid of the Wood, having satisfied herself that Sir Harald would recover, took her place on the lion's back next to Sir Godfrey. Where it had merely accepted him, it welcomed her with loud purring.

Meanwhile, Arthur's two knights had come all the way into the building, along with Garth, Tamba, and such other people as could fit and dared arrange themselves in the room, all at a respectful distance from the lion. The younger of Sir Letron's pages, the one who had shot the rabbit and later been saved from the mother bear, quietly sank to his knees and stared round-eyed at the lady and the lion throughout the entire ensuing scene.

"I think," Sir Godfrey went on, "that he already began to suspect, that morning I stood before him at my own castle's gate, suing for admittance."

Staggering halfway up, Sir Harald sat on the edge of the dais, buried his head in his arms, and said nothing.

"But if thou knewest who thy brother was, recreant knight," Sir Labigodés inquired, bewildered or politely pretending to be so, "how dared thou strike that blow?"

"Or, at the least, deliver it so unrestrainedly?" Sir Letron qualified.

Sir Harald's shoulders may have shaken a little, but he neither lifted his head nor answered a word.

"Let him be on this point," Sir Godfrey said, rubbing his beard. "I proposed the game, I gave him the first blow, and I think he struck hard so that I would strike the harder."

"There might be hope for the fellow yet!" cried Tamba.

"Hush, Tamba," Sir Letron told him, "before I change thy status from page to fool." But he and Sir Labigodés exchanged a glance that said they might be persuaded to share Tamba's theory.

"Nonetheless," Sir Labigodés objected, "there remains his attempt to usurp your castle and property."

"Your Worships," Garth put in, "might I speak as to that?"

Sir Godfrey said, "Speak, Garth."

"Well, as for trying to sit on the Quiller Couch, my lord, that was what kept telling us all you must still be alive. And he's kept your castle well these years, my lord, and all of us with it. Whether he was keeping it for himself or for you, I don't see how it makes that much difference, now you're home again, after all. And then, that day I met you and these other noble knights on the road, I guessed who you were, too, but I never told him anything about my suspicion, to my shame. And that morning you came suing for admittance, sir, didn't he ask you then to doff your hood, and didn't you refuse?"

Sir Godfrey nodded. "I had vowed never again to show my face by daylight or firelight until I stood once more within my own walls. In all justice, had I broken that vow at my brother's behest . . . But, my lords, we forget the main matter!" he cried, his voice hardening again like red-hot iron plunged suddenly into cold water. "Let it never be forgot how he seized a maiden journeying alone, to imprison her by force, against her will, here . . . in *my* castle!"

"The Aloof Fair One!" exclaimed Sir Letron.

"Yes, by my beard!" Sir Labigodés added, looking around. "Where is she? Is she still safe and unharmed?"

Speaking for the first time since she had called Sir Godfrey by name, the Maid of the Wood laughed merrily. "Perfectly safe, though you may have to play Go Seek for her. But aren't all of you forgetting something else? Sir Harald is my prisoner, not yours! He made his surrender to me."

"By his own words," Sir Godfrey reminded her, "he did not do it to escape the punishment that is justly his due."

The Maid of the Wood looked at the left-handed knight, who throughout all of this had made neither sound nor movement, save for an occasional small trembling of the shoulders. (In those days, no one considered it unmanly to weep, in appropriate circumstances; and no one would have called the circumstances anything but appropriate for this knight to weep a little just now.)

Sir Letron was fretting, "And should not our noble King Arthur, through us his poor representatives, take precedence as rightful gaoler and judge of all criminal offenders?"

"Precedence even over that of a free and noble maiden?" replied Sir Labigodés, for once at a loss on a matter of courtly protocol. "I'm not sure. . . ."

"Sir Harald!" said the Maid of the Wood. "Would you transfer your surrender to any of these others? Or would you rather remain my prisoner, whatever advice I might take about what to do with you?"

In answer, he half raised his head at last, knelt before her with bowed back, and presented her his folded hands. When she took them between her own, she turned them far enough to put a very humble kiss upon her ring finger, even though it bore no ring. Then he stood and left the hall without a word.

"I think that settles that!" the Maid of the Wood said in triumph. "He remains my prisoner, sirs! Leave him alone for now."

And, nobody disputing her claim, and not a few of the castle people—especially the ones so young that they hardly remembered Sir Godfrey—feeling more divided in their loyalties than clear as to what it was all about anyway, they left him alone.

He went directly to his own apartment, where he shut himself in for two days and two nights, refusing everything except bread and water.

Meanwhile, they finally located the Aloof Fair One and her three serving-women, who had been so busy moving again from one set of rooms to another that they had remained utterly unaware of the storming and conquest of the castle. As soon as she recognized in Sir Godfrey the palmer alongside whom she had traveled for a few hours prior to her abduction, she repaired with him to the enclosed garden, where they sat in pleasant conversation, accepting all the dainty refreshment that the castle had to offer.

The Quiller Lion remained a lion, although it could, when it pleased, lie for an hour or two as quietly as any couch, and rarely raised its spines unless provoked. Fortunately, it had become as calm as a housecat and as amiable as a puppy—unless deliberately aroused—and by

dinnertime that first day the castle folk had grown accustomed to having it pad curiously about the place. In time,
one grows accustomed to almost anything.

On the second day, Sir Harald requested three things:
the chaplain, a razor, and a bowl of red paint.

"He is wrestling with his angel," said the Maid of the
Wood. "Let him have the razor and the paint."

"And the priest, my lady?" said Garth, who had
brought her the message.

She looked surprised. "Why, of course, the priest! It is
not for me or anybody else to come between spiritual
counsel and anyone who requests it."

Sir Godfrey and the Aloof Fair One were still conversing alone with each other in the garden.

On the third morning, Sir Harald emerged at last. He
paused in his doorway when he found the Quiller Lion
resting there; but it only purred at him and licked his
ankle, so he stepped cautiously around it and proceeded to
the busier parts of the castle.

He had shaved his beard off for good and all, and he
had altered his device a little, painting the top half of its
bend bright red, with a deliberately jagged line where it
met the still-black part a little above the center point of the
shield. He carried it with feigned carelessness as, wearing
a face half defiant and half diffident, he prowled
Quillerstone until he found the Maid of the Wood playing
chess with Tamba in the open kitchen garden, the Aloof
Fair One and Sir Godfrey still being in occupation of the
small enclosed garden.

Going down on one knee before her, he said in
Tamba's presence, as he had been prepared to say in the
presence of any witnesses whatever, whoever, and how
many soever: "My lady. I am rightly called Folgeste, for my
mad and foolish deeds, as when I shut you in with that
fierce beast—as he had always shown himself to me. But
when I saw that you had taken no harm from my rash
anger, it was as if a small bird sang into my heart a note
of purest joy. If you will, pray allow me to call you my Lady
Joiselette."

"Of course," she answered, taking his hands between
hers for the second time. "It's a lovely name—one of the
best I've ever worn. And I like what you've done to your

shield, though I suppose, by the rules, you probably ought to have begged my permission first."

When Sir Godfrey and the Aloof Fair One reappeared at last, it was to announce that she had told him her true name, although, following that ancient custom, neither of them would impart it to anyone else until after their wedding. The news that Quillerstone was finally to have a real mistress again somewhat comforted its people for losing the only master they had known these last six years . . . for it had been arranged by now, with the agreement of those good knights Labigodés and Letron, that Sir Harald might have the rest of his year's grace to find the Knight of the Black Chevron or otherwise win, if he could, the ransom price of the horse and arms he owed Sir Kay, before presenting himself at King Arthur's court.

Joiselette, as everyone had been calling her by dinnertime of the same day, would travel alongside him, and Tamba alongside Joiselette. The career page had proposed to Sir Letron that his transfer to her service would relieve the imbalance in the combined parties of the two courteous champions even more handily than his serving them on alternate days had done up until now.

Taking his trueborn brother a little aside, Sir Harald said, "Forgive me, Godfrey. This was not the homecoming I had planned for you, those first several years."

To which Sir Godfrey replied, "Always take care what you vow, dear brother! Had I been able to show you my face earlier, our exchange of buffets might never have taken place. And then, your worst crime brought me a bride!" (Though this last was not said within hearing of the Aloof Fair One.)

He then released Garth into Sir Harald's service permanently, with a promise to do as much for the faithful serf's wife and children, if and when the hour should come. He also made Joiselette a present of the lion, which further comforted the people of Quillerstone, since, tame though the beast seemed as long as the Maid of the Wood remained in the castle, none of them could feel entirely sure of its temper once she had gone away.

They left the following morning after Mass and breakfast: three men; half a dozen assorted mounts and pack animals, including Sir Harald's great black charger Goblin; and the Quiller Lion, on whose smoothened back rode Joiselette. Saying—and no one argued long with the Lady of the Animals—that it might be safer to resemble a monk than a fine maiden, she had returned her borrowed finery to the knights who had lent it from their emergency provisions, and wore the palmer's cast-off robe, which the priest's wife had cut down to fit her. Only, in the fine weather, she left its hood thrown back upon her shoulders.

And as they departed, her song drifted back:

> "Oh, Everywhere, Whose mercies fold
> And wrap us all against the cold,
> Reveal Thy ways to meek and bold!"

Sir Letron and Sir Labigodés, however, stayed for the wedding.

PART THE SECOND:
The Mirror Truth

They were sitting about their fire in the twilight, eating cakes hot from the embers of a campsite oven and sharing the crumbs with the small animals gathered around Joiselette, when Tamba inquired conversationally, "What way shall we turn tomorrow—south, west, or north?"

He did not name east because Quillerstone lay behind them in that direction, although they were by now well beyond the lands Sir Harald and his serf Garth had known all their lives. Therefore—and also because the page was looking to Joiselette—the left-handed knight said nothing.

He was not, however, to escape so easily. Passing Tamba's glance along to him, the spritely maiden said, "It's your quest, after all, Sir Harald."

While by the rules of chivalry he was at present her prisoner, in her great courtesy she never so named him except when necessary to curb some new foolish impulse of his. These impulses were very cumbersome for a man who disliked making a fool of himself. It was one matter to wear the surname "de Folgeste," quite another to be laughed at for meriting it.

In answer to his lady's implied question, he stood, frowned all around as far as eye could see in the gathering gloom—which was not far, surrounded as they were by forest—and said, "Well, one of us may dream about the Black Chevron Knight tonight. That's as good a way to choose our direction as any."

"Spoken like a true alchemist," Tamba approved.

They settled their supper with such entertainment as they could furnish one another in lieu of jongleur or minstrel: The career page could recite many a courtly romance, the serf recount selections from his store of rustic anecdotes, the Maid of the Wood lead them all in melodious songs of Compline, and her pets of the evening amuse them with various affectionate antics. Then, an hour after eating, they laid them down to sleep, Joiselette gently pillowed on the Quiller Lion.

When they woke next morning, it was she who began by asking, eagerly, "Well, good Garth, what did you dream?"

"About the great tournament at Tenebroc," the serf said shortly. "At least, it must have been. It seemed to be south of here. But I never saw my lord of the black chevron."

"And I," said Tamba, "dreamed of Sir Labigodés and my old master Sir Letron, deferring to each other about possession of a certain map, both of them insisting that the other should take the high honor of pointing out to us where lies north, as if that much we could not easily see for ourselves. But of the Black Chevron Knight I fear that I saw no more in my dream than I have ever seen with my own two sparkling eyes whilst awake. And you, good my lady?" he added to Joiselette. "What dreamed you?"

"Only what I always dream."

"Which is—permitting your humble page to hazard a guess—about your Everywhere?"

She nodded, smiling, and sang:

> "Of Everywhere, and everyone,
> And every race that can be run,
> And every thread that can be spun,
> But words to tell it, there are none.

"So it doesn't seem to help us very much, I'm afraid," she added sadly to Sir Harald.

He sighed. "The rogue never showed his shield in my dreams, either. But there were two maidens. One of them seemed to be wearing armor—that was strange. And there was some sort of cave or long cavern filled with reflecting pools or mirrors. The second maiden, the one without the armor, walked through them and came out wearing a coronet of thin gold and flowers on her head. Then she turned and said, 'West,' and started singing . . . except that the singing was yours, my lady," he told Joiselette.

"And a gentler awakening than any rooster," Tamba put in. "Or any songbird of the woods, come to that! Well, sir, I should call it clear enough that our way lies westward."

❖   ❖   ❖

Westward, then, they rode, in three days encountering four separate knights along their way. Two of these knights were riding on missions for their various lords, and two were white-armored virgins in their first-year tours of errantry. Sir Harald jousted with and was unhorsed by each of the four in turn, but won three of the ensuing bouts of swordplay. So he would still have come out ahead, except that he had prudently fought all four encounters in friendship and for pure love of arms alone (that is, to keep in practice), agreeing ahead of time that there should be no question of spoils or ransom.

On the fourth day, they came late in the afternoon to a wide, purling river. There they made their camp for the night, to wake at dawn in a strangely comfortable silver mist that rose from the river like a great, swansdown cloud seeking its wonted place in the heavens. As the fog wreathed itself away into the blue sky above, they wound northward along the bank until they found a shallow ford, marked with bright sparkles where the water glanced and dimpled over a track of river pebbles.

A mounted figure waited on the far bank, as if guarding the ford. Sir Harald started on seeing that it was a beautiful woman with long dark hair and piercing, steel-gray eyes, a haughty smirk, and a breastplate in the ancient style, who sat astride a buttercream steed, with mane and tail like sun shining on milk, as proud as her rider.

"Lady," Joiselette called out to this personage, "will you let us cross today?"

The Warrior Woman grinned, saluted the Maid of the Wood—who sat, as usual, amidst a traveling court of wildlife—and answered, "Lady, that depends."

"Depends upon what?" Tamba made bold to inquire.

"Upon whether you really want to cross, whether you pass the test, and how badly you want to fight me."

Sir Harald rode Goblin into the ford up to his hind fetlocks and replied, "Madame, you may want a fight, but I will not give you one!"

"Afraid?" she asked with a mocking smile.

Sensing the anger that coursed through his rider, Goblin snorted and tossed his head.

"Afraid? You'll find me ready and willing to defend

myself. I think the Code of Chivalry allows me that much?"
Sir Harald added that last with a glance at Joiselette. "But
knighthood forbids me to raise arms against any woman.
Garth!" he went on, turning Goblin back toward the bank.
"Give me my shield and hold my sword for me."

"Good answer," said the Warrior Woman. "Garth, don't
bother."

Tamba took the word again. "But as to that first provi-
sion of yours, brave madam, do we really wish to cross
today? And, if so, why?"

The Warrior Woman said in reply, "Oh, I don't know.
Maybe because of the tournament."

"Tournament?" Tamba asked eagerly. "What tournament?"

"The one the new lady of Wisten of the Mists is holding
in hopes of finding herself a worthy lord."

"I have no interest," Sir Harald said, still smarting from
the matter of the Aloof Fair One and Quillerstone, "in
becoming lord of any strange new lady's heart and lands."

"Did I ever say any knight had to accept the grand
prize, whether he won the tournament or not? The new
lady of Wisten isn't interested in forcing any man, just in
seeing what kind of talent her little tournament turns up."

Sir Harald looked around at his companions. Garth,
who had never seen any tournament except the one of
Tenebroc, was valiantly trying not to lick his lips at
thought of more such sausages, pasties, and good ale.
Tamba made no effort to conceal his readiness for the
sights and sounds, thrills and glory of a gathering of
knights whom he, as professional page, had only to watch
with an educated eye. The Quiller Lion was tossing his
mane and pricking his paws like a kitten whiffing catnip.
As for Joiselette, she only smiled and said, "It's your decision, sir."

Looking again at Garth and Tamba—avid, each in his
way, as two little boys at Yuletide—Sir Harald decided: "I
have no reason to enter this tournament, but we might
find the Knight of the Black Chevron there." Turning back
to the Warrior Woman, he went on, "Very well, lady, if
fighting you is not the test, what is?"

"Don't worry," she replied, "you passed it."

Saluting again in their direction, she moved her mount

out of their way. But as they finished fording the river, she cast her gaze up and down Sir Harald from head to stirrup and back, grinned once again, and said, "First take a good look at the lady, my friend, and then make up your mind about entering the tournament."

Respectfully saluting the Guardian of the Ford, they passed on in search of the castle, Joiselette accompanied by a new cluster of wild creatures—her former coterie, even the birds, having remained on the other side of the river.

After a mile or two, as the path was leading them through a narrow strip of pleasant meadow, with woodland on one hand, on the other a great rockface somewhat screened by a clump of leafy bushes, and ahead of them a rolling rise in the road, Sir Harald said, "At least the story of my shame seems not to have beaten us here; she did not seem to know my shield. But what was the test, and which of us passed it?"

"I should guess," responded the cocky page, "that yonder Warrior Woman let us pass thanks to the presence among us of my own good Lady Joiselette."

"The Guardian of the Ford?" said a new voice; and, looking around, they beheld a knight with a gold lion on his blue shield, just emerging on foot from the clump of bushes between rock and road.

"Good my lord Sir Ywen, son of Urien!" exclaimed Tamba, who could recognize every knight of King Arthur's Table Round at once by his shield. "So this tournament has drawn you, too."

Sir Ywen shook his head. "I knew nothing about it until by chance we happened upon the ford back there and learned of it from the Warrior Woman, as you call her. Who gave me—" he grinned ruefully "—I fear, a most spectacular fall."

"You fought her?" Sir Harald asked, amazed.

"Why, that was what I understood the lady to demand, and does not the Code of Chivalry require of a knight that he please a lady in all things she demands?"

"In all *lawful* things," Sir Harald protested, blushing a little to reflect how he himself had lately ignored the Aloof Fair One's lawful demand to be let free.

"Oh, as to that," laughed Sir Ywen, "when a lady is as fully armed and prepared to do battle as is she of the river crossing, I take the acceptance of her challenge to be a very lawful thing!"

"Yet she let you pass, my lord, after giving you a fall," Tamba remarked. "As she let us pass after no passage of arms at all."

"As I said, I believe in my vanity that it depends on whether or not she herself judges one worthy. Although she did lay upon me the condition," Sir Ywen added, "that I swear on my honor to undergo the trial of the Cave of the Mirrors of Ultimate Truth, which lies behind these bushes."

"Indeed, my lord?" Tamba asked delightedly, craning his neck in an effort to peer past the bushy screen. "May we ask further details?"

"No," Sir Ywen told him shortly. "Nor would I advise anyone, man or woman, child or even dumb beast, to approach this place without being so commanded. Unless, perhaps, it were such a splendid creature as this fine lion whom you ride, my lady," he went on with a bow to Joiselette, "and for whose sake, much more than for that of the imaged beast on my own shield, I hereby vow henceforth to honor any and every other lion I may ever encounter as long as I live. But my squires and horses await me beyond yonder rise. Join me, and we can ride on to the tournament together, the best of friends until the time comes to joust, and then again afterward, providing we both survive." Seeing Sir Harald's hesitation, he added, "Or could I, perhaps, enlist you in my own party for the mêlée?"

With a great sigh, Sir Harald shook his head. "I do not fight at all this time. I have come this far only in hopes of finding a cowardly knight, with a shield bearing a black chevron, whom I have already defeated, but who fled from me rather than arrange his ransom."

"A knight whose shield bears a black chevron," Sir Ywen repeated slowly and thoughtfully. "No, I regret that I have neither seen nor heard tell of any such champion. But come, my lady—may I call you, as I think I overheard your page call you, Joiselette? Come, all my friends, and join me in the repast that my squires ought to have ready by now."

They were willing enough to join King Arthur's knight, both at the midday meal—which his two squires were happily able, with the help of Tamba and Garth, to lay out for seven in place of three—and in the ride onward to Wisten of the Mists. Neither Sir Ywen's squires nor anyone in Harald and Joiselette's party brought up the subject of the Cave of the Mirrors of Ultimate Truth again, even Tamba curbing his curiosity, seeing that the matter had been forbidden. No such rule of courtesy denied them the Knight of the Black Chevron as a subject for conversation, but they did not dwell on him unduly, nor at the expense of any pleasanter topic.

Less than an hour later they came to Wisten town, and found it a lively place, its mists quite blown away by the afternoon sun and breeze, fresh and clean beneath the festive clutter of a fair setting up to take advantage of the morrow's tournament, and clearly accustomed to prosperity as an everyday matter of course, for it even had its own jeweler.

This jeweler had set a canopied booth up in front of his house, where he already had a shelf full of wares out on display. Catching sight of it, our friends dismounted and crossed the square for a closer look, leaving Garth and Sir Ywen's junior squire in charge of their animals; only Joiselette kept the Quiller Lion close by her side, not out of inquietude, but because, while he seemed to inspire much less surprise than might have been expected, the townsfolk were nevertheless watching him with wary respect.

The jeweler was a happy-faced little fellow of advancing years, with a pleasant squint and a tongue as nimble as his fingers. The court knight, senior squire, and professional page examined the fruits of his labors with educated discrimination; the country knight with silent effort to educate his discrimination; and the Maid of the Wood with simple delight.

"What lustrous metals! What lovely pebbles and pearls!" Joiselette exclaimed, and burst out into another song:

> "Thanks to the Everywhere, for strewing
> Earth and sea with gifts so fine,
> And for the jeweler, who, accruing,
> Works them with such rare design."

"And thanks to you, my lady, for sharing your good taste in such an attractive ditty," the jeweler replied with a smile and a glance around at all the potential customers her song had attracted. "Pray let me present you with this enameled pendant of my own rare design, in token of my appreciation."

He handed her a teardrop shape the length of his thumb, hung on a long thong of blue-dyed leather. The pendant's brightly enameled surface depicted a pelican on whose breast, as she tore it open to nourish her young, three tiny carnelians stood for drops of blood.

"It's truly lovely," Joiselette answered, puzzled, "but what shall I do with it?"

"You might let your knight wear it as his tournament favor from you," the jeweler suggested helpfully.

"I am not her knight," Sir Harald said in a stiff, guarded voice. "I am her prisoner. And I have not come to fight in this tournament."

"Oh?" said the jeweler. "I grieve to hear that, my lord, for two reasons. First, because the prize—the official prize—is a costly golden collar of my own rarest workmanship, set with rubies and hung with a pendant on which I, myself, will copy the victor's shield in my brightest enamels. And, second, because only the contestants and their entourages may lodge in Wisten Castle this week."

Sir Ywen said, "Good man, rare and most highly desirable as this official prize most undoubtedly is, we have heard that there is a second prize, less official but infinitely farther beyond price."

"Indeed there is, good sir! That prize is my lady's hand and the lordship of Wisten of the Mists . . . although only if the arrangement should meet the satisfaction of both parties involved."

"Ah!" Sir Ywen nodded. "In that case, nothing at all holds me from striving for the chance to see you enamel my own device upon the pendant of that fine gold collar, and meanwhile enjoying all the comforts of yonder castle."

"Go on up, then, my lord," cried the jeweler—overeager, perhaps, to take advantage of the press of people crowding forward to examine his wares, "and present yourself to my gracious lady. And you, sir," he added to the left-handed knight, "why not go up there with him, at least long enough to introduce yourselves? And if my lady and my collar don't make you reconsider, come back and let me host you myself, in my own house, for my Lady Songbird's sake."

Tamba had a fancy to spend a shilling or two on some

small eye-pleaser for a certain damsel-in-waiting of Queen Guenevere's, and Sir Ywen would not refuse his junior squire a fair chance to view this jeweler's splendid array. The rest of our friends retired to hold the horses, where Sir Harald growled at Garth, "Remind me again why I'm not entering this tournament."

The sturdy serf obeyed. "Because you're in quest of the Black Chevron Knight, my lord, whose horse and arms you won already. But until you find him and make him give them up to you, your own arms and Goblin rightly belong to my lord Sir Kay, and aren't yours to risk losing again."

"Thank you," the knight replied—not, it must be confessed, very graciously; but he did his best to remedy that by adding at once, "Now take your own chance to look at the pretty trinkets." Then, turning to Sir Ywen, "Well, sir, you just heard it all."

"Indeed," said Sir Ywen, who had up until then heard only that his new companion was looking for the mysterious knight and did not intend to enter this particular tournament, but neither the relationship between those two facts nor the straitness of Sir Harald's circumstances nor—unless from other witnesses of Tenebroc—his debt to Arthur's seneschal. "Indeed, I must offer my deepest sympathies to anyone owing such a debt of honor to our sweet companion Kay of the Surly Manners and the Rude Tongue! But as for your Knight of the Black Chevron, good friend," he went on, remounting his palfrey and rising in his stirrups, the better to peer around the square, "I have not yet seen anything of any warrior answering to his description. Might he be already at the castle?"

"If he is, give him my regards and tell him—No, tell him nothing. Let me say it myself when I see him tomorrow."

"Do you not, then, ride up there with me now?"

"No, I do not."

Sir Harald had faced down the temptation of the tournament three times already that afternoon. Besides that, he was inevitably dubious about whether his name might already have been blackened by some party who, while having no occasion to pass the news along to the Warrior Woman at the ford, felt eager enough to share it at the court of Wisten of the Mists.

"Since you plan to enter anyway," Sir Harald went on

with great effort to Sir Ywen, "why not beg to carry my Lady Joiselette's favor yourself?"

After a searching look to satisfy himself that the other was in earnest, Sir Ywen said, "My dear friend, I thank you most heartily!" Then, bowing to Joiselette, "My lady, seeing that as yet I have no fair one's favor to strengthen me in this present passage at arms, might I beg the privilege of carrying yours?"

"It's really more the jeweler's favor than mine," she replied. "I'd say your own skill and practice and good health have done more to strengthen you than this ever could. But, as long as Sir Harald has made up his mind . . ."

"I have," Sir Harald said shortly.

"Then there's no reason you shouldn't have the use of it, Sir Ywen." Joiselette tossed it to him.

He caught it neatly, saluted her, and slipped it around his neck just as his junior squire, Tamba, and Garth rejoined the group, which needed only their arrival to split once again into two separate parties.

Tamba was annoyed by this new development. "What authority," he grumbled under his breath, "decrees that my Lady Joiselette and I should not go up with my lord Sir Ywen and see this enticing lady of Wisten at once this afternoon, simply because the bastard of Quillerstone takes a bee in his bonnet to subject himself to no more temptation than absolutely necessary?"

The only ears that overheard Tamba's plaint belonged to Garth, who, as a serf, would have been left in the court-yard with the horses and could therefore afford to wax philosophical about his companion's lost opportunity. "We will all have our chance to see Her Ladyship tomorrow at the tournament," he pointed out, "and have more time this afternoon to see the rest of this pretty town."

So they saw and admired it while Sir Ywen and his squires went on up to the castle—or, at least, after lodging their other animals in the town stables, Joiselette, Garth, and the lion admired the rest of the fair and prosperous town, with Harald following along in glum silence and Tamba consoling himself by fingering the little silver ring he had bought for his favorite damsel-in-waiting at half what it would have cost in Caerleon or Camelot or any other city where King Arthur customarily held his court.

What further consoled him was noticing, bit by bit, how popular his Lady Joiselette's jingle about the jeweler was becoming among the residents and visitors in the town. As more and more of them whistled, chanted, or quoted it on every side, Tamba began to join in, correcting a word here, embellishing a few notes there, even offering a few emendations and amplifications of his own, until he grew cheerfuller than if they had spent the entire afternoon watching Sir Harald collect his due from the Black Chevron Knight—whom, unfortunately, they spied nowhere—or gazing their fill at the lady of Wisten.

That same lady, for her part, welcomed Sir Ywen with delight. "One of King Arthur's own knights!" she exclaimed happily. "Have you really come here to take part in our little tournament, sir?"

"Nothing would give me greater honor, my lady," he replied, casting his glance around the hall. "All the more so, if you should have here present a certain knight whose shield bears a black chevron on a field of vair." Sir Ywen said this with the pure thought of helping Sir Harald in his search.

The lady frowned, shook her head, and raised her voice to carry throughout her hall. "Has anyone seen a knight with a black chevron on his shield?" When it appeared that no one had, she went on to King Arthur's champion, "Will it make any difference to your decision, Sir Ywen?"

"None whatsoever, madame." And, in fact, the Black Chevron Knight was nothing to Sir Ywen personally.

"Good! And may I offer you my favor?"

Sir Ywen flashed his most courtly smile. "Many thanks indeed, gracious lady, but I should fear to flaunt the appearance of your favoritism before actually meriting the same."

"Oh, that's nothing," she answered. "If I follow what you just said. . . . Most of the contestants will be wearing my favor. I had the tailor make me up a whole chestful of sleeves and scarves, and any knight may wear one who wishes."

"Ah!" Sir Ywen bowed deeply. "In that case, dear madame, it pains me more than I can well describe to refuse you. The truth is, I already carry the favor of another

lady." And he held Joiselette's pendant out a little way
from his chest.

"Oh, very good! That's all right, then. It's the work of
our own town jeweler, isn't it? Well, Sir Ywen, let me wish
you good luck in winning the collar to go with it."

"Thank you again, my lady. But do you not repeat that
wish to each and every man who enters?"

"Of course I do," she assured him with merry solemnity.
"And I sincerely mean it, every time. Haven't you ever heard
that wishes grow better and better with repetition?"

"In that case, my lady, your tournament promises to
give us excellent sport indeed!"

When Sir Harald's party had seen all they could of the
town, fair tents, and tournament ground, and nowhere
found either the Black Chevron Knight or anyone who had
seen or previously heard of him, they returned to their new
friend the jeweler, who, having done a brisk afternoon's
trade thanks in large measure to Joiselette's attractive
ditty, was delighted to welcome them back, feed them, bed
them, and set the final seal of proof on his friendship by
breathing not one more word about the tournament itself.
Not, at least, in Sir Harald's hearing.

Of course, in order to make certain that his nemesis of
the black chevron was nowhere in the immediate vicinity,
Sir Harald had to torture himself by going next day in the
capacity—as he intended—of a mere spectator to watch the
tournament along with the rest of his party, their host, and
their host's family. Barely had they reached the grounds
before the little jeweler, proud of hosting even a noncom-
batant knight in his humble household, prouder yet of
hosting the Maid of the Wood, and privileged to approach
the lady of the castle by dint of having crafted the official
grand prize for her tournament, begged leave to present his
guests to her face to face. Tamba's curiosity was satisfied
at last.

The Lady Gavrielle of Wisten was a pretty, perky,
chirky, cheerful-faced young blue-eyed blonde who wore a
coronet of thin gold wires interwoven with many kinds of
white and blue flowers to set off the honey-russet color of
her hair. While not quite of a loveliness to rouse envy in the
breasts of the famous beauties of King Arthur's court, she

could at least have held her own amongst them, if only by virtue of her insouciance.

"Are you really not going to fight today?" she asked Sir Harald, eyeing his shoulders with admiration. "I still have half a dozen scarves. You could have your pick of one to wear for me in the lists."

He looked around for Garth, whom Joiselette had insisted on drawing along to the dais but who—caught in the strange role of serving in lieu of squire to a knight whose own position was somewhat ambiguous and reputation in doubt—stood hidden as much as he could manage a few paces in the rear. From there, he obligingly whispered, "Remember, sir."

Turning back to Dame Gavrielle, Sir Harald replied, "It is not disinclination, lady. I have my reasons."

"I'm sure you do! Well, would you like to join my marshal and help officiate? And I *love* your lion!" she added to Joiselette, patting the great beast on its shaggy head. Somewhat to Sir Harald's surprise, it purred and nodded at her gentle touch, seeming to grin like a huge, happy hound, and never raising a single spine.

Fortunately, Sir Harald was not half so taken with the lady of Wisten as I am, or nothing could have kept him from throwing prudence to the four winds and entering the tourney after all. But, still convalescent as he was from his frustrated expectations of the Aloof Fair One (or, more accurately, of the idol he had idealized before he actually kidnapped her), and relieved that his reputation was not yet blackened hereabouts, he agreed with minimal gruffness to help the Wisten seneschal order, judge, and generally officiate. And, truth to tell, he did not do the job badly. Though he had never until now marshaled a tournament, he understood the principles well enough from having been marshaled, and he knew what he as a combatant liked and did not like in a marshal's actions, and he had served six years as judge and magistrate over the petty disputes of Quillerstone, castle and town, in his brother Godfrey's absence.

But what it cost him to ride about that field as referee, armored and helmeted to ward against misplaced blows during the mêlée, his sword bound, daintily and symbolically, into its scabbard with a thin white thread, and a white pennant fluttering from the lance that he must use only to signal that he saw some rule of combat being infracted . . . imagination can perhaps detail better than description.

One further nettle in his skin was the reflection that as marshal he might have been excellently placed to claim his rights from the Black Chevron Knight if that nemesis had only had the courtesy to show his shield at Dame Gavrielle's little tournament; although further reflection reminded him that the Knight of the Black Chevron could have told the most damning part of the Aloof Fair One episode, and told it in such a way as to make his own intervention appear a rescue attempt, casting the entire blame back on Sir Harald.

Joiselette, clad in finery lent her for the occasion, watched the sport from a seat close beside Lady Gavrielle's, with the Quiller Lion lying easily between them and Tamba at her other hand. Garth was allowed to find his place among the crowd of cheering peasants, enjoying his fair share of sausage, pasties, and good ale. It was a splendid spectacle, but I see no great point in filling long pages with detailed descriptions of the jousts tilted, spears broken, blows struck like flashing lightning, helms cracked and shields dented like crashing thunder, and general raining down of buffets all around the field. From that storm, only one knight could possibly emerge the victor; and it must have been perfectly plain to every reader from the outset who—even if our friend the recovering villain had entered—that one knight must be.

"Well, Sir Ywen!" said Lady Gavrielle as he knelt before her to have the rubied gold collar clasped about his thoat. "Congratulations, and may you wear this in good health!"

They exchanged a long and penetrating glance, having reason to feel even more aware than anybody else there present of the second and greater, though unofficial, prize. But after a few heartbeats they mutually smiled and shook their heads very slightly at one another.

"Good and gracious lady," said he, "I still belong to the court of our good King Arthur."

"I think you do, sir," she replied, "and I hope someday you find a lady who can love you as you deserve to be loved.

Now, be sure and have our jeweler enamel this with your device before you leave us."

Then, raising her voice, she surprised the entire assembly with the announcement: "All of you have fought remarkably well today, both offensively and defensively. We haven't seen anybody killed or even badly wounded, praise Heaven! So any and all of you who want to stay with me, will be more than welcome in my castle guard. And, to make sure that every knight has what he needs, I myself will ransom or replace all arms and horses that any of you have lost to anyone else!

"That goes for you, too, Sir Harald," she added, turning to him where he sat on Goblin at parade rest, with his helmet in the crook of one arm and his mouth hanging open.

"You haven't even seen me fight!" he snapped back at her.

"No, but you made an excellent marshal, and you must have pleased my friend at the ford—"

"Pardon me, Your Ladyship, but I cannot stay for the feast. I have wasted too much time here." Clapping his helmet back on his head, he turned his horse with knee signals and departed at a fast canter.

"Sir Harald!" Joiselette called after him in a rare fit of annoyance. "Harald de Folgeste! Sir Harald de Folgeste!" But in the presence of so many strangers she never added the telltale word "prisoner," and though the Quiller Lion added a roar, Sir Harald never turned his head, but simply nudged Goblin from a canter into a gallop.

Since Sir Ywen's squires were holding his charger only paces away, he was able to excuse himself and set off in pursuit almost at once, although it was a slow pursuit, because his poor stallion, having borne far greater brunt of action than the marshal's steed, was battle-weary. By the time Joiselette and Tamba had made their courteous apologies to the chatelaine, collected a confused Garth from the crowd that had largely obstructed his view of the events at the dais, and saddled all mounts save the lion, both knights were long out of sight.

Sir Harald rode fast and hard, rapidly outdistancing the last of his coherent thoughts though not, unfortunately, the dudgeon that infected and spurred his sensitive horse on better than any rowel of mere sharpened metal could have done, until they drew within sight of the rocky and bush-screened mouth of the Cave of the Mirrors of Ultimate Truth, where they had yesterday met Sir Ywen.

And where, today, an even stranger encounter awaited them. For, as Sir Harald recognized the spot and reined in a little with a vague, instinctual sense that it might be as well to allow his reason some small chance of catching up with his brainpan, he heard a lusty if somewhat thin male voice bawling out to a rough and ready tune:

> "I'm Jokesir the Puissant,
> Greatest knight errant!
> Lone and lonely champion,
> Righting wrongs for everyone.
> For the best knight errant,
> Call Jokesir the Puissant!"

"What now?" Sir Harald wondered half under his breath, bringing Goblin to a standstill until they should see the answer to his question.

Out from the forestland there came riding a scrawny little knight in ragtag armor, bearing a shield too battered for anyone to read its device and a broken lance bound together with a bit of cord, mounted on a mare more bones than muscle.

"*You* are 'Jokesir the Puissant'?" Sir Harald demanded in the opposite of awe.

"*Sir* Jokesir the Puissant," the other made answer, drawing himself up proudly. His helmet, if helmet it could be called, was an old-fashioned leather cap with protruding earpieces, covered in overlapping iron plates of which several were absent and most of the rest dented. It would have disgraced a common foot soldier, and it covered none of Sir Jokesir's almost boyish face—a face that would have been more nearly triangular if it had been better fed: his nose narrow; his chin almost pointed; his cheeks almost hollow; and his wideset brown eyes, perched between high cheekbones and spare brows, wearing beneath the braggadocio an almost melancholy cast.

This melancholy, however, Sir Harald was still too wrought-up in his own grievances to notice. "How in God's holy name did you get past that she-devil who guards the ford?" he demanded.

"Oh, she laughed and let me pass with no argument whatever. No, not like that," Sir Jokesir added stiffly, for Sir Harald was laughing, too—though not, alas! the cleansing laugh either of fellowship or of appreciating a joke on oneself. "*Her* laugh was friendly."

"And admiring, too, no doubt!" said Sir Harald. "I suppose she could afford it, now their little tournament is safely over."

"What? You've had a tournament here? I mean—you did not wait for Jokesir the Puissant, who has ridden so long and so hard to grace it with his prowess and mighty feats of arms?"

"Be glad you failed to get here in time," Sir Harald said cruelly. "They would have cut you to ribbons."

"Ribbons, indeed! I see by that white ribbon on your lance that you were the marshal. You might have held the proceedings up until my arrival."

"I almost regret missing that chance. You would have given us something to see. Better than a born buffoon! But how could I or anyone else sense that you were—"

Harald broke off because Jokesir, angered by his insults, came charging at him full tilt.

Not that this much endangered the left-handed knight. As the skinny youth spent most of his might trying to kick his poor little mare into a canter, Sir Harald simply signaled Goblin to stand firm and swung his shield up to meet the blow.

Surprisingly mighty that impact was, but with a power that rebounded back upon the one who struck it. The bit of cord gave way and the crudely mended lance fell apart again, but not before the vibration, carrying from point to grip, knocked Sir Jokesir himself from his saddle onto the greensward.

And then, I am ashamed to record, Sir Harald did what he would not have done had he been in a better frame of mind: Leaping from Goblin's saddle, he dropped his own unused lance, drew his sword with a little snap of the decorative marshal's thread, and gave battle to Sir Jokesir the Puissant on foot, man to man.

Though foul, Sir Harald's mood was not yet murderous.

Wanting violent exercise more than blood, he instinctively aimed his blows at his adversary's shield—even when Sir Jokesir's ineptitude made hitting shield instead of head or torso an awkward reach—and he struck with the resounding flat rather than either the edge or the point of his blade.

Nor did Sir Jokesir prove completely without resources: What he lacked in strength and expertise he made up in energy. He would not have lasted two blows in a deadly serious combat, but he met this merely exasperated sparring with so much gallantry, resilience, and fortitude that they were still hard at it when Sir Ywen, having twice allowed his horse a brief rest and once followed a wrong turning, eventually rode over the rise and found them.

"Is this a private mêlée, Marshal?" Sir Ywen inquired, reining up. "Or may any knight join in?"

Sir Harald paused, panting. "Ask Sir Jokesir the Puissant, here. He started it."

"On severe provocation!" Sir Jokesir protested. "Don't forget how severely you provoked me, Sir Knight-Marshal of the Bend Sinister!"

"He blames me for failing to hold the tournament up until he could join it," Sir Harald explained to Sir Ywen. Then, to Sir Jokesir: "You silly pup, just how long do you think you would have lasted against Sir Ywen over there, King Arthur's own Round Table knight, who won the tournament?"

"How long have I lasted against you, Sir Proud Knight? Hey? Did you think I could give you such a battle when we began it, Sir Vainglorious? Surprised you, didn't I? Worn you out, haven't I? For all your crowing!"

"The only way you've worn me out, Sir Young Idiot," Harald growled at him, "is with the effort to keep from wounding you seriously."

"If that's what you have to think to comfort yourself," Sir Jokesir noted with a resolute shrug. "Come on, then, Sir Ywen of the Table Round, help him out! I'll let you fight me both at once!"

Sir Ywen smiled and bowed slightly in his saddle. "Many thanks, good Sir Jokesir, for your gracious offer, but I am overweary with fighting too many lesser knights today and, even were I fresh, I should quake with fear at the prospect of facing your puissance in open field."

At this juncture, Joiselette and her companions, along with Sir Ywen's two squires, appeared atop the rise.

"Ah!" exclaimed Sir Jokesir. "An audience—even a lady fair, riding a lion! Come on, then, Sir Proud Marshal, if you aren't overweary, too!" So saying, he bounced up and, with a tiptoe spring and an overhand swing, struck Sir Harald a blow that almost, though not quite, dented his helmet.

It was the final grain of a very gritty day. With one blow, Sir Harald had him backed against the nearest tree. The second blow sent Sir Jokesir's blade flying. The third, his shield. Sir Harald swung his sword up for the final stroke—

And with a great roar the Quiller Lion sprang between them, Joiselette still on its back, her arm flung up to protect Sir Jokesir.

His swing already begun, Harald caught it back with such a painful wrench that the sword tumbled harmlessly out of his numbed fingers.

He staggered back several steps, turned, tore off his helmet, and hunched over with his head bowed and his right hand alternately clutching his left hand and left shoulder.

White-faced, Sir Jokesir found his sword and shield, came shakily forward, and laid them on the grass before Sir Harald. "Well, Sir . . . Whoever You Are," he acknowledged, "you gave me the fight I asked for, and I'd have to say you won it. My horse and arms are yours."

All that Sir Harald said was, "I am still a villain."

"Hadn't you better let me decide that?" asked Dame Gavrielle, who had arrived with a few attendants shortly after Joiselette's party. "I'm the mistress of Wisten, after all. And I'd hate to think I just had a villain marshaling my first tournament."

Sir Harald got to his feet, made her an awkward bow, and stood silently staring at the grass. Nobody else said anything, but somehow they all got themselves arranged for a sort of impromptu court, while the lady of Wisten rode downslope to a conveniently central spot, where she could sit, judgelike, looking down from her fine gray palfrey.

"Now, then," she went on, "I only got here in time to see the tail end, so you had better tell me all about whatever just happened here. I am sorry I missed it. It must have been as exciting as anything that happened in the regular tournament!"

Sir Jokesir stepped forward, gazing at Dame Gavrielle with something that looked very much like adoration. "Your Ladyship, I am Sir Jokesir the Puissant, most errant of knight champions. When I found out I'd come too late to enter your tournament, I insisted on challenging this knight, your late marshal. I still don't know his name, but he kindly accepted my challenge and, I'm afraid, amazing as it seems, he beat me—or would have beat me, with a few lucky strokes, if this good lady and her lion hadn't intervened. So now my horse and arms belong by right to him and you behold me, dear and gracious madam, penniless but proud to stand at your service."

"I don't want his horse and arms," Sir Harald protested. "I would not take them even if they were worth taking. I never should have accepted his challenge, and he would have been ashamed to challenge me if he had known that my name is Harald de Folgeste."

"Well, what of it?" Dame Gavrielle asked as Sir Harald paused. "I've known that much ever since our jeweler introduced you to me this morning, and I don't see anything in your name to shame him away from challenging you if it tickled his fancy. Or to have kept me from asking you to help marshal my tournament."

Sir Harald heaved a sigh and inwardly cursed his tongue. It seemed cruel and unusual to serve as the instrument of blackening his own name but, having trapped himself into it, he bravely finished the job.

"Earlier this summer I accosted a maiden who was traveling alone, and forced her to ride with me to my brother's castle of Quillerstone, which I had been holding for the last six years, where I held her prisoner against her will. Sorely against her will."

"What happened to her?" asked the lady of Wisten.

"By now she will be happily married to my brother, who came home and claimed his castle just in time."

Dame Gavrielle relaxed. "Oh, that's all right, then. But you really ought to have told me!"

"He is under my charge, lady," Joiselette explained, "and he has been behaving himself beautifully—"

"Until now," Sir Harald muttered.

"Would it have made a difference?" Joiselette went on.

"Probably not," Dame Gavrielle replied, "only it would

have been nice to know the whole story ahead of time. Did my good friend at the ford ever ask about it?"

"Madame," said Tamba, "if you mean that bold Warrior Woman, I should find it hard to credit that she could ever comprehend, understand, or sympathize with the plight of any damsel carried off against her will!"

"You don't know her as well as I do," Dame Gavrielle answered with a smile. "Well, Sir Harald, if she passed you through without question, all I'm going to ask of you now is that you go spend an hour in the Cave of the Mirrors of Ultimate Truth over there."

Sir Ywen murmured, "'All'?"

"Your Ladyship," Sir Harald protested, "it seems too light a sentence."

Arthur's knight said, "Wait until you have tried it, my friend."

"My lord Sir Ywen there," Sir Harald argued, "came out of that cave to win the tournament hands down."

"Be that as it may, sir," Dame Gavrielle repeated, "my sentence stands. One hour in the Cave of the Mirrors of Ultimate Truth—no more, no less."

"My lady?" he appealed to Joiselette.

But she only ratified the judgment of the lady of Wisten. "No less and certainly no more, Sir Harald. You mustn't be too greedy."

"Of course," the lady of Wisten added, "you can rest overnight and go in tomorrow morning."

Sir Harald's only reply was to drop his helmet, march forward, and disappear behind the bushes.

"My lady," said Sir Jokesir, speaking for the first time since he had owned himself defeated and offered up his horse and arms, such as they were. "When I told you I had insisted on challenging him, I didn't . . . Well . . . I understated things a little. What actually happened—I sort of charged at him. Twice. I, er, didn't give him a fair chance to refuse my challenge. Either time."

Tamba grinned, and Garth let out an audible sigh of relief. Sir Ywen nodded as though deeply satisfied to learn that his new acquaintance was not so lost to knightly honor as willingly to fight any man so plainly the weaker and inferior in arms; although, no doubt in consideration of Jokesir's feelings, he refrained from voicing this sentiment. Joiselette smiled and said, "Sir Jokesir, thank you for explaining it to us."

Then they all looked at Dame Gavrielle, who frowned a dainty frown and judged, "It doesn't make any difference in Sir Harald's sentence, seeing that—whether you were aware of it or not, Sir Jokesir—he had already broken a rule or two before you ever met him today. But maybe you'd better go in there, too."

Nine paces inside, Sir Harald met a wall of blistering heat.

He fell back a step and considered the situation. Ahead of him, he saw nothing save such vague rocky outlines as what dim daylight seeped through the bush-screened cave mouth still had power to limn. Reaching forth one mail-mittened hand, he felt nothing across his path except the fiery sizzle. Drawing his hand quickly back, he stared at the glowing links.

Enchantment was obviously at work here, or his flesh already would have been in serious pain, rather than merely prickling at him. For a moment, he toyed with the idea of sitting down where he was and waiting the rest of his hour out right here. That, however, did not strike him as quite in the spirit of his sentence; moreover, it promised more boredom than chastisement. Besides, instead of cooling, his ring mail began to glow brighter and hotter.

Sitting down on the narrow cave floor, he wriggled out of it, a tedious enough process, but one that *could* be accomplished without assistance. Grunting to notice that the metallic fabric cooled as soon as it was off his body, having left only a few scorch marks on his surcoat and gambeson, as well as some reddened patches on his exposed skin, he rolled it up and placed it carefully near the cave mouth. Then, slipping surcoat back on directly over gambeson, he turned toward the interior.

Without his suit of mail, he passed safely through the invisible curtain of fire, to find himself moving in an enclosed atmosphere of intense, moist, yet mildly pleasurable warmth. A few more paces through this soupiness, and he discovered that what he had mistaken for the continuation of the tunnel was simply a vein of darker stone, where in fact the tunnel branched off right and left.

No one had instructed him what to do in such a case. If he had lingered awhile longer outside, would Her Ladyship of Wisten of the Mists have provided more detailed directions? He shrugged—rubbed his sore shoulder—and, rather than return outside and ask, took the tunnel to the left.

At the turning of the now-distant cave mouth, he soon lost the last kiss of light and had to grope his way onward in warm and sticky darkness. The ceiling sloped lower and lower, until he had to stoop and, finally, crawl on all fours long after a less stubborn man might have gone back, reasoning that he ought to have taken the other turning.

At long last, after what seemed more like months than minutes, a speck of light appeared in the far distance. Encouraged, Sir Harald crawled faster.

The ceiling grew no higher: He was still, perforce, on hands and knees when he reached the light and found that he had taken the correct branch, after all. A golden frame set with great milky pearls stood like a round doorway in the tunnel, and an enameled plate on the lower edge of this frame bore in bright colors the words: *Harald de Folgeste. Mirror the First.*

He looked in, and saw a face much like his own, but younger—ah, God! so much younger!—weary beyond belief, and . . . a woman!

The face swung back and became one part of an entire scene: The very young woman lay abed, a man bending above her and another woman bundling bloody rags up at the back of the room. In the man, Harald recognized his own father, the late lord of Quillerstone, mature but with no silver hairs as yet—little older, in fact, than Sir Harald himself was now.

The woman with a face so much like Harald's own smiled weakly up and moved one hand to pull a corner of swaddling blanket away from the tiny head that lay on her breast.

"Ugly little half-serf bastard," the man said, laughing; and though he spoke in tones that would have made the vilest insult sound in a dog's ears like the fondest endearment, still the words rankled in Sir Harald's heart. "Why weren't you a girl, eh, little villain?"

"My lord," murmured the woman, "don't forget your promise."

"Oh! no fear of that, sweeting," he reassured her, stroking back her sweat-dampened hair. "A bastard daughter with thine eyes would have been easier to marry off well, but this one will be raised side by side with my own trueborn son, who should be—"

"My lord Sir Warin!" cried someone at the door. "My lord, your lady is brought to her childbed!"

With one quick, final pat to his paramour's damp locks, he turned and hurried from the room.

"So," muttered Sir Harald. "It would have served you well, Father, if the daughter you wanted had been born in Godfrey!"

He had known the outlines of that night, of course, but never until now so many of its details. He had remembered his mother with his heart only, not his mind, dying as she had a scant two years afterward—in childbed, ironically, with a stillborn daughter. But never had he pictured her so young, so very young, scarcely more than a child herself!

"Mother," he murmured, reaching out for her hand. But as Sir Harald crawled through the frame toward her, she melted away, along with the rest of the room, and, rising to his feet, he had just time to see his surcoat drenched in blood, before the rocky tunnel darkened again around him.

He pulled off the wet garment. The gambeson beneath it seemed dry. By now he suspected that whatever enchantment bound this place would eventually, in its own good time, restore the surcoat to him, so he left it lying there on the floor while he groped his way onward through darkness illuminated only by memories. Being an honorable man, the former lord of Quillerstone had kept his promise in spirit as well as letter, even after his paramour's death, raising both sons almost side by side, the bastard— and elder by several hours—only a little in the shadow of the trueborn.

After what seemed not too unbearably long an interval, another light appeared in the distance. At the same time, the ceiling sloped down again, but not as much as before, forcing him now, not to crawl, but only to walk at a stoop.

This frame was silver set with sapphires, stood waist high, and bore its enameled plate at the top, reading: *Harald de Folgeste. Mirror the Second.* When he knelt the better to look in, the face that met him was his own, but many years younger—eighteen or twenty years younger—a beardless boy barely old enough to observe fast-days as yet.

Frowning as if deep in his own thoughts, unaware of the man on the other side of the mirror, the boy bowed his head and the scene swung out as the earlier one had done, letting Sir Harald see that his younger self sat at a table, a book propped up before him while he awkwardly and painstakingly strove right-handedly to copy letters onto a set of wax tablets. (For knighthood was not the universally illiterate state we moderns sometimes suppose.)

So, thought the man. *This would seem to be when I was already a page, but had not yet given in to my weakness. The other hand, boy! Try it with thy left hand.*

And, stepping through the silver frame, he found himself once again in the child's body, slowly transferring the stylus from his right hand to his left. . . .

Godfrey, also a child again, burst into the room. "Brother! Where is our sire?"

"Seeing to our guests, I suppose. Wherever they are."

"Help me to find him."

"I am not to leave this room until I have my tablets filled up with letters that do not bring tears of laughter into his eyes."

"Brother, three of the visiting squires are sitting on the causeway prising the shells off turtles and casting them down onto the rocks still alive!"

Harald the page struck his stylus down so hard he embedded it in the wax, and followed his brother out of the room at a run. Harald the knight thought, *Yes, this comes back*, and made no move to stop his younger self.

Three squires just newly graduated from pagehood, the three most junior members of the visiting lord's party, they looked very young to Harald the man; but to Harald the boy, still years away from a squire's estate, they looked almost as large as full-blown knights. Nevertheless, after one glance at the dead and writhing turtle remnants that bloodied the rocks, he strode straight up to the eldest of the three, where he squatted working his blade between his next victim's upper and lower shells, and rammed his fist hard into the hand that held the knife.

Not until the older boy squealed and dropped the knife

did the younger boy see that, despite all his teachers' best training, he had reverted to using his left fist.

"Hello!" cried the second squire. "Here's the Devil's-handed serf bastard, flushed out to the rescue."

The third squire thrust yet another turtle, which he had just pulled from a net where they were keeping them, up at Harald's nose and cried, "Here, little bastard, pay attention and let me teach thee the difference between a turtle and a damsel in distress!"

Harald answered them only with kicks and fisticuffs, until the three of them picked him up bodily and threw him—not onto the rocks; they were, after all, more mischievous than murderous—but out into the waters of the lake.

Floundering up to the surface for the second or third time, he saw that Godfrey, who had beat a retreat at the end of the causeway, had finally succeeded in fetching their father.

"Rogues," Sir Warin was telling the squires, "you had leave to make a good catch for our supper, not to waste it for your own idle pleasure. Now be off to the kitchen with what's left, and make sure the cooks get them all complete, if you hope to escape the punishment you deserve." Then, climbing down the rocks, he knelt and extended his right arm. "Here, son. Catch tight hold."

Harald reached out left-handed, and Sir Warin jerked his arm away. "Not the Devil's hand, boy! God in Heaven, use the hand we've taught thee to use!"

With a great effort and splashing that involved all four limbs and his trunk as well, Harald brought himself a few inches closer and strained out again, stubbornly, with his left hand and arm.

"God's nostrils!" Unblushing to utter such a terrible oath, Sir Warin gave in and caught hold just as his bastard began to sink again. "Very well, boy, use whichever hand pleases thee, and the shame be on thine own head!"

Even as Harald caught hold of his father's arm, it melted away, and he found himself standing once more alone in darkness, the cavern floor beneath his feet, its walls close on either side, and his quilted gambeson many times its usual weight, because it was sopping wet. He peeled it off, let it drop, and moved on in his shirt and breeches, which the enchantment had preserved still dry, at least for the present.

He suspected that Sir Warin would not have honored those words drawn hastily out under the duress of the moment, but for his lady, Dame Genevieve, who retained primary supervision of both boys as long as they were still pages, and who thenceforth honored the promise on her husband's behalf, insisting that his paramour's son might copy letters and do whatever else he chose with either hand. He owed much to his sire's long-suffering wife, even though he had never been allowed to call her anything save "madame" and "my lady"—unlike Godfrey, who in tender and private moments was privileged to address her as "Mother." In a double twist of irony, she had died much like Harald's own mother, about ten years after the incident of the turtles, in childbed with a stillborn daughter.

Twice they had almost had a sister, before Joiselette's coming.

Walking upright now, with no further downslope of the surface above him, he came at length to the next frame, a simple one of beaten bronze, inset with emeralds green as grass, and having on its west side a plaque inscribed: *Harald de Folgeste. Mirror the Third.*

The face he beheld this time on looking in was very nearly his present one, lacking only a few years, a few lines, and a few very small scars. And it was gazing, not back into his own eyes, but far beyond him, into the distance, with an expression of melancholic nostalgia and dreamy ambition, all mingled together.

The angle swung round, allowing him to view the same vista as his slightly younger self: Sir Godfrey riding away with the crusader's proud red cross on shield and banner. Sir Miles and Sir Joffrey—the castle's entire complement of fighting knights, save its new lord's bastard half-brother alone—rode at Sir Godfrey's back, along with all the squires and pages, several of the men-at-arms, and various other manservants. Every one of the departing lot likewise bore the crusader's cross.

Sir Harald remembered the moment now. Their father, growing somewhat careless after the death of his wife and latest infant daughter, had permitted himself to sustain two serious jousting wounds. He rallied and lived long enough to see both sons dubbed knight by his own hand in full ceremony, then faded and died soon after Yuletide of that same year. The following spring, after scant months of ruling Quillerstone, Godfrey had heard a sermon and let a fever of fervor carry him off to the Crusades.

Knowing what must come next, this time Sir Harald did not step through the mirror into his former self. He stood simply and watched as Godfrey reached the forest edge and turned for one brief wave of farewell, as the reflection of a younger Sir Harald lifted his left arm to return the salute from his place on the battlements, as Sir Godfrey turned forward again and disappeared among the trees, followed by all his retinue.

Sir Harald went on watching, as passively as possible, while his younger self came down from the battlements and looked about with something like smug satisfaction at those Quillerstone people who, having remained at home, had begun trickling back in from the causeway after waving their own goodbyes to their lord and his dear companions.

The older and very, very slightly wiser knight watched, shuddering inwardly but outwardly making no move either to influence or even re-enter the past. That day's thoughts were keen enough in mere memory. Not that he had wished his brother anything but well. Far from it! Such prayers as he sent up would always include Godfrey's name, and already stray inspirations for the homecoming banquet in, as they supposed, three or four years at most, marbled Sir Harald's plans for the more immediate future. But until that homecoming he, the bastard son but also the elder, knighted with equal validity, and having, as the event had just made clear, a greater sense of responsibility to his home, was in charge of it all: island, castle, causeway, village on the mainland, and all the rim of territory pertaining thereto. It went far toward tempering the loss of his brother's companionship.

Cringing, he now watched his then self cross the court-yard with unjustifiably jaunty stride, approach the small Hall of the Quiller Couch, and take the key from its hook beside the door. He neither summoned an audience nor sought to escape one, but whistled as he unlocked and opened the door in full sight of those castle folk who were already gathering to witness his experiment.

Boldly he went in, not even closing the door behind him. The Quiller Couch stood quiet, innocent, enticingly beautiful, like a long tray of thick, downy cushion covered in tawny velvet with silk-cased pillows to match, its arms of burnished gilt rising at either end like great, graceful handles, the whole resting on four slender legs of the most finely turned and gilded wood, all as tranquil and calm as the sunset of a cloudless, windless day in June.

He mounted the dais with confidence, stroked the smooth wood of the nearer arm, pressed the cushion and felt it yield pleasantly beneath his fingers. All was still peaceful, obedient to him; and he fully expected it to remain so. Was he not, until his brother's return, for all practical and legitimate purposes the true lord and holder of Quillerstone, its people his to judge, command, and protect?

Turning around to face the open door, Sir Harald sat on the tawny cushion.

Next instant, he was sitting on the dais steps and, an atom of time after that, wrestling the Quiller Lion for his very life.

He had not even worn his sword—whether in false confidence that the couch would behave for him, or in reluctance to risk damaging one of Quillerstone's unique treasures—but might have found himself unable to draw it in any case, so hard the lion bear-hugged him with its huge, claw-y paws. It was touch and go for some moments, but at last he broke free long enough to half sprint, half roll through the door, which someone—Garth, he saw when his head cleared—at once slammed shut in the lion's roaring face, and dropped the bolt into place.

The new acting lord of Quillerstone leaned shakily against the thudding door, his garments sliding in rapidly crimsoning shreds off his shoulders, and looked at the familiar faces gathered around at a distance just great enough to maintain the semblance of respect. At first they seemed fearful but, bit by bit, as they saw that he was only—only!—disgraced and bloodied, not seriously damaged in body, their anxiety turned into smiles, smirks, and outright grins. Several in the rear ranks laughed aloud.

"Perhaps our trueborn lord is still too close at hand! Try again tomorrow, sir, but next time take your sword!"

someone near the back, whose voice Sir Harald chose not to recognize, suggested much too merrily.

Garth, who folk said had once been like a younger brother to Harald's mother, muttered sympathetically, "Or perhaps it's his for life, my lord, however far he might be from where he belongs."

"I will overlook disrespect this once," Sir Harald said to the voice near the back of the little crowd. "Mark you, only this once!" Then, seizing gratefully on Garth's suggestion, he added, "Let this test serve to reassure us, from time to time, that Sir Godfrey, wherever he may be in body, is still alive and with us in spirit. But, mark you all again, and mark you well: It is a test for myself alone. For myself, and no one else!" He emphasized his words by relocking the door, which still shook beneath the lion's onslaughts, and then deliberately, if with still-trembling fingers, placing the key, not on its former hook, but in his belt.

The free-tongued old cook who used to boast of having been his mother's special friend grunted, "Well! If any of our earlier lords had thought to do that, we'd be the richer today by more than one young brat. Come on now, sir, and let us bind up those scratches for you before they fester."

Touching the shoulder, not of the knight beside her in the mirrored scene, but of the one who stood on the other side, she drew him in, after all, to find himself again in darkness, with his shirt, like his poor dignity, hanging in sticky wet shreds.

He finished tearing them off and proceeded, shivering, in his breeches alone.

Of the large iron frame set with blood-red rubies, identified in a plaque on its east side as *Harald de Folgeste. Mirror the Fourth*, I will say little more, seeing that you will already have read most of it in Part the First of this present chronicle, and what you can have read (if at all) only between the lines, concerned Sir Harald's intentions—or, more accurately, his frustrated hopes—regarding the Aloof Fair One, and left him with nothing to cover his nakedness save Adam's fig leaves.

It was a relief mixed with deep dread when, after groping along again in darkness for either a very long or a very short time—he never afterward could so much as guess which—Sir Harald reached the mother-of-pearl frame set with huge, sparkling diamonds and read in large letters on a screen of latticework and heavy velvet across its face: *Harald de Folgeste. Mirror the Last.*

After two atoms of hesitation, he pulled the screen away and beheld—

Sir Jokesir the Puissant—

Who, having taken the turn to the right, had passed through his own mirrored memories, to reach the mother-of-pearl frame and pull its screen away on his side at exactly the same moment, and in exactly the same state of dress, as his erstwhile adversary.

The two men gaped at each other for three heartbeats and two panting breaths. Then, both at once, they began to laugh.

They laughed long and hard and healthily, until at last they fell forward onto each other's chests, turned, and stumbled together down a tall passageway illuminated with wax candles, that had suddenly opened up for them on one side—they never noticed whose—of the diamond-set frame. They went arm in arm, never speaking a word, at first staggering, but still from time to time breaking into chuckles, giggles, or downright laughter; and after every such pause walking on more and more steadily, until, by the time they reached the entrance and found all their garments, whole, clean, and fresh, waiting for them in two neat piles atop their armor, their strength was as firm as it had been on the morning after their last truly refreshing night's sleep. The very aches and bruises of their last battle, down to Harald's wrenched shoulder, were healed and cleared away as though they had never been.

Helping each other re-dress, they quit the cave, to find Garth waiting just beyond the bushes. A few paces away, Joiselette sat cushioned on the couchant lion, in comfortable conversation with Dame Gavrielle, Sir Ywen, Tamba, and—rather to Harald's surprise—the Warrior Woman of the Ford. Sir Ywen's squires and Dame Gavrielle's attendants were beguiling the time with a game of Hide and Seek at the edge of the forest.

"My goodness!" cried the lady of Wisten. "Has it been an hour already?"

Sir Harald replied, "To me, my lady, and—I suspect—to

my friend Sir Jokesir as well, it seems more nearly a life-time."

Sir Ywen nodded knowingly. "Did I not warn you that no one would be well advised to enter that cave without direct and specific orders to do so?"

"Which orders they had, of course." Joiselette stood and approached her prisoner, holding something out in her hand. "Sir Ywen has given me back my favor, Sir Harald, since he only borrowed it for the day. Would you like it now?"

He took the enameled pendant into his palm and held it tenderly fisted for a moment, meanwhile regarding Sir Jokesir and Dame Gavrielle. The slight-framed knight stood holding out his heart in the gaze he aimed at the lady of Wisten; and she looked back, if not in kind, at least in willing friendship. While some hint of amusement flavored her regard, it was amusement of warm and graceful kindliness.

"My lady Mistress of Wisten of the Mists," Sir Jokesir said at last, "will you accept a formerly errant knight into your service, even one who didn't get here in time for your tournament?"

"I thought so," the Warrior Woman remarked with an attractively skewed smirk.

At the same moment, Sir Harald pressed the pendant back into Joiselette's hand and wordlessly jerked his head toward Sir Jokesir. The Maid of the Wood smiled, nodded, resumed her seat on the lion, and slipped the piece of enamelwork to Dame Gavrielle as quietly as if they enjoyed a prior understanding.

"I accept your service, Sir Jokesir the Puissant," said Dame Gavrielle. "And, even if you didn't make it here in time to be a contestant, I hope you'll take this for your badge anyway. It was worn by the knight who won my little tournament, but he won't stay here. He has too many prior commitments."

Sir Jokesir kneeling before her, Dame Gavrielle dropped the pendant on its cord around his neck and took his hands between her own. Then she looked across at the Warrior Woman and said, "There! You see? At least it got me one new knight, after all!"

The Warrior Woman cocked her head to one side and

lifted one brow, as much as to say it was probably just as well that Sir Jokesir had missed the tournament.

But here we must leave Wisten of the Mists and its people, who have no further part in our present story.

Sir Harald had fallen into what Garth considered the very bad habit, for a knight, of helping pitch the tents and otherwise make camp every evening. Their first night away from the lands of Dame Gavrielle, however, much to Garth's satisfaction, he left all the work to serf and page, while he sat apart with Joiselette and privately told her his adventure in the Cave of the Mirrors of Ultimate Truth.

After finishing, he added, "But Sir Ywen went in alone. At least, he came out alone. Who did he see in that last mirror?"

"Only Sir Ywen himself could tell you that. It must be different for everyone. But in any case, I'm sure his experience was just as enviable as yours."

"Enviable?" Sir Harald repeated. "I take it that 'enviable' does not always mean 'pleasurable.'"

"No more than 'pleasurable' always means 'enviable.'" With that, Joiselette broke into another song, as if unable to stop herself, although this time she sang as softly as the gathering twilight:

> "One special envy for each soul,
> One private quest, one precious goal,
> But all our lifetimes make the whole.
> Why envy someone else's need?
> For friends and family we may bleed,
> But none can for another feed.
> Enough alike to sympathize,
> To read the face with mind and eyes,
> But in the difference lies the prize."

"Whose prize?" asked Sir Harald. "Mine, or Jokesir's?"

"Both of yours, sir. This prize belongs to everyone."

PART THE THIRD:

"The Fearful Picture of a Vision . . ."

(Scott, *Ivanhoe*, ch. XLIII)

"I wish Your Worship wouldn't do that," Garth grumbled. "It isn't fitting work for a knight!"

Having already tended his noble charger Goblin, which was the only work Garth recognized as befitting a knight about the campsite, Sir Harald was helping Tamba put up Joiselette's pavilion.

"You came to tolerate my freaks last summer," Sir Harald replied, driving a tent peg into the freshly flowering soil.

"Last summer was last summer." Even as late as last autumn, Garth's new master—for legal as well as practical purposes—might still have been feeling too chastened to relax of an evening and watch his inferiors perform all the work that properly belonged to them; but the loyal serf had hoped that the winter would have knocked some of that nonsense out of Sir Harald's knightly head.

Instead, as the season of Pentecost moved farther and farther beyond the actual Sunday of the feast, with each new shoot and flower serving as another reminder that the time drew near when Sir Harald must either pay his debt to Sir Kay—his arms and beloved horse, if their ransom could not be found—or be branded triply a traitor, his mood grew more and more subdued. Pounding another peg into the ground, he answered Garth: "Even your great Sir Gawen must do all this for himself whenever he goes questing completely alone."

"Maybe," Garth conceded, "but not when he has attendants to do it for him."

Joiselette, who sat amid her usual cluster of birds and small animals mending a tear near the hem of her black robe (nobody had ever considered needlework too menial a task for even the finest lady in the land; and, indeed, she had spent part of the winter re-embroidering the design of her knightly prisoner's surcoat to match his revised shield), interrupted her song long enough to say quietly, "Let him alone, good Garth. He has my permission."

Tamba merely chuckled, which was his preferred manner of partaking in these little squabbles between master and man, meanwhile accepting all the assistance he could get from either of them. Then, suddenly, he stood straight and shaded his eyes against the westering sun. "But who comes here?"

All paused and turned to see what the page saw. A lone rider was approaching on a little brown donkey: a slim, slumped individual in broad-brimmed brown hat, brown cape over russet tunic, and baggy brown trousers with plain brown hose tied below the knee.

"Hail, friend!" Joiselette called out, breaking the short silence. "Be welcome!"

The brim of the hat rose slowly, disclosing a beardless, white, and very weary young face. One leg jerked out to bestow a weak little kick on the donkey's flank. The patient beast ambled onward a few paces more before pausing to let its rider slump out of the saddle completely and roll prone into the half-concealing grass.

All four companions—along with such of Joiselette's furred, feathered, and scaled friends as could adjust to the crashing hurry of the larger beings—rushed to the fallen rider. Joiselette reached him first by a few heartbeats, checked quickly, and pronounced, "It seems to be pure exhaustion, nothing worse. Let him have my bed."

"No!" Sir Harald protested at once, meanwhile gathering the unconscious stranger into his arms. Standing up with the limp form cradled against his chest, he blinked once, glanced around with a puzzled frown, and declared: "He can have my tent. It never hurts a knight on quest to sleep under the stars."

Not because Joiselette—who ate of anything offered her—had ever asked them to, but rather because they found they could hardly bear to take advantage of the trusting creatures who flocked to her in every place, the men had fallen into something resembling a perpetual Lent, eating other foods heartily but flesh only when they happened upon some furred, feathered, or scaled creature newly dead of mishap, or when the Quiller Lion took pity on them and dragged back to camp the remains of some large kill of his own. The lion, who had been out hunting his daily fare when the stranger arrived, brought nothing back today, thus demonstrating that though he had many remarkable gifts, prophecy was not always nor necessarily among them. Garth, however, so far broke their usual custom as to catch a trout from the clear stream they had followed all that afternoon; and Tamba, who had spied out some of the mysteries of cookery during his days with Sirs Letron and Labigodés, stewed it up with barley, wild onions, and various seasonings into a heartening broth for their unexpected guest, using a little kettle he chanced to espy hanging from the said guest's saddle, and thought somewhat better in quality than their own slightly battered stewpot.

"Call me David ap Gwillam," the youth told them when sufficiently revived. "I travel in search of my older brother, who has fallen into the clutches of the Knights of the Blue Flame."

"I have never heard of them," remarked Tamba.

"Nor I," Sir Harald slowly affirmed. "Do you fear for your brother's life, David ap Gwillam?"

"I fear . . . I fear that if he is not saved soon, sir, he will be lost to us forever! These Knights Keepers of the Blue Flame have taken to worshipping a proud dame who rides upon a dragon. So cruel has she made them, that they condemn to bitter death any other lady or woman, damsel or girl, who might dare venture into their land."

"That cannot conform to our good King Arthur's law!" cried Garth.

"To say the least," Tamba agreed, "a fearful waste."

Sir Harald asked, "Where is their land?"

"If I knew that more exactly, I might have reached it before hunger and weariness overcame me. It is said to lie three leagues, or sometimes three hours, or, again, three days, north of Despair."

"Ah!" said Tamba. "Instead of a map, a riddle."

"A riddle that we must help solve," Sir Harald said, reaching forth in the firelight to rub the lion's head, which made the great beast purr. Over the months, they had passed from wary truce into alliance bordering on friendship, so long as the knight kept his hindquarters at a respectful distance from the lion's back, which consented to bear nobody save Joiselette.

"What about your own quest, master?" Garth wanted to know.

"We might as easily find the Black Chevron Knight on the way to these Keepers of the Blue Flame as in any other direction." Then, suddenly recollecting that he was still the Lady Joiselette's prisoner, he cast her a glance across the fire.

She smiled and nodded. "It may lie as little as three hours north of us, if this place where we are now sitting counts as David's despair. But if we succeed in finding the land of the Blue Flame Knights," she added lightly, "I trust you will not blame me for waiting at the border!"

Next morning they crossed a grassy rise, came to a wide river, and saw on the other side a vast wasteland where, as far as met the eye to east, west, and north, the forest lay charred and blackened by fire, only a few stripped trunks of once-proud trees still sticking up here and there like begrimed and broken bones.

"Let me suggest," proposed the ever-resourceful page, "that east or west along this side of the river would give us pleasanter searching, besides sparing us the danger of crossing so wide and white a reach of water."

"The country of the Knights Keepers of the Blue Flame lies somewhere to the north," David insisted.

Sir Harald looked the river up, down, and across. "Goblin could swim it. Although I wouldn't ask him to carry me and my armor both."

As a rule—and except when playing the lone villain—Harald de Folgeste copied the sensible custom, while traveling in company through reasonably civilized country, of leading his charger while his chain mail rode a pack horse and he himself a good hackney. David's news concerning the Knights Keepers of the Blue Flame had led the party to suspect that they might no longer be in reasonably civilized country; and so today he was riding on the great black warhorse, both of them fully armed, in case of encountering some fierce foe too deficient in chivalry to wait while an intended victim armed and re-mounted. In this desolate place, however, with open field behind them and burned-out woods before, the worst things to fear were hardly such as the best mail could guard against.

"Say that Goblin could cross, Your Worship," Garth protested. "What good would it do us to have you on that side of the river and the rest of us still here on this side? Trust me, Goblin might be able to swim it, and a few of our other beasts—but not all of them, not even leaving most of their loads behind."

"Abandon whatever else you will," quipped Tamba, "but bring along my store of spices—even at risk of seasoning the river."

"You wouldn't ask our poor lion to wet his paws, surely?" Joiselette teased them, then added, "Why not see if we can find a boat or bridge?"

It may have been a mere suggestion, but Sir Harald immediately took it as a command, turning Goblin's head westward to lead the way along the riverbank.

It was not long before they found both bridge and boat; but the boat was moored on the far side, and the bridge was a perilous-looking old thing of frayed ropes and moss-covered planks, suspended so low over the water that the highest waves lapped up to glister it with spray.

"I think," said Tamba, "that I am the lightest man of us, and my Firefly the lightest little horse. Let us be the ones to cross that bridge and bring back the boat."

"No," David protested in a husky voice. "Surely, good page, I have less weight than even you, and all of you have been so kind as to choose your path for my own and my brother's assistance. Let me make the attempt."

"*That*, you will not!" exclaimed Sir Harald. And, without waiting to hear any further discussion, or even to ask his lady's permission, he rode Goblin forward to the bridge.

"Sir Harald!" Joiselette called after him.

Having reached the bridge, Goblin hesitated briefly; but, at a tchuk from his rider, lifted one great hoof and set it down firmly on the second plank.

"Sir Harald!" Joiselette called again, this time adding, "Prisoner!" for emphasis. "At least listen to your own words of a little while ago, and take off your armor first!"

So bidden, he recollected his somewhat ambiguous position in the party and backed Goblin onto solid ground again, though still blocking anyone else's access to the bridge. "My lady! Having stripped, may I take this danger on myself, as befits the one knight of the company?"

"*Now* he remembers what befits a knight and what doesn't!" Garth grumbled under his breath, no doubt thinking about the tent pegs.

"Sir," Tamba still tried to protest, "what is a page but a very lightweight knight?"

"No," Joiselette said firmly. "Sir Harald has requested the danger, and he may have it, provided he doesn't ask that bridge to bear him, his horse, and his armor, all three."

If Tamba had been a young page on his way to squirehood, he probably would not have dared speak as he sometimes spoke to the duly dubbed—even if not so very long ago renegade—knight; but in fact he was actually Sir Harald's elder by a year or two, and such grown-up gentlemen as Tamba, who had chosen of their own accord to remain pages for life, occasionally developed a certain cheekiness that might better have befitted the court fool. It was an occupational hazard.

As for Joiselette, she might have pointed out that she was surely the lightest in weight of any of them, and crossing the bridge on foot would be the safest way for whoever went. But she had amassed enough experience of her traveling companions to know that such an offer and such an observation would only have been met with time-consuming counterarguments. Scrupulously though they bowed to her preferences or supposed preferences in other matters, they could all—her prisoner foremost—be depended upon to rebel whenever they thought it was a question of her own safety or comfort.

Meanwhile, while I've been taking the time to offer you the above commentary, Garth and Tamba have already helped Sir Harald strip off his armor, and our knight, without even stopping to throw his surcoat back on over his gambeson, has jumped back upon his strong steed and started across the elderly bridge.

It swayed and groaned beneath Goblin's weight. Its groans and creaks worried them more than its swaying and tipsiness—since even Sir Harald could exercise caution when occasion absolutely demanded, and Goblin was one of those animals from whom "horse sense" received its name. Clearly comprehending the gravity of the situation, he lifted each massive hoof in turn with great care and set it down again one pace farther forward so gently that, had the planks been eggs, only his weight and not in any way his movements would have cracked their delicate shells. Yet, for all their care, the farther they progressed from the bridge's anchored end, the more deeply it bowed beneath them. Bit by bit, step by step, it came in increments closer to the river's far from glassy surface.

At last, when they were about a third of the way over, the entire middle portion dipped down below the rushing waves, so that it became a bridge under water . . . and, at the same time, an increasingly steep one, those planks still above the actual surface growing ever wetter and slicker with the spray and dashing foam.

Goblin paused. They could see his great muscles begin to bunch, even as his rider leaned forward in the saddle.

"Sir Harald!" Joiselette cried. "Don't—"

Too late. Losing horse sense in the giddying slope of the downward curve, the mighty charger made his leap.

Had it been from cliff to cliff, solid surface to solid surface, all would have been well. The stallion landed squarely on that part of the bridge that first emerged beyond the submerged length—and crashed right through.

"Ropes and all!" cried David.

"Aye, God be praised for that much!" said Garth. "Or they'd have been snared."

"Instead of merely drowned?" fretted Tamba.

"No!" Joiselette exclaimed, pointing. "Look there!"

First Sir Harald's head, then Goblin's, broke the surface as man and horse bobbed back into sight—at least the top parts of their bodies—moving toward the far bank with such purpose that the onlookers knew the knight had not boasted idly in claiming that his charger could swim it.

Reaching land, the great warhorse hove himself ashore with one powerful surge of his forelegs, followed by some little scramble on the part of his hindquarters. He then waited long enough for Sir Harald to slide off before shaking himself so that drops flew from his glistening black hide like diamond sparkles in the sunlight—a strange, small instant of beauty against the stark background of burned woodland. By the time they could look away from that shower, Sir Harald had reached the boat.

Actually less boat than barge, it proved large enough to ferry the animals across one at a time. Sir Harald and Garth, as the two strongest human members of the party, manned the long poles that fortunately still resided in the craft, while Joiselette stood at each beast's head in turn to hold it tranquil amidst the roiling eddies, Tamba watched the four-footed ones still waiting to be ferried, and David gathered them as they arrived on the farther bank. Goblin, of course, had the longest wait and, it must be said, bore it the most patiently, considering that there was not a single blade of green grass to be nipped anywhere from the blackened sward, but only puffs of pale ash squirting up from every spot on which he set down a hoof. The dust of that vast burning still lay heavy over everything, cool but recent enough that no breeze had as yet blown it away; nor did the seared earth as yet show any sign of the fire having fertilized it to bring forth fresh growth.

"Where is God in all this?" Sir Harald asked, not in rage, but in somber bafflement.

"Hidden," Joiselette answered sadly, bending to shed a tear over the burned remains of some small creature who had failed to gain the river in time. "Deeply hidden. Very, very deeply." And, as sometimes happened, her song took on a solemn and mournful tone as they picked their way through the wasted forest.

> "Oh Thou, Who here, as everywhere, must be—
> Yet far too subtle for our eyes to see!
> Lend us the trust to use in place of sight,
> And lead us by the hand through our dark
>   night."

Yet even the Maid of the Wood soon fell silent as they stumbled through that charred black and ashy white wasteland, where no living wild things remained at all to flock about her in welcome.

All the rest of that long day they traveled through burned-out forest until, toward evening, dry, dusty, and blackened from brushing against charred limbs, they came to the edge of a vast fen.

"Here we camp," Sir Harald said as wearily as though

he had ridden that day in his armor, which in fact he had never put back on: little enough chance of surprise attack in this dreary waste. Bleak though the campsite was, nobody disagreed, since both behind them and as far as they could see ahead, the prospects were still bleaker.

The lion left them awhile, as usual, though what he could hope to hunt was beyond any of them to say. Nevertheless, after they had finished tending their other beasts, raising their tents, and scavenging enough half-charred fuel for the small campfire that they needed without this time really desiring; and as they sat around it thinking moody thoughts whilst watching Tamba cook them a broth of barley and spices in David's good little kettle, the lion returned proudly dragging the ready-roasted but still recognizable carcass of a boar.

Garth lost no time in carving out five of the choicest pieces. Joiselette accepted hers with gratitude, but David demurred, shaking his beardless head and lifting not one finger to receive the meat.

"You need strength, lad," Garth protested, and Tamba added, staring out at the morass ahead of them, "Between two such days as today and tomorrow, we all of us need as much strength as we can beg, borrow, or steal."

"With all my thanks," David insisted politely, "this dust and destruction have sickened me somewhat, and my stomach feels more in need of rest than of food. With your kind leave, let me content myself with Tamba's good barley soup."

"Even monks that have sworn off all flesh set aside their vow long enough to swallow a little strengthening broth at need. How if I were to mince a little of this wild pork and add it to the stew?" Tamba suggested.

"I beg you, do not take so much trouble," the youth replied a little hastily.

"To refuse good pig?" Garth grumbled. "Anyone might think you were a circumcised dog of a Jew!"

He had meant these words in jest, to cajole David into eating a few bites; but as soon as they were uttered, suspicion fell on the camp like a net of sharp steel wires weighted with lead. The horses, mules, and donkey continued quietly grazing on what grasses they could find along the margin of the unburned marsh, and the lion, with even less knowledge than an ordinary beast of the bitter generations that already in that golden time lay between Gentile and Jew, sat between David and Joiselette looking puzzled and somewhat saddened. But for a moment the silence lay heavy upon all the men.

Then Sir Harald said, "No. God's Blood, I'd stake my life, David is no more circumcised than I am myself! Let him eat or not eat whatever he wishes."

Joiselette rubbed the lion's head. He gazed at her, then turned to David and laid one paw on the lad's knee as if at once begging pardon for his offense and inquiring what it was.

David shook his head and said: "No. Thank you, sir, but I must not impose on your kindness any longer. My father's name was not Gwillam, but Joseph. I am indeed of the children of Israel."

Joiselette said gently. "Joseph. Joseph of Arimathea was a good Jew. As were Joseph of Nazareth, and Mother Mary, and Ihesu Himself."

"And my brother," David added as if anxious that there should be no further appearance of deceit. "Nor have we ever abandoned the creed of our fathers and mothers." He rose and turned to take his departure.

"David!" Sir Harald cried, likewise rising to his feet. "Don't go! Pardon us! Tamba, let him have as much of the barley as he can eat."

David turned back, and they could see a tear glistening on his smooth cheek. "Thank you, sir. Thank you, all of you. I will accept a little of your barley. And, if you will permit me to sleep here tonight, I will relieve you of my presence in the morning."

"What in God's holy name has changed?" Sir Harald demanded. "You and your brother still need help, and these Flaming Blue Knights have still broken King Arthur's laws, and I still have to search *somewhere*."

Joiselette added, as though teasing the entire company, "How great can all these famous differences really be, if it took us so long to sniff out your shocking secret?"

Taking his cue from the lady whom he officially served as page, Tamba argued, "You seemed willing enough to accept our help yesterday, never asking what *we* were."

And Garth, sounding a little ashamed of himself, said

gruffly, "Besides, this country we're in, nobody should go stumbling around in it by himself."

So they set out next day across the bogs: three good Christian men—even if the chief of them had been a villain—one staunch Jew, and . . . what, exactly, Joiselette might be, they had all of them assumed without questioning. And if one or more of them began to ask himself, now, whether she might ever attend other rituals as eagerly as theirs, he kept that thought locked well within the coffers of his own brain. In any case, it was clear that she would shun both blood sacrifice and sins of the flesh; therefore, if she had ever attended Hebrew ceremonies, they must, despite all rumor, have been innocent of such.

Today Joiselette led the way; or, rather, the birds, snakes, frogs, and other denizens of the unburned marshlands showed her the safest paths for heavy equine and human feet, and she relayed their guidance to her companions. Again today, Sir Harald rode unarmored—for obvious reasons, with sucking bogs on every side.

From midmorning until midafternoon, they were on a path so narrow that two missteps in either direction might have drawn them under. They had no space to make their usual midday stop for rest and a full meal, but must content themselves with such mouthfuls of hard journeybread as Tamba could dig from the saddlebags and pass around hand to hand. The horses, mules, and donkey found rich browsing here, as they progressed slowly along, but small wonder if they still felt ill-nourished from the day before, when they had had nothing from riverbank to marsh-edge, save precious oats from the saddlebags.

About the middle of the afternoon, the party came to an island of solid ground only just barely large enough for them to dismount and snatch a few moments' relative ease while debating whether to take a belated respite here or press on at once in the hope of finding enough ground to make full camp before nightfall.

As they talked, the pack horse who bore, among other burdens, Sir Harald's armor, tried to reach some succulent-looking weed several paces distant, and in doing so stepped off the firm path and at once became mired. Panic-stricken, the poor beast strove to pull free. His hind hooves slid in after his forefeet. He tried to lunge forward and only slewed in deeper and farther from solid ground, all the while sending forth one horse scream after another.

Shouting "God's Blood!" Sir Harald plunged in after the beast before anyone could stop him or even fully understand what was going on. And hard on Harald's heels went David.

"Pretend it's water!" Joiselette cried after them. "Swim! Get a rope," she added to Garth and Tamba, meanwhile shedding both her black wool robe and white linen shift.

David flopped forward in an effort to follow her advice. Harald, however, was already thigh deep. "Easy to say!" he panted back as he struggled with the rapidly sinking beast. "The straps!" he shouted to David. "Damn! Loosen the harness!"

Snatching the rope's end from Garth, Joiselette dove naked into the bog and began, true to her own advice, swimming toward the trapped trio. David was hacking at the horse's harness with his belt-knife—in those days, everyone carried such a knife to cut his or her meat at mealtime—Harald scrabbling for the girth, and both of them in danger every heartbeat of being crushed under by the frenzied thrashing of the very beast they sought to save. Joiselette's arrival ended that threat, at least. Quickly calming the creature with a murmured song, she managed to secure the rope around its sturdy neck. The horse quieted, Harald and David succeeded at last in freeing it of the load that had been bearing it down all the faster.

By the time the packs vanished completely into the mire, Garth and Tamba had the other end of the rope fixed round Goblin. Appearing to bunch every muscle in his strong body, the great charger first planted all four feet firmly, then began to back, step by careful step, Garth at his head pulling with him while Tamba and the lion tested the ground behind him to make sure of his continued solid footing. Hand over hand on the rope, Joiselette and David helped each other back to safety, while Harald, by holding to the pack beast's mane, finally brought his own legs near enough the surface to kick a little as though swimming.

And then, at last, they were all safe again, three sodden people and a shuddering, bare-backed horse . . . and the two men who had wisely helped from firm land shivering in something even more than relief and exhaustion, as their eyes took in the survivors. With garments slicked and plastered tight against flesh, Harald and David seemed more closely stripped than did Joiselette, with the mud covering her nakedness.

And, for all her curious maturity of mind and spirit, Joiselette still had the body almost of a child.

David did not.

Tamba broached the subject at last, that evening, as three of them rested beside their campfire safe out of the bogs. "I think that we can no longer call you 'David.'"

For answer, the Jewess pulled her cloak more tightly about herself and then sat with her head buried in her arms, while Joiselette tenderly rubbed her shoulders.

Sir Harald and Garth were some paces away, using up the last of the failing daylight in an activity that must have appeared very strange to a chance passer-by, had there been any, who did not know the circumstances. All the remainder of that afternoon, the knight had been abnormally silent—they feared him either stunned or controlling himself with superhuman effort—while his loss sank in. When they finally stumbled to safe and solid ground, it was obvious to all that he must release his feelings somehow; and, since he would strike neither living beast nor fellow human—even though the heedless pack horse could have been held chiefly to blame, and both Garth and Tamba bravely offered their own backs for failing to have tethered the animals securely—and since Joiselette strictly forbade him to injure himself even at secondhand by striking rocks or trees, and since after losing everything the one beast had carried they could hardly afford the destruction of any further supplies . . . Garth was building up hard-packed dummies of earth and turf, which his master immediately demolished with foot and fist, from time to time peppering his efforts with a bloody oath or some such comment as, "A turtle without its shell!" or "Not even mine to lose!"

This did not cease until he had physically exhausted himself and the night was complete. Then, finding the campfire by its own light, since the moon had not yet risen, he sank down between Joiselette and Tamba, and let Garth rub his shoulders for a moment or two before remembering that the serf must be almost equally weary, and bidding him take his own rest.

Tonight the lion had brought back the whole carcass of his freshly hunted deer, and did not drag the rest away for his own meal until after Tamba had carved out four choice shares for hungry humans—the Jewess again praying to take vegetable nourishment only, which the page took for a sign of penitence. So far had the hardships of the road eroded the company's sense of mannerliness that the maidens and page had already eaten, he heartily and they sparingly. Now, as knight and serf settled down at last, Tamba offered them generous if very well roasted slices, still on the spits.

Sir Harald shook his head. "Not yet. For God's sake, Garth, get back your strength!" he added, seeing the serf hold back despite his hunger. "I'll eat in a little while."

"Then how will you prefer it, Sir?" Tamba wanted to know. "Cold, or burned to charcoal?"

For answer, Harald seized his share, spit and all, and then sat staring at it, turning it moodily back and forth in the firelight. Garth, however, gratefully began to eat.

"Deborah," said the Jewess, lifting her head.

"What?" Sir Harald replied.

"My true name is Deborah, the daughter of Joseph."

"Maid Deborah." The knight's nod was as guarded as his voice. "It is a beautiful name. And . . . is he truly your brother?"

"Forgive me. He is truly my betrothed."

Sir Harald's sigh was almost a shudder, but all he said was, "I guessed as much."

"Jew, woman, and betrothed!" said Tamba. "What other surprises do you have in store for us, Maid Deborah, daughter of Joseph?"

She shook her head.

Joiselette put in, "She could hardly have told us he was her betrothed without revealing her gender."

"But why, my damsel, may I ask with all due respect, should you conceal that, against God's law and Nature's own?" the page persisted, blithely ignoring the fact that his own lady was currently faring abroad in the cast-off robe of a male pilgrim.

"Why," said Joiselette, "if I had to follow my lover into

a land where they burn every woman they find, I'd pretend to be a man, too!"

"Yes," Tamba argued, "but as a fair maiden, she might have found a dozen heroes to champion her cause."

"In place of one poor, left-handed, half-reformed villain," Sir Harald said bitterly. "Forgive me, Maid Deborah. I have already failed you. What good is a knight without armor? A turtle without his shell!"

"Sir," Deborah whispered, "your noble heart has not failed me."

"You did very well this afternoon, Sir Harald!" Joiselette assured him.

"I should have done better."

"That load would have sunk our poor beast before Goblin could pull him out."

"If I had held onto it myself—"

"Then it would have sunk you."

"The helmet, at least. . . . It was the same helmet you brought back to me, that morning we first met."

"Of the three of us, sir," Joiselette told him with the hint of a twinkle, "you, me, and the helmet, I would rather lose the helmet."

"Damn!" he exclaimed. "It was not even my armor to lose! It was Sir Kay's! How can I hope to ransom it and Goblin now?"

"When we find your Knight of the Black Chevron," Garth suggested, "the Quiller Lion may decide him to do what's right."

Sir Harald shook his head in bleak discouragement. "We won't find him."

"Prisoner!" Joiselette said, catching up his half-forgotten cut of roasted venison and holding it beneath his nose. "Eat your supper."

Silently, he began to obey.

"For the matter of that," Tamba said reflectively, "there is something that has been weighing a little on my mind. How many do they number, these Knights Keepers of the Blue Flame?"

"Some say sixty-six," Deborah confessed, "and some say six hundred and sixty-six. All that I have ever seen with my own eyes were the six who bore away my . . . betrothed."

"Let us say a mere six," Tamba reckoned up. "How much could a single knight, with or without mail, do against even a mere six other armed and armored knights?"

"A good deal," Garth grunted, "if he were Sir Gawen."

"I said a knight," Tamba replied, "not an archangel!"

Having finished his meal, Garth was ready for debate. "If need be, we can stand and fight with Sir Harald."

"With all respect, my friend," said Tamba, "you are brave and sturdy, but you as a serf have never been trained in the finer points of fighting, and I as a page have never been trained in the hardier. Even as makeweights, we would be of limited use against armed knights on their destriers. The Quiller Lion, now, if he could be persuaded to continue with us at cost of abandoning our Lady Joiselette at the border—"

Swallowing a half-chewed mouthful, Sir Harald said suddenly, "Even villains may have some sense of honor. Or at least of fair play. I still have sword, shield, and lance." (The sword and shield had been ready to hand on his riding hackney, and therefore safe; the lance was the one burden besides his own harness and saddle that they permitted Goblin to carry on the road.) "I can challenge them as I stand, to either lend me armor for the combat, or send their champion as poorly equipped as the challenger. And the same terms for the Black Chevron Knight!"

"Now you sound more like yourself, Sir Harald!" Joiselette exclaimed, bouncing up briefly to brush a kiss across his forehead.

"Well!" Tamba murmured. "Now that we have that matter comfortably settled, it only remains to regret that one of our pavilions and part of our bedding have also been lost. And, whoever the armor was, the pillow was mine."

"Be glad, anyway," Garth muttered in answer, "that your spices were on one of the mules."

Joiselette and the grateful Deborah shared the shelter of the remaining pavilion, but what cushions and coverings the party still possessed were divided up as equitably as possible—or, rather, as equitably as Sir Harald would allow, for he insisted on his prerogative as a knight on quest to sleep with a cloak his only blanket and a saddle his only pillow.

Setting the demands of the journey above all differences in rank and station, Tamba and Garth slept beneath the same blanket. As Tamba had privately pointed out to Garth while setting up camp, if Joiselette could sleep beneath the same cloth roof as a Jewess, it ill behooved her page and Sir Harald's serf to call themselves strange bedfellows.

In the middle of the night, wakened by Garth's snores and wakening him in turn to make him stop, Tamba added in a soft voice, "But how much assurance have we, truly, that these Knights of the Blue Flame are indeed villains?"

"They have stolen a man against his will."

"A Jew. We know nothing of what he may have done, nor whether they may not mean to convert him."

"They murder poor ladies."

"For that, we have only the word of a Jewess."

After a moment, Garth said slowly and sleepily, "I know Sir Harald was a villain, because he admits it himself, and he stole that Aloof Fair One against King Arthur's law. And he shouldn't have said he wouldn't give up his horse and arms to Sir Kay. But our Lady Joiselette believes the Jewess, and Sir Harald believes our Lady Joiselette . . . and even if he didn't, he'd have to obey her until she releases him. And he's my rightful master now."

"But suppose our Lady Joiselette should be mistaken this time? Suppose that once again your master has chosen the evil side?"

Garth, however, was snoring again, as if the problem that bedeviled his comrade meant little or nothing to him.

Yet it was either a brief nap, or a pretense meant to silence the page; for after Tamba had quieted and begun once more to breathe with the smooth rhythm of slumber, Garth opened his eyes and peered anxiously, by the light of glowing fire-gleeds and the nearly full moon that had risen now, at the form of Sir Harald, who lay nearby with his back to them.

"Master?" Garth whispered cautiously.

There was no reply, neither by word, sound, nor movement . . . only a little raggedness in the rise and fall of the knight's shoulder, and Garth thought he might have imagined this. To be on the safe side, he added in as soft a whisper as before, "It was only sleep-talk, Your Worship. Don't pay him any heed."

Then, hoping his master had heard nothing of any of this, the good serf slipped back into slumber for the rest of the night.

And had Sir Harald overheard? If so, he never betrayed it by word or sign; so let us leave him his privacy in the matter.

❖　❖　❖

They woke next morning to mist that muffled all things in moist obscurity. Breaking their fast as best they could, and packing up their camp more by feel than by any other sense, they took their lead from the lion, with Joiselette on his back—trusting his wild instinct, despite his having spent the greater part of his existence to date as a piece of furniture doubly enclosed in castle and hall.

Even though they had to ride closer than usual in order to follow the dim and blurry forms going ahead, so thick was the enveloping fog that they felt far more isolated, almost closeted, in their ones and twos, than when they rode at greater distance apart in bright sunlight.

Still dressed as David—for this small party had lacked the foresight and packspace to carry along full sets of women's garments against emergency; and besides, they were still riding north, as they hoped, to the land where women met fierce welcome—Deborah rode immediately behind Joiselette, an arrangement the two had settled between themselves. After some hours, when the way seemed wide enough, with no more trees looming like thin dark towers to left and right, Sir Harald began to close the interval, step by step, gradually so as neither to outdistance those who followed him nor—he hoped—to excite their undue attention, until his hackney and Deborah's donkey walked abreast.

Thinking perhaps that he meant to reopen their break-fast debate concerning the order of march, she began in soft tones, "Truly, sir, I feel safer between the lion and you, than I could feel between you and your good attendants."

"My damsel, I have no wish to argue the point with you again . . . only to ride side by side awhile. With your permission?"

"Sir," she answered with a small catch in her throat, "you honor me by asking it."

Taking that for an affirmative, he rode on at her side for some moments before at last resuming, "My damsel . . . I do not know how it is among your people . . . but among us, it is no dishonor for any good woman to have . . . another knight or two in readiness . . . in case of misfortune—which God forbid!—to her husband or—"

"Sir Harald." She seemed to turn her face toward him, then look away again. "Good, noble . . . may I call you friend?"

"With all my heart!"

"Even when I have confessed that there does still remain one more secret that I have not yet told?" After a brief pause, she went on, "Sir . . . my betrothed went with them willingly, because they lured him with the golden promise of something that he could gain no other way in this world. We, too, play at jousts and tournaments, when we are little children. . . . They lured him with the fair promise of knighthood."

Beneath their mounts' hooves, the ground began an upward slope.

After a moment, Sir Harald replied, "It makes no difference in anything I have said."

"But for that," she added, "by now we should have been in one of the Moslem lands across the sea, where Jew, Christian, and Musselman live freely side by side. My love was schooled as a physician, to save lives rather than take them."

"Who am I to blame any man for aspiring to knighthood? But I know," Sir Harald went on steadily, "dear Maid Deborah, I know with all my heart that I would never have left such a betrothed bride, not even for a place among Arthur's own knights."

The slope grew steeper underhoof. Joiselette's song was a soft series of notes drifting down from above the ghostly flag of the lion's tail ahead of them, the voices of Garth and Tamba were a low murmuring in the mists behind, and neither pair's words distinguishable to the ears of the other pair.

"Sir," Deborah said softly, "among us, betrothal is as binding as marriage itself, but even if that were not so . . . Gentle Gentile, have you thought, in your great generosity, of what would happen to you among your own people, were it known that you had even made such an offer to a Jewess?"

"I have thought of little else since the night before last."

"Since two nights ago?" She paused long enough to reckon it up and remember. "Since the night you learned that I am sprung from Abraham? But it was not until the following day that you discovered my sex!"

He shook his head. "I guessed that much the first evening you came to us, when I picked you up limp from falling off your mount."

"You guessed . . . and said nothing? For surely it was surprise I saw in the faces of your two men yesterday! Was it not surprise?"

"I am sure it was. I held you cradled to my chest," he confessed, "that first evening, a little longer and more tenderly than perhaps I should have. . . . Small doubt my Lady Joiselette guessed as well. But to Garth and Tamba, I am sure you were simply a young lad handsome enough to turn any maiden's head."

She smiled. "And from Tamba I heard a tale or two that could prove useful in helping me maintain my disguise."

"It might be better to avoid repeating those tales among men who murder women."

The slope grew steeper yet. Indeed, they were climbing a rise both long and high.

Serious again, she resumed, "Dear friend . . . my very dear, good friend . . . among us, betrothal is as binding as marriage, and I would not have it otherwise, for I love him with all my heart. . . ."

"Who could question that," Sir Harald said gently, "seeing what you risk for him?"

"And yet . . . and yet . . . there is a part of me that wishes, somehow, I might be two women. And one of them a Christian. Sir, you cannot truly have thought how you would be shamed and outcast from your own people—"

"For all I know, I am that already! And for the sake of a lady who is to you as a river pebble to a pearl. No," he tried to unsay his assessment, "she is, after all, my brother's bride."

"I do not understand."

"Hasn't Tamba told you that tale?"

"No."

He gave a grunt with a question mark at its end. "I understand Joiselette and Garth leaving it untold, but . . . well, ask them about it when you have the chance." Dropping behind again as if offering Deborah the chance to ride forward and question Joiselette, the knight muttered to himself like one in a position to judge, "That betrothed of hers is doubly a fool, not to have recognized his own good fortune. God's Blood, I could wish myself a Jew!"

Sir Harald was but one man; and yet, had Deborah and the Aloof Fair One ever been able to sit down together and compare notes, it is clear that Joiselette herself would have had a great deal of difficulty persuading them that they were talking about the same knight.

Meanwhile, acting on Sir Harald's hint, Deborah urged her donkey forward until she rode almost abreast of Joiselette, who was singing:

> "In muffling mysteries of mist—
> Gray, foggy daylight of the soul—
> Remind us, God, of all we've missed,
> And after action make us whole."

Deborah cleared her throat and opened her mouth, but before she could begin to ask what had happened between her protector and his brother's bride, they topped the rise and found the fog suddenly half-clearing to reveal two bulky forms that faced them only a few yards away.

One was a white warhorse carrying a knight in black armor, with a white plume to his helmet and on his arm a shield with a wide black chevron cutting through a field of black and silver vair. The other was a great, blood-red dragon bearing on its back a woman clad in simple white silk girded with gold, and having over her shoulders a rich blue mantle spangled with silver stars and collared in its turn with the fringe of her long, flowing golden hair, which was itself crowned by a plain gold chaplet set with huge emeralds and rubies, sapphires and beryls—every one of which seemed to match the color of her eyes.

At sight of the dragon, the lion first snarled and then gave a mighty roar, starting up on his hind legs with his forepaws reaching out to strike. Tumbling off—or possibly sliding on purpose—Joiselette cried, "Sir Harald! Look out!" already too late.

At the lion's roar, Sir Harald had spurred his horse forward to join them at the crest. The Black Chevron Knight couched his lance—*left-handed*, they saw with horror—and charged. Sir Harald drew his sword and tried to maneuver the terrified hackney to a sidestep, but the Black Chevron Knight, as if noticing that his opponent was not prepared for a joust, lowered his lance and pierced the poor beast through the chest.

It fell screaming, its rider leaping clear just in time. It thrashed twice or thrice and lay still in merciful death. Meanwhile, wheeling easily about, the Black Chevron Knight seized Deborah from her donkey's back. His two squires, galloping up out of the remaining veils of mist, seized Joiselette while her lion was still facing off with the dragon, and bore her kicking and pummeling back into the fog after their master and his captive.

The woman on the dragon lingered long enough to block pursuit. Shouting and brandishing his sword in black fury, Sir Harald ran forward to join the lion. The dragon reared up, presenting them with a breast and belly covered in overlapping scales broad as trenchers and hard as diamonds. Sir Harald slammed his sword on them with all his strength.

The blade shattered.

The Dragon Lady's laughter burst down on him sharp and hard as the fragments of his sword itself. Next she turned her scaly mount and retreated after the others into the shrouding fog.

Roaring again, the lion sprang after them and chomped down at the dragon's tail. For a second, it seemed he had the wyrm . . . but the beast slid through his teeth and was gone as though gulped down by the gray mist.

"Traitor! Monster! Devil!" Sir Harald screamed after the kidnappers, trying vainly to find names vile enough.

"Master!" cried Garth, finally reaching the top of the rise; and Tamba, hastening behind him, added, "What's happened?"

"They've stolen them! Both!" Sir Harald cast his broken sword to earth with such force that it sank to the hilt and stuck fast. "God's Blood! To slay a poor hackney and steal two maidens!" Catching Goblin's reins from Garth, he threw himself onto the saddle and plunged into the fogbank after the lion, who had seemed to wait only for him.

Sir Harald now had nothing left save horse, shield, lance, and his old enemy-turned-ally the Quiller Lion. Who, feline of magical origins that he was, appeared to have a tracking nose almost the equal of any hound's, and continued leading the way, uphill and downdale, all that day as surely and unhesitatingly as though there had been no shred of fog and the quarry were still clearly visible rather than as thoroughly out of both sight and hearing ahead of them as Garth and Tamba behind.

Indeed, thick though the mist had been in the morning, it was thrice as thick now, so that Harald felt as though they moved through heavy combed wool, with nothing around him on any side, nor above, nor even below. He could barely see Goblin's ears. They followed the lion largely by the roars it gave forth from time to time for their benefit. Well for them that there were no more bogs across their way, nor any cliffs just here—although, to be sure, Goblin would have stopped short had he noticed any such danger in time. Harald now depended more than ever upon the wisdom of his warhorse, having lost his spurs along with his armor . . . the same spurs fastened to his feet years ago, on the day of his dubbing, by his sponsor, Sir Joffrey le Châtain. (Sir Joffrey was one of those knights who had gone with his brother Godfrey on crusade to the Holy Land but, unlike Godfrey, had never come home again.)

Twilight turned the mist around them from gray wool into blue, and finally velvet black; but, now accustomed to moving sightlessly, they scarcely slowed their pace. Then the blackness brightened to silver, showing that somewhere above the fogbank the moon shone full and clear. If this failed to hearten them to any very great extent, it may have been because by now they were all three—man, horse, and lion—more hungry than weary and more weary than hungry. Yet still they kept on.

And then at last, as they reached the top of another broad hill, the mist dissipated again—this time for good and all—and in the bright silver moonlight they saw a terrible sight waiting, as if prepared on purpose to rack Sir Harald's soul:

At one side, Joiselette, still in her black pilgrim's robe, lay bound hand and foot atop an ancient stone altar, the white-sheathed Dame of the Dragon holding above her a blade that gleamed like oil in the moonlight, and, at the dame's back, her huge and scaly beast. Far to the other side Deborah, still in her masculine garments, stood tied fast to a tree, the Knight of the Black Chevron near her on his white horse, with his lance in hand ready to swing at either her or her would-be rescuer.

"Sir Harald!" Joiselette cried in tones of strict authority. "*Save David.*"

Thus commanded, he couched his lance and rode for the first time in his life left-handed against a living foe and not a mere practice dummy.

Sir Harald heard the lion roar and glimpsed it springing away toward the dragon, but he needed all his concentration for the Black Chevron Knight bearing down on him in full armor, while he himself had no other protection than his shield and his experience earlier in the day of this same knight's cowardly treachery. Seeing his opponent's point dip down toward the horse, Sir Harald knee-signaled Goblin into a swerve and flashed his own lance up to strike the Black Chevron Knight's out of the way while galloping past.

They turned their horses, paused a moment to study each other, and charged again. This time the Knight of the Black Chevron held his aim true. Each man's lance struck squarely on the other's shield—and both lances shattered.

But the Black Chevron Knight was once again near Deborah's tree, and one of his squires, unnoticed until now, dashed out from behind the foliage and handed his master a second lance.

Sir Harald slid to the ground, dropped the butt of his broken lance, and gave Goblin a slap to order him out of harm's way—no shouted command could have made itself heard above the din and clamor of the battle between lion and dragon on the other side of the hilltop. The Black Chevron Knight spurred his charger toward the unmounted man. Sir Harald hunkered down, holding his shield with both hands, moving it here and there as the Black Chevron

Knight's aim seemed to waver and change in the moon-light. His mind recognized that all must be taking place quickly, but his senses felt them as if they were happening with the slowness of poured honey.

Lance struck shield. At the instant of impact, Sir Harald half rose, tilting his shield and throwing his weight upon it so that the tip of the lance slid down into earth and caught there, quivering. The Black Chevron Knight, failing to let go in time, sailed out of his saddle to describe a perfect arc in the moonlight above his adversary's head.

He struck the ground with a hard clatter and—burst apart like a sack of grain hurled against stone.

Sir Harald snatched up the butt of his broken lance and hastened over to club his foeman if need be.

He found the armor absolutely empty.

There was neither corpse nor fragment of corpse any-where, not within hawberk, nor helmet, nor gauntlet, nor anywhere on the ground. It was as if he had been battling a hollow suit of mail.

There was blood, but he presently discovered that it came from his own leg, which the tip of the Black Chevron Knight's lance had raked open during its passage from shield to earth.

But he could waste no more time in astonishment. Catching up the sword of the Black Chevron Knight, he turned to the stone altar.

That, too, was empty now, both Joiselette and the Dragon Lady vanished . . . though it took him a few blinks to be sure of that, for looming behind the hewn stones lay the huge corpse of the dragon, with the lion standing atop it, bleeding; mewling piteously; and staring now into the distance, now at Sir Harald, and again into the distance.

"Go after them!" Sir Harald called up to him. "Find her!"

Leaping down from the dragon's back with a curious, clumsy limp, as if he were slightly wounded in the paws, the lion had disappeared before the knight finished speaking.

Himself both limping and bleeding, Sir Harald turned and clumped as hastily as he could to the tree where Deborah had stood bound. For a few sickening heartbeats, he thought that she had vanished, too; but one of the Black Chevron Knight's squires, either seeing which way the wind suddenly blew or allowing some native humanity to reassert itself in his heart, had already unbound her and sat with her on the ground, chafing her bruised wrists and ankles.

Goblin, approaching from the other direction, reached the squire and the Jewess at almost the same moment as the knight, to stand over them snuffling gently.

"Oh, Sir Harald!" Deborah cried. "They are gone! We are in their land, and she is still in their power!" Having kept herself conscious long enough to tell him this much, she fainted away.

The squire took up the explanation. "This lad is unhurt, sir, only exhausted with the fear and suffering. My delightful Dame of the Dragon whistled my former lord's horse over to her and took your maiden away on that while your lion was finishing the dragon. That, my lord, was a very noble fight! My former companion, the Black Chevron Knight's other squire, went with them. They will be taking her to the keep of the Knights of the Blue Flame. Who will surely burn her, sir, but not for some days yet. They must hold a trial first, to make all fair and just in their own sight."

"Do you know the way?"

"The Dame of the Dragon described it well to us, sir. It is not far from here."

"Can we trust you?"

"I think, sir, that you must. Far enough, at the least, to let me bind up your leg. My name, Sir Knight of the Bend Sinister, is Alaron de Sableblanc."

"Very well, Alaron de Sableblanc, prove yourself." Cradling Deborah tenderly in his arms, Sir Harald gave up to the way the whole world wavered all around him as well as within his head.

Now, unlike his erstwhile fellow squire, who had pledged a second loyalty to the Dame of the Dragon when she bade them follow the Blue Flame, Alaron de Sableblanc had kept his faith whole and undivided for the Knight of the Black Chevron alone, and thus was free to pledge it elsewhere instantly on that knight's demise. True, as you may have noticed, he had actually pledged nothing at all to Sir Harald in so many words; but he had offered his name, and that implied the promise of standing by them through the present crisis. But even if he had harbored any evil intention, no doubt he would have thought better of it beneath Goblin's watchful eye.

Morning found Sir Harald feverish and mildly delirious.

"Why did you not wake me?" Deborah cried, flinging off the cloak—his own—with which Alaron had covered her.

"You had just gone through an ordeal yourself," said Alaron, who still believed her his fellow in sex and, being to all outward appearances a commoner, somewhat beneath him in station. "Besides, Master David, what could you have done for him that I have failed to do?"

Lifting the blanket—once the Black Chevron Knight's—that covered Sir Harald, she inspected Alaron's work on his wounded leg. "It is well wrapped. How did you dress it?"

"With whatever rust I could scrape from the lance that made the wound. There may not have been enough, for I was a good squire who kept his knight's gear clean and polished; but I made up the deficiency with a little dirt that the point had gathered from the ground," Alaron explained, equally proud of his squireship and his resourcefulness.

Deborah listened without blenching, for the remedy was indeed an ancient one and at one time recommended by renowned physicians. But she said, commencing even as she spoke to unbind Sir Harald's leg, "We must try another specific. Bring me clean water and more bandages."

"Are you a leech?" he demanded.

"I have been apprenticed to one," she replied, expressing truth in terms that he could instantly understand, "and I have a sovereign specific for open wounds here with me."

"If that is so, perhaps I begin to understand why he saved you in place of his lady. No matter what she may have ordered him, I should always have put a female's safety above that of any male."

But he left for the water and bandages; and Deborah, relieved that the squire had guessed none of her secrets, opened her pouch and brought out the small silver box of precious balm that she always carried, for safety, about her person. The pouch had of course suffered a thorough miring two days before in the thick bog, and some of its contents had had to be discarded as beyond salvation, but, thankfully, this box had both survived and, with its tight-fitting lid, kept its priceless contents quite safe.

Sir Harald's incoherent mutterings were growing louder, and he was beginning to thrash a little, so, lest his delirium wax violent, she carefully removed his mealtime knife from his belt and looked about for a place to secure it out of harm's way. It was then she became aware that Goblin was nowhere to be seen . . . only his saddle, bridle, and other harness, lying piled neatly on the ground.

"Where is his horse?" she demanded of Alaron de Sableblanc as soon as he returned with the water and clean wrappings. She spoke in a soft voice, but Sir Harald jerked and moaned almost as though he understood.

The squire stood and examined the scene with care. "I tethered him to that limb—and it was sturdy enough, for his tugging has left it in place. But I hardly dared hobble such a horse as that. It would have seemed an insult. I have known many of my fellow men who showed far less intelligence. Well, let me go after him at once. Do you know his name?"

"It is Goblin. But stay long enough to assist me with his master."

Deborah needed the squire to hold Sir Harald down while she washed his wound thoroughly, anointed it with the balm—which, while not magic, might appear so to the simple and unlearned—and bound it up again in fresh wrappings.

From time to time in his delirium, Sir Harald called out various names, among them not only "Joiselette" and "Garth," but also—very often—both "David" and "Maid Deborah." Who Joiselette and David were, Alaron de Sableblanc knew, or thought he knew; who Garth and Tamba were, David could tell him. "Deborah" David described as that mysterious lost love Sir Harald had mentioned, his brother's bride, whose story she had not quite had the chance to learn from Joiselette. Except for "Goblin," the other names he uttered were equally strange—or, occasionally, like "Sir Kay" and "Gawen," well known—to both his nurses.

By the time they had finished he was almost calm, and Alaron could go in search of Goblin. Deborah sat alternately moistening a cloth to cool his forehead, and washing the former bandages as best she could for re-use. "If only Miriam's balm was applied in time," she murmured. "Oh, Lord of our father Abraham, he has lost everything else except his shield. Let him keep his life!"

After about an hour, Sir Harald sank into a restful slumber. Deborah spread the laundered bandaging out in the sun to dry, kindled a small fire, found some wine and other provisions in the saddlebags Alaron de Sableblanc had left, and began preparing broth for her patient to drink whenever he should wake. A few hours later, Goblin reappeared, leading Garth, Tamba, and the rest of the party's surviving animals. While they were still greeting Deborah—with honest joy, be it noted, for her late peril had had the effect of making even Tamba forget some of his prejudices—Alaron returned to report failure, and was dissatisfied only with Fate on discovering that, had he struck out southwest instead of southeast, he might have reported success.

Such explanations having been made all round as could be made (though Deborah had had time to warn her old companions not to reveal her sex), Tamba took Alaron somewhat to task—for, albeit merely a page, he was a dozen years and more the squire's senior—for failing to raise the Black Chevron Knight's pavilion last night, as if sleeping beneath its cloth roof might have prevented Sir Harald's fever. Alaron replied that helping his former master kidnap two people had not made for the most restful day of his life, and at its close he had been too exhausted himself to put the pavilion up without assistance. Deborah tried to make peace by reassuring them that Alaron had dressed the wounded leg as well as any physician could have done; but, not being Joiselette, and also still being bound by her disguise as David, she managed little more than making them keep their voices low, and then shaming them by setting out with Garth to raise their own party's remaining pavilion.

Instructed by example, page and squire soon had the black tent up as well. Garth and Tamba then set about the rest of the work of making camp, while Deborah, refusing to see her patient moved until after he had awakened of his own accord, returned to her place between him and the little cookfire. As for Alaron, he set himself at last to the task that had awaited him since midnight, and started gathering up the armor of the Knight of the Black Chevron.

"I had long known that my old master was but the hollow shell of a man," he mused, holding up the empty hawberk. "I had not fully guessed *how* hollow!"

"If not for my Lady Joiselette," said Sir Harald, "your Knight of the Black Chevron might have been myself."

Deborah gave a small cry of gladness and gratitude. He had awakened quiet, free of fever, and . . . if his waking sentence failed somewhat of making perfect sense, at least it was a clear response to Alaron's words, and no less irrational than that of anyone freshly surfaced from the dreams of ordinary sleep.

After drinking broth, and being moved into one of the pavilions, and sleeping once more, and wakening again, Sir Harald begged all four of them to come close, and said to Garth:

"You are no longer a serf. Tamba, Alaron, and . . . David are witnesses. I set you free."

"Have I ever asked for freedom?" Garth replied. "What would I do with it?"

"Much what you have been doing with serfdom. Put your hands between mine and swear me your continued service. Only, should I be killed, you will have your own choice of new masters."

"As your serf," Garth argued, "at direst need I could serve you as ransom for Goblin."

Sir Harald shook his head. "That bargain, I hope and trust, would be rejected by any knight of King Arthur's, even Sir Kay. Nevertheless, in event that I am mistaken about that, it is the very outcome I wish at all costs to prevent. No, pledge your faith to whomever you will—Sir Gawen himself, maybe—or, better still, go home again to your family, but do so as a free man henceforth."

So Garth, argued into it at last, put his hands between Sir Harald's and pledged.

The fortress of the Knights Keepers of the Blue Flame was still a new construction in the land, and its walls were stout wooden staves, sharpened at the high tips, save in one corner where a new stone watchtower had replaced the former one of wood.

Nevertheless, for all its newness, the cell beneath this tower was such that not even Joiselette could find any songs therein. The Maid of the Wood sat mutely shackled on the damp earthen floor, in preference to the pile of straw that must already have been moldering when this deep cellar was dug, and listlessly stroked the heads of the rats and mice who, instead of stealing her meager supper, tried to augment it by carrying crumbs to her from their own small stores.

Although reasonably roomy, occupying half the area beneath the tower, with a bolted door at the top of a flight of stairs, the place was almost an oubliette, and had no window at all to the sky, not even the traditional high, tiny, and barred one. Day and night, its only light came from a little lamp filled with ill-smelling oil, placed well beyond the prisoner's reach, and replenished from time to time by the wordless gaoler when he brought her dry bread and stale water. Once, the flame flickered out between his visits.

As Joiselette sat there on what might have felt like the fourth afternoon or the fortieth night, but was in fact late on the first morning—the Keepers of the Blue Flame having sent their gaoler often in order to create the impression of many passing mealtimes—a young knight of their order came down, lighting his own way with a wax candle.

He gave a start on seeing her. "They have even chained you!"

"Your lady insisted."

"Unpardonable!" He strode across the floor—first mice and then rats scurrying away at his approach—knelt beside her, and, having set his candle at a safe and convenient distance, took a scarf from his neck and wrapped it around hers as a cushion against the rusty iron collar, which had itself been salvaged from some older dungeon.

"Pardon her anyway," Joiselette told him, a little animation coming back into her eyes. "Remember how upset she must be over losing her poor dragon."

"It has always angered me that we should ban all other women from our land and choose that one, of all others, to worship!"

"You are very handsome," she observed. Then, curiously, "Is this meant as some sort of temptation?"

"No. I cannot help the way I look, but at this moment I do not feel handsome. I have come to warn you."

"I already know that they mean to kill me. Although I certainly never intended to break their foolish law."

"They will not burn you without first staging a trial. Demand a champion."

Gazing into his eyes, she nodded. "I see. Bless you. Do they know that you are here?"

"They think I came to taunt you."

"Won't leaving your scarf like this rather undo that impression?"

He winked. "I will tell them that, instead of taunting, I tried to tempt. . . . Indeed, lady, I would far rather serve you than my proud Dame of the Dragon!"

"I think you already have a truer damsel than either of us, do you not?" When he blushed and bowed his head, Joiselette added, "Good! Never forget her."

"Lady, what stops me from serving you both?"

"Her and me—nothing at all. But her and the Dame of the Dragon, or the Dame of the Dragon and me—you would find it very difficult indeed."

After the young knight had regretfully taken his candle, lest his comrades have too much cause to suspect him of kindness, and left her to the feeble ministrations of mice and rats, Joiselette sighed and murmured, "Poor Sir Harald!"

Nevertheless, after a few more moments she began once again, seeming hardly aware that she did it, to sing:

> "Oh, Everywhere, Who feeds on love,
> And for Whose love all creatures yearn,
> Remind us, even in our loss,
> What love You feed us in Your turn."

She had not much longer to wait before another knight, much less kind, and assisted by two squires still less considerate than he, and two rude servants who showed signs of barely constrained cruelty, arrived to take her to trial, unlocking the collar that held her by a chain to the wall, but leaving her wrists shackled as if five men could not otherwise have escorted one maiden, whether docile or desperate, a few paces across a fortified courtyard.

Yet perhaps their precautions were less extravagant than might first appear, for scarcely had they stepped out into the sunlight than a great lion, glimpsing them through narrow gaps between the staves, commenced to hurl himself with tremendous roars against the wooden palisade, until it shook beneath his assaults. His front paws, when they struck, sounded hard as metal.

"Watchman!" the knight in charge of Joiselette's guard shouted up to the man-at-arms on the tower. "Where in the Devil's name is your bow?"

"No!" Joiselette cried, running to the wall as though the five men around her did not exist. Reaching it, she thrust her small hands through the gaps as far as they would go and began fondling the Quiller Lion as best she could. He quieted at once; and, strange to say, not only did the watchman obey her in preference to his proper master, but the knight refrained from repeating his implied command to shoot the beast, growling instead, "Do you know this animal?"

"We are old friends," Joiselette replied, "and his paws seem to be hurt. Let him in, so that I can bandage them, and I promise he will not so much as threaten one of you."

"Let him stay outside," returned the knight, "where he may threaten all he wishes, until we tire of it and shoot him, for his pains, as full of arrows as a hedgehog is of spines."

Joiselette rose to her full height, which was not at all tall but somehow seemed in that moment much taller than it was, and said steadily: "I think that you are about to try me for the crime of being a woman in your land. This lion can bear witness that I did not cross your borders willingly."

A knight with a grizzled beard, who stood close enough to have seen and heard the entire scene, demanded, "Can this be true, Sir Baalzob?"

"As to whether it is true or false," the knight of Joiselette's guard grumbled, "I cannot say."

"In that case," the older knight declared, "allow the lion in with a safe-conduct, pending his good behavior, and bring her whatever she needs to tend any injuries she may find on him. And remove her fetters. Let no one ever again be able to say with justice of the Knights Keepers of the Blue Flame that they failed to offer anyone less than justice. I will go and inform the court of this small delay."

The older knight was a man of high authority in the Order of the Blue Flame, and the others followed his command to the last jot and tittle. Some among them whispered afterward that the lion's wounded paws had looked very strangely injured indeed before the girl bandaged them—less like badly burned flesh than nubs of charred wood. None of them knew the Quiller Lion's history.

The lion limping less than before, and Joiselette walking with one hand lightly in his mane, they were led at last into the great hall of the Knights Keepers of the Blue Flame.

Two thrones stood side by side on the high dais, and in one of them, the taller by dint of a dragon's head worked in gold on its back, the Dame of the Dragon sat holding in her hand a scepter of silver wrought with golden salamanders. Beside her sat the Commander of the Blue Flame: an old knight with straight shoulders and a silver beard cut neatly at the collarbone, who held in his hand an orb with an artificial tongue of fire worked atop it in blue enamel on silver. The actual Blue Flame burned in a little lamp set on a silver lampstand between the two thrones. A scribe with his recording materials sat at a small table below the lady, and the knight with the grizzled beard, he who had ordered the lion let in, stood half a pace behind the throne at the commander's other shoulder. It might have been observed, from time to time, that the Dame of the Dragon cast angry looks upon this grizzled knight, which appeared to glance off him like wasps attacking armor.

"Why is she not shackled?" the Dame of the Dragon demanded.

"Because I saw that her shackles were senseless and unnecessary," replied the knight with the grizzled beard, "and because she needed full freedom of her hands in order to bind up her lion's wounds."

"They ought to have restored the shackles to her wrists before bringing her into Our presence," said the Dame of the Dragon. Then, turning to the commander, "Bid them restore the shackles!"

He, however, after gazing slowly around at all the knights, squires, pages, men-at-arms, and serving-men of the order, who crowded the hall and who numbered, in all—counting himself and his grizzled lieutenant, though not counting the numerous serfs—sixty-six, finally shook his head. "I, too, judge it needless."

"As for that lion," the lady went on, stamping her foot impatiently, "it is the very beast that slew my noble dragon!"

Joiselette spoke. "Only in my defense. He was trying to save me from being carried into your land against your law and my own will."

"Is this true?" demanded the commander.

The lion roared.

"Nay," the commander declared, "we cannot accept the uncorroborated testimony of a brute beast." And again his gaze searched the population of the hall.

At last the Black Chevron Knight's second squire, he who had fled with the Dame of the Dragon, stepped forward and confessed, "It is true, my lord. I saw and witnessed it all."

The lady threw on him one of her bitter glances; and, unlike the knight with the grizzled beard, the poor squire seemed to wither beneath it, shrinking back with a shudder into the ranks of onlookers. But the commander, ignoring this byplay, said in tones of judgment:

"This being so, the case against this maiden for breaking our ban on all her sex is dismissed. Since she is here against her own will, let her simply be escorted back across our borders and there released, along with her lion, who has our trusted lieutenant's sworn safe-conduct and, moreover, offended against our lady only in defense of his own."

"*No!*" cried the Dame of the Dragon; and then, as all looked at her, she went on: "That is not the only charge, nor even the more serious. Else why would you suppose I should drag her here against her will? Of course against her will, for she knows well what she is, and therefore what she must justly fear. My lords, she is heretic!"

A sigh went through the great hall.

"Heretic?" Joiselette asked in astonishment. "How? In what way?"

"Aye," agreed the commander. "How heretic, and in what

way? In behooves us to hear this charge, and you, my honored lady, to explain it."

"The creature is never grave, as befits honest piety, but always laughing and singing."

"I grieve in season," Joiselette protested. "Only, my seasons may not always coincide with the calendar."

"Nay," the commander instructed her, "you must be silent while we hear the full accusation. Leave to speak will be granted you in due time and course."

"She consorts," the Dame of the Dragon continued, "with whomever she will, never asking beforehand what they are, of what creed or morality."

The grizzle-bearded lieutenant said, "So did our Lord Ihesu, as I have read it in the Book."

"You twist the text to your own purpose!" the Dame of the Dragon snapped, looking as though she might accuse *him* of heresy next.

"You must hold your peace too, for now," the commander told his lieutenant. "Have you any further charge, honored lady?"

"Aye, and the heaviest of all! Scarcely an hour ago, when in misguided charity our newest knight dared to visit her in her cell, she tempted and attainted him."

"She did no such thing!" cried the handsome young knight who had visited Joiselette.

"Did she not?" returned the Dame of the Dragon. "Then will you be so good as to inform us as to what really passed between you, Sir Tophit?"

Stymied, he was silent.

"These are indeed heavy charges," the commander agreed gravely. "Where are your proofs?"

"For the first: Was she not singing even in her cell within moments after Sir Tophit left her this very morning? For the second: That Knight of the Bend Sinister with whom we found her traveling, and who slew my poor Knight of the Black Chevron before he had his chance to grace your brotherhood with his great valor, had earlier villainously abducted a virgin journeying alone, as my Knight of the Black Chevron might have testified, for he had tried to rescue her. For the third charge, my proof is the same as for the first, and it is also verified by Sir Tophit's own silence before this court."

The lion gave a second roar.

The commander looked at Joiselette. "These are telling proofs, but you may try to answer them, if you think it possible."

Joiselette laughed. "For the first and third: If I sang, it was because at least one human soul here had finally shown me kindness, and I suppose he stands silent now because you seem to disapprove of that kindness. For the second: It is true that my Knight of the Bend Sinister did indeed steal a maiden traveling alone and attempt to seduce her against her will, but certain other knights had better success in rescuing her, and, since I happened to be with them, he chose to offer me his surrender, and has been my own prisoner ever since."

The commander nodded. "These answers are not wholly unsatisfactory and, while they do not demolish the case against her, they at least leave it in doubt."

The lieutenant broke his silence to ask, "But what, my lord and lady, is the exact nature of her alleged heresy?"

The commander looked at the Dame of the Dragon.

With a smug smile, that lady suggested: "Ask the creature what she thinks, right at this very moment."

"I think," Joiselette answered softly, "how the greatest wonder of all is that God is everywhere, even here, even now, loving every one of you with equal love, at this very moment, and always."

"You hear it, my lords!" the Dame of the Dragon crowed. "Everywhere, is He? In the very cesspits, too, I suppose?"

"Even in the very cell where you imprisoned me."

"And loving all creatures, down to the rats and toads?"

"Down to you and your dragon," Joiselette replied steadily, matching the lady gaze for stare.

"And loving all equally!"

"How else could the Everywhere love, being pure Love Itself, save to love every creature in the same perfect measure, wholly, entirely, and beyond any degree?"

"You have heard it, my lords!" the Dragon Lady repeated in triumph. "Out of her own mouth she has convicted herself!"

"In the cesspits, too?" the commander mused, rubbing his chin and shaking his head, both at the same time, which made rather a bird's-nest of his beard. "The rats and toads equally with ourselves? Damsel, damsel . . . these are very strange thoughts!"

"If they are heresy, my lord," said Joiselette, "let God decide. I claim the right of trial by combat."

"We cannot deny it," the commander said before the Dame of the Dragon had time to speak. "Name your champion."

"But name none of our knights or squires!" the Dame of the Dragon cut in at once, looking around fiercely. "Lest he be tainted with thy heresy. Sir Tophit!" she added, her glance settling on that hapless young knight. "Thou shalt prove thine own innocence in this matter by serving as my champion for this court!"

"I have been hastily trained and newly knighted, my lady," he stammered in protest. "I lack experience—"

"The outcome of any trial by combat," ruled the commander, "depends solely upon the will of God. This being the case, our newest and least-trained knight is fully as fit as our most experienced for the holy work. Let it be so!" He struck his orb once, gavel-like, on the arm of his throne. "Nor may thy lion serve thee, child, as champion. We will allow no such trial between man and beast."

Joiselette looked around the court in her turn. "May he serve me as messenger, then?" Her gaze settled on the grizzled lieutenant at the commander's shoulder. "May I write an appeal and tie it round his neck?"

"This request is certainly just and reasonable," said the lieutenant. "Nor could any fair and impartial judge object to it."

"It is pointless, however," said the Dragon Lady. "God can as easily raise her up a champion with no message sent or received at all, so let the trial take place this afternoon."

"Nay," the commander said slowly, casting a sidelong glance that some later called apologetic toward the Dame of the Dragon, "we must allow even God a little space in which to work His wonders. Fetch her parchment, pen, ink, and a little pouch to tie it up in around her lion's neck, and let her have three days' grace."

"My Knight of the Bend Sinister is wounded, my lord," said Joiselette. "How badly, I could not see."

"Nor can this court abide the convenience of any one particular champion," said the commander. "Three days."

His lieutenant coughed. "Forty days is the customary term of grace, my lord."

Perhaps the old commander wished to reassert his own authority, for he repeated as his final word in the matter: "God can as easily raise her up a champion in three days as in forty."

"And in three days," cried the Dame of the Dragon, "let her burn as a heretic, if not as a woman."

Joiselette protested, "Rather than burn alive, let me fight as my own champion, if no other appears."

"Damsel!" the commander exclaimed in shock. "It defies all the laws of chivalry, as we understand them, that a woman should bear arms on the field of honor."

"Because she might be injured?" Joiselette could not forbear a little laughter. "If you fear hurting me, my lords, why that sunless cell, this trial, and all this talk of burning?"

Strange to say, several of the men present laughed with her, including the grizzled lieutenant, who said, "Now that it has been put like that, my lord, if worse comes to worst, I can find no reason for denying her horse and arms, permitting her into the lists against our young Sir Tophit, and leaving the rest to God."

"Aye," the commander grumbled, looking from his lieutenant to Joiselette to the Dame of the Dragon and back again to Joiselette. "Put like that . . . some of the smaller squires' armor might not prove too impossibly large for her. . . . But first let her pen her message."

"And after that," said the knight with the grizzled beard, "I give up my own room for three days to be her new prison, and let us feed her well, and weigh her down with no chains of any kind. It must never be said that we purposely sent any champion to our field of honor wan, weary, and starved."

"No," the commander acknowledged with a sigh. "When the irregularities of this business come to be recounted, let that, at least, not be among them."

So for the next three days, the Keepers of the Blue Flame allowed Joiselette greater comfort than they gave their own knight. For he, being in their eyes the champion of Truth and Right, had various fasts and purifications to undergo; while she, whom most of them already considered on the word of their Dame of the Dragon to be a lost soul in any case, was granted every luxury and liberty available within the fortress walls—except that of exchanging words with any member of the company save its commander and its lady, who were alone considered beyond threat of corruption.

Moreover, she had no worse to fear than fiery death, while as for what Sir Tophit had to fear . . . my pen would prefer not to detail it, but only to remark that it could not have been what he had in mind when he bade her, before the trial, to demand a champion. Surely he had trusted in God to defend the prisoner's cause, with no matter how new and green an instrument!

The fatal day dawned as clear and bright as though no tragedy impended. The lists waited ready in the wide field just below the fortress, with the stake on an overlooking knoll, faggots piled high around it; even if the accused heretic were to die in battle defending her own innocence, they meant to burn her body lest it corrupt the earth. Meanwhile, at the bidding of the grizzle-bearded lieutenant, they brought out a chair with arms, a high back, and several cushions, that she might wait at her ease.

On both sides of the lists stood tiered benches for the witnesses, with a blue awning above the scaffold of honor, where the most important Keepers of the Blue Flame sat: the Dame of the Dragon and the knight commander in their own thrones from the great hall; the grizzled lieutenant; Sir Baalzob; and a few others on camp-chairs. The sounds of all this construction had echoed up through the wooden walls into the fortress for the past two days, providing the principal players with a rhythmic background for their preparatory meditations.

As witnesses and spectators, there were only those members and servants of the Blue Flame as lacked more active roles in the day's festivities, and such peasants as could be forced to tend the flocks and till the fields without the assistance of womenfolk. These, however, sufficed to fill up the benches well before Joiselette was led out, in simple white tunic and surcoat long enough to hide the squire's breeches she wore in case of having to don mail and take up arms in her own cause.

Against that eventuality, a suit of training armor designed for a young squire and almost small enough to fit her had been piled near the stake, along with the lightest weapons that could be found and a warhorse old enough to be judged sufficiently placid for a small and untrained female. No one present seriously expected a real knight to come riding over the horizon in time to champion her, but there was quite a bit of secret betting as to whether or not she would actually put on the armor and fight, or opt at the last moment for the softer mercy of confessing her grievous sin and being strangled before the flames were lit.

"We sentenced her," said the commander, "with three days' grace to find a champion, just before our midday meal three days ago, which was somewhat delayed by reason of the trial. Let the sentence be carried out just before our midday meal today, which will be served at the same time as it was that day."

Sir Tophit, who sat ready armed on a pure white horse—once the steed of the Black Chevron Knight—before the judges' scaffold, said, "Good my lord, might I humbly beg leave to approach the prisoner with the arguments of reason?"

"She will only tempt him with her blandishments," the Dame of the Dragon told the commander. "At worst destroying and at best weakening him."

"Nay, my lord!" the young knight argued. "I pray you, permit me to prove my loyalty."

The lieutenant leaned forward and murmured something into his lord's ear, after hearing which the commander lifted his orb and pronounced:

"If the witch should weaken him in body or will, it will make no difference, for in the ordinary course of nature an untrained damsel could never outmatch even a weakened knight; and, moreover, we depend not on arms and the ordinary course of nature to decide our cause, but on God, Who can give the victory wherever He will. But, in any case, to ride into battle against a maid feeling that he might have eliminated the need for such combat with a few timely arguments would weaken him more surely than any blandishments of hers might do. Therefore, let Sir Tophit salve his conscience by making the attempt, but prove his loyalty by returning at once to his post here before us the very moment our herald summons him with a blast from the silver horn."

Before the Dame of the Dragon could change his commander's mind, Sir Tophit bowed in the saddle, turned his horse, and rode to Joiselette, startling away all the creatures gathered with her, save for two squirrels and a snake who hid behind her feet, and a wren she was stroking with one finger. But perhaps the young knight had practiced a touch of duplicity in failing to specify what arguments of reason he would employ, or where, exactly, his loyalty lay; for when he had brought his charger close enough that he could speak to Joiselette without being overheard even by the two masked executioners who sat throwing dice in the shadow of the stake, he said:

"Dear child, spring up behind me and let us escape together!"

She looked around the field, at guards and archers, men-at-arms and Sir Tophit's fellow knights, none of them anticipating the need for sudden action in the festal spirit of the day, but most of them ready for all that to spring into service at a moment's notice. Smiling, though with a tear in her eye, she replied, "Dear sir, how far do you think we would get?"

"I would far rather flee with you than fight you!"

"If it comes to that, sir, please remember I would far rather receive the stroke of mercy from your hand than burn alive, or even be strangled. But don't despair of having another knight to fight today—"

At this very moment, almost as if the commander suspected his champion's duplicity, the silver horn sounded. After one heartbeat of sad hesitation, Sir Tophit saluted Joiselette, turned his horse, and rode back to his appointed place.

"Though I wish," Joiselette murmured to herself, "with all my heart, I wish it could be settled without a battle between these two in particular!"

The shadows reached their shortest point of the day. "It is time," the Dame of the Dragon said with a smirk. "Let her fight, or burn at once!"

The lieutenant said, "Nay, we should wait until the hour at which we actually began to eat our dinner."

"Not so," protested the Dame of the Dragon. "This is the hour at which we raised the tables."

"Nevertheless," the commander decreed, "we will wait yet half an hour."

The shadows having lengthened by another half-hour's worth, the Dame of the Dragon repeated, "It is time!" And now neither the commander nor his lieutenant could find any counter-argument. As for their poor champion, he seemed long ago to have retreated into a sort of haze, seeing, hearing, and moving only when directed to do so, and otherwise sitting like one ensorcelled.

"Go," the commander ordered two of his people, a herald and a squire, "and bid her prepare either to fight or to burn."

They went afoot, carefully watching their toes lest they kick up too many of the meadowflowers, and the squire—who happened to be the same one that had once belonged to the Black Chevron Knight, then gone with the Dame of the Dragon, and afterward testified at Joiselette's trial—almost knelt to her, but the herald caught him in time.

"Prisoner," said the herald, "the hour has come. My lord and my lady bid you prepare either to fight or to burn."

Joiselette sighed. "Who will help me on with the armor?"

"Child," said one of the black-hooded executioners, who had come forward, "why not spare yourself both the bumps and the flames by confessing thy sin? I promise thee, I wield a quick and tender noose."

"He wears a merciful mask," growled his fellow executioner, "but the plain truth is, he has a wager on it."

Joiselette looked straight into the eyeholes of the second executioner, and laughed. "With you, no doubt! Well, I'm afraid he loses his wager and you win. I cannot deny what I am."

"Lady," said the squire, "you have never told us *what* you are!"

"Is that any reason to deny it now? But we'd better not make them wait any longer." With another sigh, she turned to the pile of training armor.

The squire went forward to help her, having been sent

for that purpose; but they had scarcely removed her white surcoat long enough to put on the gambeson, when a murmuration rising from the onlookers' benches like the sound of waves on a pebbly shore alerted them to a new development.

Sir Harald had arrived just in time, to find Alaron de Sableblanc's worst guess confirmed.

He rode with the arms and in the armor of the Black Chevron Knight, black on his great black warhorse Goblin; but he had garnished them with his own surcoat and shield, stained though they still were, one with traces of mud that had resisted every laundering technique available in camp, and the other with the scars of his moonlit battle. Spending the intervening time in idle convalescence had seemed harder to him than that battle itself, and only Alaron's continual reassurances that the Knights Keepers of the Blue Flame would certainly do nothing irrevocable for a full three days could hold him quiet enough for Deborah's salve to knit the edges of his wound back together. Even now, the swollen leg, though snugly bound, reminded him of its complaint by pressing against the armor, which otherwise fit him admirably.

Garth, Tamba, and David—since Alaron had not yet devined her gender, they hoped that she would be as safe here as themselves (however safe that was!) and safer than had they tried to leave her fretting at the border—rode behind, leading the pack animals; and, as soon as they came within sight of the lists, Alaron de Sableblanc turned his light horse and circled back to join them, leaving the knight to head the procession.

Sir Harald led it to the end of the lists, where everyone else stopped except Garth, who, carrying the Black Knight's lance and helmet, followed to the very foot of the judges' scaffold.

Staring up at the silver-bearded commander, the new-come knight demanded: "What in God's holy name is going on?"

"Did not the lion reach you?" asked the commander.

The knight shook his head. The Dame of the Dragon smirked.

"Sir Harald!" Joiselette exclaimed, running forward in

her breeches and gambeson, joy in his appearance over-coming all other considerations for the moment. "My lord commander—here is my champion!"

"God's Blood!" Sir Harald cried softly, reading from her stranger-than-usual attire, and the pile of arms he could see beside the stake, that she had actually been about to fight for herself. The image of what could have happened had he arrived even the quarter part of an hour later made him feel more hollow than his late adversary's armor when it struck the ground.

But they were dragging her back again to her armchair before the stake, for all that she waved and clearly wished to tell him something further. As for Sir Harald, rage against these Flaming Blue Knights flooded every part of him that had felt hollow only a heartbeat ago. For once in his life, he said nothing—did not trust himself to open his mouth—but, allowing the anger to bear him like a tide, clamped his teeth, held out his hands for his helmet, set it on his head, then accepted the lance in its turn from Garth, settled it into his right hand, took a firmer grip on the shield in his left, and cantered to one end of the lists, ignoring the marshal who was trying to point him to the other end.

Never had he so much as glanced at his opponent-to-be, the champion of the court, mounted on the horse that belonged by right of conquest to Harald himself.

The commander signed his marshal to let it be and allow the newcomer his choice. Indeed, while the lists had been erected as fairly and with as little advantage to either combatant as possible, the end that Sir Harald had chosen with so little examination beforehand was very slightly the worse. Mechanically as a quintain, poor Sir Tophit put on his own helmet, accepted his lance, adjusted his shield, and took his place at the better end.

Although, the lion never having reached them, Sir Harald and his group knew nothing about the charge of heresy, they had known all along about the Blue Flame Knights' custom of burning any woman who entered their land. So he had had all the time since Joiselette's abduc-tion to consider the various disadvantages he would be at in such a combat as this, from his lefthandedness to his leg wound, and plan his course accordingly. But now all his plans boiled down to a point of rage directed against the Knights Keepers of the Blue Flame, in the person of their armed and anonymously helmeted champion.

Meanwhile, David (as I shall call her while she is here disguised in Blue Flame territory) could not help tearing her attention between Sir Harald, Joiselette, and the benches of spectators . . . where, failing to find one face in particular, she looked again at their champion, and pressed her hand to her mouth.

At a signal from their commander, the heralds sounded their horns. Having waited only for that call, Sir Harald couched his lance and charged. He had planned to concentrate on keeping his seat and saving himself for the swordplay, in which he would stand a better chance, but now that strategy was forgotten in such an intensity of desire as he had never before known to unhorse his opponent and be done with it.

Take care what you wish.

Sir Tophit had seemed sluggish, almost hesitant. Not until the other was actually bearing down on him did he heed the heralds' horns, set his own lance in its rest, lower his shield into place, and begin spurring forward. This hesitation cancelled out whatever slight advantage the lay of the land might have lent him.

They crashed together near Sir Tophit's end of the lists, and, for once in his life, Sir Harald had the satisfaction of keeping his own seat whilst seeing his adversary topple.

Reining Goblin to a stop and a turn, he dropped his lance and dismounted, drawing his sword and hastening with a scarcely noticeable limp to where the champion of the Blue Flame lay still.

"Rise and fight!" Sir Harald shouted.

The other knight made no movement.

"Or do you surrender, then?" Sir Harald demanded, holding his sword to the fallen man's helmet.

The commander stood. "Knight of the Bend Sinister, the battle is yours."

The Dame of the Dragon began, "No! It is not yet—"

The commander seized her scepter and deliberately dropped it onto the field. "We declare, stranger, that you have won. Your lady is proved innocent in our eyes and set at liberty, on the single condition of leaving our land within the day." To his attendants, he added, "See to Sir Tophit's injuries."

But before they could descend, David raced onto the field, knelt beside the fallen knight, and removed his helmet. "Tobias!" she cried.

He looked very young, very pale, and very still. There was no blood, but his large black eyes stared up fixed and motionless; nor did he give any sign of seeing, hearing, or otherwise sensing anything around him; nor could they detect any rising or falling of his chest.

Putting out one arm to hold back the attendants of the Blue Flame, Sir Harald told them, even now remembering to maintain the Jewess's disguise, "He was this lad's brother." Then, taking off his own helmet and pushing back his mail coif, he got down on one knee beside the fallen man and said huskily, "I did not know."

But even if he had known, what could he have done differently?

David was quietly sobbing on the downed man's breast. Repeating aloud, for the benefit of the Blue Flame company, "Brother. My friend's brother," Sir Harald stretched out a trembling hand and closed the staring eyes.

As he lifted his fingers away, the eyelids opened again, not with a snap but a flutter; the eyes moved with intelligence; and, discovering who lay sobbing on top of him, Tobias sat straight up and wrapped her in an embrace that might have given everything away to the Keepers of the Blue Flame, had their attention not been diverted just then by the arrival of yet another new company.

Here came the Quiller Lion, paws unbandaged and whole again, leading the great Sir Gawen himself, flanked on the right by his good cousin Sir Ywen and on the left by Arthur's trusty if crusty seneschal Sir Kay, and with our old friends Sirs Letron and Labigodés bringing up the rear like the last two points of the golden pentacle.

At sight of the lion, the Dragon Lady let out one short scream of annoyance. She never explained it to any of those present, but I can tell you now that she had caused another heavy mist to blanket a certain steep and rocky riverbank midway between the Fortress of the Blue Flame and the hill where she had left Sir Harald. When the left-handed knight appeared without the lion, she assumed that her plan had succeeded, causing the tawny beast to miss its footing in the fog and die in the river. But, whether sensing the trap or for some other reason, the lion had no sooner been out of sight of the fortress than he turned in the opposite direction and found King Arthur's court as quickly as if he had somehow known that it was presiding a day and a half away (perhaps this enchanted beast had some trace of precognizance, after all). And because even a magical fog can last only so long, it had long ago dissipated, so that Sir Harald and his party had followed Alaron de Sableblanc across the river that morning on the only bridge, with no undue difficulty.

Sir Gawen led his little troop to the foot of the judges' scaffold, where, when they had all removed their helmets and saluted, he began courteously:

"Sir, we are the advance guard of King Arthur's court, and I see that we have come in time to save you from lighting your fire and thus incurring both God's wrath and that of our good monarch, who forbids any such action on pain of his mortal displeasure."

"Hear, hear!" said Sir Letron, actually letting his previous acquaintance of Joiselette get the better of the mannerliness that ought to have kept him silent at this moment.

"Sir Gawen," the commander of the Blue Flame answered with equal courtesy, "for I see that it is you by your shield, which every good knight knows as well as his own, in one sense you have come too late, after all, for the matter has already been decided and we would not have kindled our fire in any case, the damsel's champion having by the grace of God fairly defeated our own."

This made half of them look at Joiselette where she stood stroking the lion, which had run to meet her in her latest return from the stake; and the other half at the far end of the lists, where a small group including Garth, Tamba, and Alaron de Sableblanc had already gathered around David, Tobias, and Sir Harald.

"I think I know that man," muttered Sir Kay.

"As do I, my lord," Sir Ywen remarked, "having had the pleasure of making his acquaintance last year at Wisten of the Mists."

"By God's big toe," Sir Kay went on, "if it isn't the same knight I unhorsed at Tenebroc!"

"Harald de Folgeste, my lord?" Sir Labigodés said by way of verification, with an effort redirecting his glance from Joiselette now that he had reassured himself as to her safety. "You must know, that is the identical poor bastard of whom we told you," (in those days, "bastard" could as well be a plain and simple statement of fact as anything else, and therefore no discourtesy even from the most courtly mouth) "who abducted a maiden traveling alone, and tried to steal his trueborn brother's castle."

"Of both those misdeeds," Sir Ywen murmured, "he has acquitted himself, in my estimation at least, rather handsomely."

Out of courtesy, Sirs Labigodés and Letron had dropped Sir Harald's intention to renege on what he owed Sir Kay from the list of his crimes, since by the time he bade them adieu last summer that much had changed.

"The same man, is he?" said the sensechal, who kept less perfect account of his personal affairs than of those pertaining to his kingly foster brother. "Curse me if his name hadn't gone clean out of my head. Harald de Folgeste!"

Among the inconveniences of storytelling is that, no matter how many things happen all at once, the poor, harried narrative can follow only one thread at a time. Since a great many things have been happening all at once on this field of honor and festivity, I must go back now, by just a few moments, and unravel one plain and simple strand from the glittering tangle.

Sir Harald's emotions on discovering he had killed Deborah's first love and then on finding that the man was still alive after all, the reader can imagine better than the writer can describe. The same might perhaps be said of what happened next to our knight, but this time, because it was less expected under the circumstances, I must make the attempt.

Nothing changed for Sir Harald, and everything changed. There were no lights, no sounds, no visions . . . only the sudden understanding of why Joiselette sang. He felt the kiss of God, and for a timeless instant the Divine Presence lay thick and airy Everywhere.

The sense of it faded at once, but in the afterglow he went on resting motionless on one knee: He remained as aware as ever of what was going on around him, but it demanded no further activity on his part until he heard Sir Kay call his name. Then he rose stiffly and limped forward, supporting himself with the black knight's sword. Joiselette and her lion joined him between Arthur's knights and the judges' scaffold.

"We congratulate you, Sir Harald de Folgeste, on your fine victory," Sir Gawen greeted them, "and we rejoice, sweet Lady Joiselette, on your blessed deliverance from danger."

And, though it might not have been the time or place for the reminder, Sir Kay added, "By the way, I believe that the year is up."

"By some days, I think," Sir Harald acknowledged, bowing his head formally. "Forgive me, sir. We were caught up in these events."

"They seem important enough to excuse the delay, but I'd appreciate full payment now."

Sir Harald turned and looked his question up at the commander, who replied, with a shake of his head:

"Sir Tophit's arms are not his own, but, like the arms, horses, names in chivalry, and other gear of every Knight Keeper of the Blue Flame, the property of our order. Nor were they included in this trial by combat, fought as it was for holy purposes rather than mundane glory and profit."

Joiselette asked, "But the Knight of the Black Chevron hadn't formally joined your order yet, had he?"

"No," admitted the grizzled lieutenant, "he had not."

Sir Harald turned back to the seneschal. "Sir, by misfortune I lost my own armor in a bog, and my arms in battle. But I can give you these that I stand in, and, as ransom for my horse, that of the late Black Chevron Knight, all of which I had already won before today's combat . . . Where is it?" he asked, looking around the field.

The white warhorse had disappeared; and so, they suddenly saw, had the Dame of the Dragon.

While squires, pages, and servitors ran about in search of them, the knights turned their immediate attention to other matters. Tobias, whose name in the order had been Sir Tophit, came forward with David and said:

"My lords, I am no longer Sir Tophit, but plain Tobias, a Jew, who should never have been dubbed a Knight of the

Blue Flame. Let me hereby renounce both my knighthood and my membership in the order."

"This is ungrateful of you, Sir Tophit," said the commander, "after we have allowed your scruples in all matters pertaining to diet and the like. Nevertheless, we will hold no man against his will."

"Nor will you ever again hold any woman against her will, my lord," said Sir Gawen. "Not if you would have the friendship of our lord King Arthur, who has commanded that all women be protected and honored everywhere, not threatened with burning for the mere fact of their womanhood."

"As to that," protested the commander, "we would have let her leave our land in safety, once it was established that she had entered it against her will. But there was also the grave suspicion of heresy, and that was the reason we had the stake prepared today."

"As to who is heretic and who is not," growled Sir Kay, "if you want Arthur's friendship, you'd be well advised to leave it to churchmen to decide!"

"But as to your request, Sir Tobias," Sir Gawen mused, rubbing his chin in pure perplexity, "we will honor your wish to change your allegiance; but I am not sure that even a Jew, once dubbed, can renounce his knighthood at will."

Sir Ywen spoke. "Sir Harald, you have fought him . . ."

"And found no dishonor in him as a knight, my lord," Sir Harald replied at once, exchanging a hasty glance with David. "Let there be no question of stripping away his rank dishonorably!"

"There is none," Sir Gawen agreed at once. "Only . . . could even King Arthur . . ."

"We'd be hard put to find even one squire willing to serve him," Sir Kay said, blunt as ever. "Unless that boy at his side . . ."

"Sir Knight," Deborah put in, "since it appears that my danger is past in admitting it here, I am not a boy, but a Jewess and this man's betrothed. Let me go away with him into Spain."

"Where," added Tobias, "if I cannot renounce my knighthood, I can at least leave it honorably unannounced, to gather dust while I practice the medicine I was trained to practice."

"Well!" said Sir Gawen, visibly relieved. "The world needs physicians as well as knights, or who would heal our wounds? Wait long enough, then, for a wedding gift to help speed both of you happily on your way, with our best wishes."

By now Alaron de Sableblanc had found and dragged forward his erstwhile companion in the service of the Black Chevron Knight, who confessed with understandable reluctance that, upon collecting his late master's white warhorse at the far end of the lists, he had led it around behind the judges' scaffold, where the Dame of the Dragon, slipping away when everyone's attention lay elsewhere for a moment, had mounted it and made good her escape. He would have followed her, but could not reach his own horse in time.

"Then follow her now, if that be thy choice," Sir Gawen said, the faintest tinge of disgust creeping into even his gentle voice.

"Nay," said the commander, "let him stay here and take his discipline along with the rest of us, in the reformation of our order. As for her whom once we called our lady, in addition to all else that she has done, it appears that she has stolen a good knight's horse."

"Though *which* good knight's," Sir Kay muttered, "is not yet completely clear."

Attempting to swallow, and finding his mouth very dry, Sir Harald bade Garth lead Goblin forward. As long as mortal life lasts, not even the kiss of God lends sovereign proof against every heartache. "My lord," Sir Harald told Sir Kay, "he responds best to a light hand upon the reins, and only the lightest touch of the spur. And, if you would allow me to redeem him whenever I can find the ransom—"

"Maybe, and maybe not," Sir Kay cut him short. This latest rudeness made Labigodés and Letron blush, and caused even Gawen and Ywen, accustomed as they were to the sensechal's tongue, to blink. But Sir Kay paid them no attention as he went on to Sir Harald, "On the other hand, I can hardly wear two suits of armor or ride two warhorses at once. Pledge me your allegiance, and you may keep the use and care of them as part of the bargain."

Sir Gawen, who knew Sir Kay better than did the others, nodded as though not entirely surprised.

Sir Harald, however, was astonished. "But . . . your own ransom, my lord?"

"I'm making other arrangements," Sir Kay said shortly, "and thank you very graciously for reminding everyone of the fall I took at Tenebroc. Well? Do you accept the bargain, or not?"

After a long pause, Sir Harald looked to Joiselette.

She winked. "The choice is entirely yours, Sir Harald. You are no longer my prisoner. I set you free with all my gratitude and the greatest of pleasure!"

He did not forget to thank her with a bow. "Yours was the easiest yoke any captive ever bore, my lady. I beg you never to release me, at least, from the bonds of friendship."

"Nicely spoken," Sir Letron murmured to Sir Labigodés.

"Well enough," Sir Labigodés acknowledged. "A different word here, a change of phraseology there. . . . Still, all in all, well enough."

"In that case, Sir Kay," Sir Harald resumed, turning back to the seneschal, "I will be glad to pledge you my loyalty, on the sole condition that it never comes into conflict with my conscience."

Sir Kay snorted. "De Folgeste, a pledge to me is a pledge to King Arthur. And from what I hear, your conscience is hardly the most reliable touchstone, anyway."

"That last remark, now," Sir Labigodés observed to Sir Letron—although loud enough for the whole group to hear, since by the long-established custom of King Arthur's court, nobody thought it discourteous to point out Sir Kay's failings, "concerning his conscience, was both gratuitous and superfluous, and therefore rude beyond measure."

"But probably kinder than I have deserved," Sir Harald said quietly, and, putting his hands between those of Sir Kay, pledged his fealty then and there.

"It only remains," said the Lieutenant of the Blue Flame, "to find a new lady for our reformed order, the old having proved herself treacherous and unworthy."

"Joiselette, sweet child," said the commander, "since it appears that our order of banishment has been rendered null and void, will you deign to remain here with us and become our new liege lady?"

Laughing in delight, she shook her head. "Why not take the Savior's holy Mother for your lady? And treat every woman as you would treat her! As for me, I've a notion to rest awhile in King Arthur's court, and see how my friend behaves himself there."

"I think," Deborah said softly, "that he will behave very well."

And if from time to time throughout her subsequent life in sunny Spain, living and working side by side with her dear spouse, Deborah called to mind the knight who had stood by her so steadfastly the last week of her great search, the kind physician Tobias never wearied of listening with lively sympathy to all she told him of that quest . . . for he felt, in some strange way he could never express, that he owed that knight something even beyond bringing his bride back to him.

They never suspected that Sir Harald might not always and invariably be justifying their high opinion. But he was still and ever left-handed; he had still his temper, his stubbornness, and his tendency to act before thinking; and he never sat at Arthur's Table Round, but always remained one of the many lesser knights attached to that good king's court.

Yet Joiselette's words that day on the field of the Blue Flame had been teasing ones, as she demonstrated shortly thereafter by singing, to the accompaniment of the Quiller Lion's purr:

> "Oh, Everywhere, Who holds us all,
> All times, all souls, in one embrace,
> And binds us all, in every place,
> To one great, glowing point of grace,
> Pray comfort each, and comfort all."

Part the Fourth:

A Mad Day's Work

"Oh, Everywhere, You season with the seasons,
And dish the world up with changing reasons
For compliment and praise—pray help us savor
This autumn's rich and thickly flowing flavor!"

So warbled Joiselette, unconsciously as usual, while the party wended its way through the motley woods.

It could no longer be called a very small party. Besides Joiselette, her page Tamba, Sir Harald, Garth, the Quiller Lion, Goblin, and the numerous other horses and pack animals, it now included Alaron de Sableblanc, who had become by mutual consent Sir Harald's squire, and also Garth's whole family: his wife Gytha, their two children, a little gray donkey given them by Sir Godfrey of Quillerstone, and the family cat.

The donkey was called, for her stolid solidity, "Mistwraith." The cat was called, more descriptively than imaginatively, "Mouser." The little boy, who was barely six—still young enough that his parents could recollect and reckon up his age, year by year, on their fingers—would someday wear his true christened name for everyday usage, but at present still went mostly by the affectionate endearment "Nubbin." By now the Quiller Lion had by and large grown almost as tame as his fellow feline Mouser, and Nubbin delighted in sharing his back with Joiselette.

But it is Nubbin's big sister Wandith who will suddenly and unexpectedly become a crucial character in Sir Harald's story.

Like most of the Round Table's important knights, Sir Kay the Seneschal held several fine properties of his own, as that era understood ownership; this meant that the properties were really King Arthur's, which he granted to various of his lieges, who in turn might grant them to various of *their* lieges, and so on down the line. Among Sir

Kay's holdings was the fair manor of Beaumarches, so called because it enjoyed a beautiful vista view of what had been, before Arthur's reign, the borders, or "marches," of some pretty little petty kingdoms. One of these borders was a broad hill where sheep could pasture the year round; the other was a wide and lovely lake.

Shortly before the great tournament of Tenebroc, Arthur's seneschal had been given grounds to withdraw Beaumarches from the knight who had held it for nineteen years. So the manor had gotten along for five seasons—one full turning of the year plus another summer—under the care of its steward, waiting for a new liege lord. This new lord of Beaumarches Manor Sir Kay now hoped he had found in Harald de Folgeste.

"They tell me," he said to Sir Harald on making him the grant, "that you governed your half-brother's castle reasonably well while he was gadding off to the Holy Land. Let's see if you can do as much for a simple manor. And, while you're at it, you had better make just as good a job of governing yourself."

To which Sir Harald could only reply, "My lord, with the help of God and our Lady, I will do my best."

Sir Kay said, "Hmpf."

First, of course, Sir Harald had to put in a month's attendance at King Arthur's court, where they soon repaired and repainted his shield good as new after his late encounters. Then, having sought and received permission, he returned briefly to the castle of his boyhood, where the Aloof Fair One—now alternatively known as Lady Elinor of Quillerstone—spent the entire fortnight of his visit fiercely closeted in her own chosen apartment, rather than either lay eyes on her erstwhile abductor, or mar the occasion for everyone else with anything worse than her absence. Of course, her absence had the effect of shortening Sir Harald's stay, which otherwise might well have lasted twice as long; but we will say no more about that just now.

In all other respects, it was a more formal and satisfying reconciliation than the brothers had allowed themselves to make the summer before. And, among its legal formalities, Sir Harald having set his loyal attendant Garth free during the aftermath of his last battle with the Knight of the Black Chevron, Sir Godfrey now freed Garth's wife and children as well, so that the whole family might freely follow Sir Harald to his new holding.

Garth's daughter Wandith had been still a child the summer her father went with Sir Harald, first to the great Tenebroc tournament and shortly afterward on his year-long quest for the Black Chevron Knight. But the turning of five seasons had wrought a noticeable change in the girl; now she might, in the right degree of twilight, be mistaken for Joiselette—and not necessarily at the lowest possible estimation of Joiselette's age, either.

Imagine, if you will, what it was for this young maid, just at the same romantic time her body was budding toward womanhood, to find herself bound upon the grand adventure of an excursion farther afield than she could ever before have dreamed of traveling in her entire lifetime, and, awaiting her at journey's end, the brave new life of a free peasant in a new place where nobody save her family and a few close others—fewer than the fingers of a single hand, if one did not count the animals—would ever have known her as a serf. Is it any surprise that the same new freedom that her father met with awkward reluctance, her mother with tempered practicality, and her little brother with only as much understanding as matched his small size, filled Wandith's heart with the heady wine of dreams beyond her station?

What might surprise us is the target that caught her fledgling fancy. With both Sir Harald himself and his teen-aged squire Alaron de Sableblanc available to nourish her virginal daydreams, where should they cluster instead, like so many quivering moths drawn to a candle flame, but around the career page, Tamba.

Perhaps already the maiden preferred maturity in a potential mate, and Tamba, having just seen his thirty-first summer, was in years the oldest man of all the little troupe, saving her father alone. Perhaps Sir Harald was a little too well known to Wandith and a little too much marred in her estimation for the role of romantic hero by what she had witnessed of the Aloof Fair One episode; and Alaron de Sableblanc at seventeen might have been too near her own age and too total a stranger; while of Tamba the few glimpses she had snatched during the preceding year had all been favorable, and now his quips and merry little tales often made the whole party laugh. Further than this I shall not speculate.

She was not too shy of Alaron, however, to enlist his services as go-between and scribe (for while literacy was far more rampant than we moderns often suppose among the medieval upper classes, the same cannot be said of the lower classes; and even as free peasants, Garth's family no more aspired to the mysteries of reading and writing than to those of alchemy). So Wandith would tell Alaron in secret what she wanted to write with pinpricks on a yellow, but still pliable leaf—for example: "By the sky above, It's you I love"—begging him as a favor to give it some courtly polish before hiding it where Tamba and nobody else would find it; and Alaron would read back to her:

"By the skies so fair and blue,
Dear my lord, I love but you,
And will rest forever true."

Each note would close with a request to "Please reply in the same place." And that evening, or the following morning, Alaron would bring her another leaf pierced through and through with characters, hold it up to the light and read, for example:

"Unknown sweetheart, kind and true,
Countless thanks I proffer you,
Whether skies be gray or blue."

And then Wandith would kiss the leaf and place it rapturously in the beginnings of her bosom, to keep it safely if somewhat scratchily until it crumbled away, while she planned what message to dictate next.

Thus it went for a fortnight across King Arthur's realm, through woodlands where nuts ripened on tree and bush, while berries tumbled overripely into their hands and mushrooms sprang up from the ground after every rainfall. More often than not they slept the night in pavilions, Joiselette making Garth's family share hers; but twice they stopped at manors, twice at monastery or convent, once at a moated castle—which disappointed Wandith, since she found it not nearly so fine as Quillerstone—and once even at that rarity for the age: an actual inn.

And during all this time, so clever were Wandith and

Alaron about it, that none of the rest of the group ever suspected what was going on beneath their noses—not her family, nor Sir Harald, nor even Tamba himself. For Alaron de Sableblanc saw no reason either to conceal the leafy messages anywhere that Tamba might conceivably find them, whether beneath his pillow or at the top of his saddlebags, or to retrieve the replies therefrom, when simply assuring the maiden that he had done so would work as well—nay, better, since it flustered no one else's peace of mind. Nor did the pinpricks spell any actual words. From Alaron's point of view, this made the whole system even neater and more convenient: pinpricking so many words on the limited surface of an autumn leaf would have been very tedious and cumbersome, whereas—so innocent was the trusting Wandith of the least acquaintance with writing—he could make a few lines and circles stand for almost anything he pretended to read aloud; having the sharp memory of a young illiterate, she never asked him to read them again later, and if by remote chance any of the leaves should stray out of her safekeeping before they finished drying up and crumbling away, nobody else would be able to make anything at all of the marks on them.

It was as well for Wandith that she slept every night surrounded by her family, the Maid of the Wood with her changing assortment of local birds and beasts, and, at the entrance, the Quiller Lion; or, when they slept beneath the roof of castle, *et cetera*, she shared the same bed with her mother and Joiselette. Such arrangements precluded any midnight rendezvous. As for the daylight hours, private though her consultations were with her supposed scribal go-between, they were of necessity brief, rarely out of sight and never out of hearing of one or more other members of the party; and by daylight Wandith could of course see very well the difference between Alaron and Tamba.

So matters stood when Beaumarches Manor greeted its new lord and master. And an unexpectedly lavish welcome this proved. Sir Harald and his company arrived to find the place ready bedecked with banners and hung with autumnal garlands, while young men turned stuffed and spitted meat—a pigeon inside a capon inside a piglet inside a sheep inside a whole beef—over a fire in the courtyard, and aromas wafted from kitchen and ovens that bespoke fresh breads, cakes, puddings, and other side dishes for the feast.

Joiselette's wild retinue tactfully took flight—winged or legged—but the humans and domesticated beasts of the party, including the lion, sat or stood gazing around them with gratified awe. Although no manor was quite a castle, Beaumarches seemed to promise a life in many ways more comfortable than the life inside one of those cold and somewhat claustrophobic stone keeps.

A fine, three-sided villa dating from Roman times, it was blessed, among its numerous outbuildings, with a tidy chapel in the latest ecclesiastical fashion, which stood at the very entrance to the courtyard and on whose single broad step waited a group of three brightly clad women and two men. The younger of the two men—a tall, rangy fellow about Sir Harald's age, of good yeoman stock (or, at least, a good yeomanly style of dress)—detached himself from the others and stepped forward to bow before the knight, telling him: "Be welcome to Beaumarches, good my lord. I am Felicitatus, steward of your manor."

Glancing beyond Felicitatus, Sir Harald saw the darkest-haired of the three women, a brown-eyed beauty in russet and white, pointing at his shield while she whispered something to the older man—obviously, by his dress, the chaplain. Noticing that the knight had observed her gesture, she jerked her right hand down to join her left in turning flowers and a kerchief over and over between her fingers, while her eyes returned his regard somewhat fiercely.

Sir Harald lowered his gaze again to Felicitatus, who was jingling his keyring as if to draw the new master's attention back to himself. "If it please my lord to retire to the hall," said he, "I think we have time sufficient to swear you our fealty, each man and woman of us, before the feast is fully prepared."

"That sounds like an excellent plan," Sir Harald agreed. "But—" and he frowned in puzzlement "—how did you know to prepare all this for today?"

"My lord Sir Kay informed us of your arrival," the steward answered smoothly.

Sir Harald's frown deepened a bit, for, competent though Sir Kay might be in all matters pertaining to his office of high seneschal, how could even he have been quite so confident as to calculate the exact number of days his leige knight might spend in reaching Quillerstone, visiting Sir Godfrey, and then traveling from that castle to Beaumarches? Especially when Sir Harald himself had hoped to spend more than a mere fortnight visiting his old home? But he did not press the matter, asking instead, "What, exactly, happened to my predecessor?"

"Did not my lord Sir Kay inform Your Lordship as to that?"

"Not in so many words."

Felicitatus shrugged elaborately. "Not being privy to my lord the seneschal's thoughts, I can but guess that for some reason Sir Almovitus failed to give satisfaction. To the best of my knowledge, our beloved Sir Kay sent him to take second command of a fortress somewhere in the northernmost marches of our noble Arthur's kingdom, but I should have thought Your Lordship would have known more than I pertaining to that subject."

Sir Harald glanced again at the brown-eyed beauty, who seemed still to be frowning with unabated ferocity at his shield. Somewhat less than perfectly at ease, he gestured for assistance in dismounting and disarming—a squirely duty that Garth had learned by now to leave to Alaron de Sableblanc, though not without the occasional visible qualm of jealousy or regret.

Half an hour thereafter, clad in a fine bliaud of furred velvet, Sir Harald sat in the lord of the manor's chair on the simple, low dais at one end of the hall, taking his new people's hands between his own and receiving their pledges of loyalty, each in his or her turn.

Sir Almovitus had had a high-backed chair fashioned for himself in imitation of King Arthur's throne, but when Felicitatus mentioned it, Sir Harald bade him leave it safe in storage, while he settled himself in the same good but simple backless armchair the steward had used while governing the manor through its lordless interim. Alaron de Sableblanc stood a pace behind the chair at Sir Harald's right shoulder, and Tamba, though technically Joiselette's attendant, stood at the knight's left to balance the picture, while the Maid of the Wood herself—whose position in the

whole tableau had become even more socially ambiguous
than Sir Harald's when he was her prisoner—unbalanced
it again by reclining respectfully a little to one side, her
back at rest on the couchant Quiller Lion, her right hand
on the manor's fiercest mastiff, and her left on Mouser,
who, catlike, had always shown more pride than rightly per-
tained to any animal living with serfs or even free peasants.
As hastily as the people had poured into the manor hall
for this ceremony, Joiselette had not found time to borrow
finery befitting the occasion, and still wore the black
palmer's robe, which was by now considerably patched.

Garth and his family, having already pledged their
troth to Sir Harald at Quillerstone, had no need to do it
again at Beaumarches. But they found places among the
other common folk, and made the most of this introduction
to their new home and fellow members of the manorhold.

All, from the steward down to the kennel boy, tacked a
few Latin words to the end of the simple oath; but only the
dark-haired beauty Sir Harald had first noticed on the
chapel step pronounced them clearly and distinctly: "I,
Procne of Beaumarches, pledge my loyalty to you, my lord
Sir Harald de Folgeste, *quam diu tu meritus eris.*"

Her hair glistened with strands of orange and gold
among the deep brown as it flowed free, except that two
thick locks, one on either side of her oval face, were drawn
gracefully back and plaited together beneath a garland of
autumn flowers. Her long, somewhat sun-browned fingers
rested between his, and he saw himself reflected in the
pupils of her cool brown eyes as she enunciated her oath.

She was the fourth to pledge it, after Felicitatus the
steward, Sir Philibros the chaplain—who was not actually
a dubbed knight, but given the title because of his priest-
hood—and Dame Iris the chaplain's wife. Maid Procne was
their elder child, and Maid Philomela, who followed her,
their younger. To outward appearance, Maid Procne resembled her father chiefly in the color of her hair, both Dame
Iris and the younger daughter being crowned with such a
fine, pale shade of gold that the silver strands were as yet
almost invisible in the mother's elegantly bound tresses.

A strange look passed between the chaplain's wife and
Alaron de Sableblanc. Sir Harald did not quite notice it, but
Joiselette and Tamba did. For that matter, as the ceremony

went on, several other Beaumarches people darted curious glances up over their new lord's right shoulder, enough so that he began to suspect his squire of wrinkling his nose, winking, or otherwise drawing attention to himself—a trick Sir Harald would more readily have expected of Tamba—but, in truth, Dame Iris was the only one whose regard Alaron returned, and that with a solemn and worshipful countenance.

It pains me to record that the worship Alaron de Sableblanc stood eager to offer Dame Iris of Beaumarches, as her willing vassal of Courtly Love, in no way modified the designs he had hatched upon the pretty little slip of a serfborn Wandith, who waited at present with her parents and little brother among the common folk, drinking everything in with greedy eyes.

After the pledging of allegiances there followed, true to the steward's promise, the feast, with meat and ale in plenty for all, accompanied by fish and fowl, turnips and carrots, beet greens and cabbages, apples and pears and fresh-picked berries, cheeses and nuts and honeyed sweetmeats, pasties and white bread. For the new lord's high table, there came an extra suckling pig served with an apple in its mouth, and a roast swan as finely re-feathered as if it had been for the king's own court, as well as a little cask of Burgundy wine.

While the tables were being raised onto their trestles, a kirtle and surcoat that the chaplain's younger daughter had almost outgrown were found for Joiselette, so that now she sat in yellow and white at Sir Harald's right, the mastiff happy to make himself a stool for her feet, which would not otherwise have reached the rushstrewn floor. With Harald and Joiselette at the high table sat the chaplain and his family. Felicitatus did them and himself the honor of serving their table, nominally assisted by Tamba and Alaron—which was proper, of course, even though so capable did the steward prove himself that the squire and page had little to do, and many were the choice morsels that Tamba popped into his mouth to tide his stomach over until he could properly partake of the broken meats in the banquet's aftermath. Alaron, however, devoted what minimal assistance he could offer in dancing attendance upon

Dame Iris, eventually putting her at some pains to continue ignoring his attentions.

For the rest, while Sir Harald thought he sensed a kind of constraint at the start of the meal, by its end all seemed for the most part merry and congenial. Perhaps it was the good wine, of which none of them partook more than just enough. Or the entertainments. Or the fact that what dumb worship Dame Iris suffered Alaron de Sableblanc to offer her with his table service, and which seemed to Sir Harald but the fledgling flights of Courtly Love toward a lady old enough to handle the situation with both tact and amused enjoyment, largely screened the knight from the sharp glances of Maid Procne, sitting at her mother's other side. Or perhaps it was the simple presence of Joiselette, who could flavor almost any gathering with good cheer.

Near the end of the feast, they brought out a great basket of fine saffron buns. Picking one at random and breaking it open, Sir Harald was surprised to find inside it a silver ring.

"What's this?" he asked, working it out of the bread and examining it almost too intently to notice the awkward pause that had fallen over the high table, one that Felicitatus dispelled by answering gracefully, "The happiest of good omens, my lord! That particular talisman represents the keyring to our manor and to our hearts."

The tradition was not unknown to Sir Harald. At Quillerstone Castle, they baked fortunetelling tokens into the Yuletide cakes. "Oh," he said, then continued, "so you use this custom for the arrival of a new master?"

"We use it, sir, whenever we find it appropriate to the occasion."

Sir Harald nodded meditatively and placed the ring on his right little finger—the only one it would fit—for the remainder of the feast, while the steward led the gathering in a cheer. There were saffron buns enough that everybody got one, and soon reports of further talismanic finds were pouring in from every table. The goose girl found half a groat and Tamba the other half of that small coin, which effectively proved the page's premature munching and caused some merriment; the blacksmith found a tiny inkpot, which caused more; one of the cotters found a miniature hive and the fletcher's wife the misproportioned bee to go with it; the stableman found a silver candle no longer than the first joint of his finger, with a golden flame no larger than the head of a pin, and the most elderly cook blushed like a maiden as she held up the miniature candlestick to match it; the kennel boy was delighted to find a little key and ran about like one of his own dogs until he located the lock in the hands of the falconer, which seemed to disappoint him until Felicitatus—who had a graciously flowing interpretation ready for all these trinkets— explained that good fortune would come to the kennel boy through one of the falcons; and Nubbin found a tiny silver feather or quill, which Wandith claimed ought to have been hers because they had squabbled a little over choosing their buns. This made eleven charms in all: an odd number, causing Sir Harald to wonder aloud whether one might have been lost. Felicitatus assured him that the two halves of the broken coin counted for a single charm, making a full set of ten rather than a dozen.

We would call such a method of fortunetelling, no matter how whimsically meant, hazardous to health as well as teeth; and no doubt we would be right. But in those rough and unhygienic times, people tended to chew their bread with care anyway, their flour being full of tiny chips from the millstones.

I mentioned the entertainments. There were no visiting minstrels nor professional fools at Beaumarches just then, nor tumblers nor jugglers nor trained storytellers; but the steward had marshaled and arranged the manor's home-grown talent so as to fill the need nicely between courses. The goose girl piped a duet with the smith's lad, who played cymbals of his own design and craftsmanship; the falconer kept three balls in the air whilst balancing a little knife on his long nose; the miller told a droll tale and the chaplain a sentimental one; the blacksmith and the manor's single man-at-arms wrestled comically until everyone's sides ached with laughing; and Felicitatus capped it all with a graceful song, accompanying his own deep voice on a skillfully plucked lute:

> "Though our love
> Needs must yield to laws above:
> Consequently we await
> Fate;

"Though the sighs
That from ardent bosoms rise
Quiver with resplendent fear
Here—

"Let us plan
Every move as best we can:
Thus our foes will but ensnare
Air.

"If we plot
Craftily enough our knot,
Two hearts we may finally find
Entwined."

As these words flowed forth from the steward's throat, Tamba thought that he glanced most meaningfully at Maid Philomela of the long, loose golden tresses. Sir Harald wondered otherwise, with a vague and misty melancholy that marred his evening somewhat. The romance struck a pleasantly double echo in Master Alaron's secret soul, while to tender young Wandith, who sat with the rest of her family near the foot of a side table, gazing her fill at Master Tamba on the far end of the hall, it could have only one personal significance.

Much later that evening, some hours after dark had fallen, Sir Harald sat alone with Joiselette, Tamba, and the dozing lion, in a little room off the master's bedchamber, admiring the dance of firelight over the old mosaic floor.

He had originally retired here with all the people who had accompanied him from Quillerstone. Having disliked seeing Garth, after so well proving his worth, seated near the bottom of a lower table, he was trying yet again to persuade the faithful freedman into a higher position, perhaps the understewardship of Beaumarches—capable though Master Felicitatus obviously was, even he would surely welcome a good assistant. With a mug of mulled wine forced upon him, Garth seemed to waver; but when Nubbin fell asleep on the lion's mane, the family made up its mind to seek its own place in one of the trusty pavilions, leaving their more permanent settlement to be decided next day.

Soon after Garth and his family, Alaron de Sableblanc also begged to seek out his bed. Tamba might have felt similarly tempted, but, already fast adoze in a pile of rugs and furs, he would have needed to wake up first.

Joiselette hummed, for once putting no words to her melody, at least aloud. As for Sir Harald, weary though he was, his heart seemed too full of many matters, mostly pleasant, for sleep to come quickly.

"These are good people," he said at length, forming words around one thought out of a teeming multitude. "I hope I will make them a good master."

"By everyone's account," said Joiselette, "you made them a good master at Quillerstone for six years."

Our knight was an unlettered man, as his era understood the term: That is, while he could read and write letters in the vernacular or common speech, he knew no Greek and only enough Latin to say his Pater, Ave, Creed, and Confiteor, and pick out a few stray phrases in the Mass and certain legal documents. Joiselette, however, seemed to understand the classical languages as well as the current ones, so now he asked her, "What do those words mean, that they all added after, 'I pledge you my loyalty'?"

She answered softly, "'For as long as you yourself deserve it.'"

"Oh. I see." He sat and turned the information around and around in his mind for several moments before repeating, "I see. They are good people indeed. My lady, thank you for trusting me with this knowledge."

At this same hour, Master Felicitatus sat with Sir Philibros, Dame Iris, Maid Procne, and Maid Philomela, in their little house near the chapel, holding council.

"We ought to have been safe enough," the steward complained. "Who could have expected or foreseen his arrival a good fortnight before the earliest date of our calculations?"

"But why would the beneficent Sir Kay have sent this knight, of all men, to be our new lord?" the chaplain wondered.

"If he is indeed the same knight," Maid Procne pointed out. "If so, how do we explain this dear maid, his sisterly companion? And there is that small but perhaps vital discrepancy in the device on his shield."

"The good knight who visited us last year might merely have forgotten," Maid Philomela said with a shudder.

"The memories of knights are rarely mistaken in such matters," her mother replied, and frowned slightly. "But the squire! I am sure he is the same one. . . . How and why should he return to us now, serving this knight, when last year he served the other?"

"In such a matter as the device on a shield," Felicitatus commented, "most courts would doubtless prefer the word of a knight to that of a squire, especially when that squire is under grave suspicion of weathercock loyalties. As for Sir Kay, kind overlord though he has ever shown himself to us, there is that one murderous blot on his name in the greater world outside, as I have heard tell, in the matter of our gracious king's ill-fated son Loholt."

"King Arthur has forgiven him, and that is all that need concern us of the affair," Sir Philibros said, thus dismissing the whole business from their consideration. (As will we, since it has no bearing on our present tale, has been told elsewhere at length far better than I could recap it, and has been mentioned here only in strict veracity to the historical record and fairness to the steward's many-sided mind). "But returning our attention to our own new lord," the chaplain went on, "who *is*, obviously, our clear and immediate concern . . . can Sir Kay have sent him to us more for his testing than for ours?"

"But if he must be tested . . ." Maid Procne began.

"Then he *is* the same one!" her blonde sister finished, shuddering again.

"Nay, my daughters, that has yet to be proven," Sir Philibros reassured them. "The four new peasants who accompanied him thither seem devoted to him, and they appear to comprise just such a good, Christian family as I could wish all folk to be."

Dame Iris repeated, "And the sweet little Joiselette clearly cherishes him like a brother."

"But even if he is not the same one . . ." Maid Philomela began.

"Then he must be equally suspect, to need testing," her dark sister finished. "And he *is* left-handed."

"If he needs testing, for whatever reason," Felicitatus said confidently, "and if our good Sir Kay entrusts the task to us, then test him we shall . . . meanwhile laying our own plans with greater care than any broody hen who hides the clutch she hopes to hatch."

"As expeditiously, my good Master Felicitatus, as you managed to explain his finding of that token," the priest nodded. "Yet I wonder which of us drew the bun holding the hand to go with that ring?"

"I did," Maid Procne replied in a carefully toneless voice, producing from her pouch a silver hand no longer than one joint of a man's thumb, part of the manor's time-worn collection of an even dozen fortunetelling favors and therefore far too valuable to throw away. "Which proves, I think, the worth of these trinkets in predicting the future," she added sarcastically.

"Well!" said her father. "It is but a foolish old game, after all, tolerated but never sanctioned by our holy faith. Meanwhile . . ."

"Fear not, my dearest one," Felicitatus concluded. "Only trust me, and, with a little skill, we will win through yet!"

Might the chaplain's confidence in the new family have wavered, I wonder, had he been watching when, at almost the same moment he uttered his words of approbation, Wandith met Alaron in a moonlit spot midway between two pretty bowers near forest on one side and lakeshore on another, at the distance of a pleasant stroll from the rest of the manor buildings.

I call them "bowers" because the folk of Beaumarches used that name for them; but in some ways they more nearly resembled the beehive cells of certain olden hermits. They were constructed of rough-hewn stone to about waist height, and from there a wattle framework supported a well-thatched round roof. A combination of living vines and plucked branches, respectively weaving their own way or woven by hand through the framework, effectively screened the interiors of these pleasant retreats; though fast browning with the season, this rustling foliage was still ample to provide as much privacy as almost any resident of that sociable era could ever desire for an hour or two.

Earlier that day, between the pledging ceremony and

the feast, while Tamba was helping raise the tableboards to their trestles and Joiselette borrowing festal garments from the chaplain's daughter, Nubbin and the lion had briefly gone missing, which lent Alaron the chance to accompany Wandith in a search for them. They had found them here, between the bowers, and appointed it in hasty whispers a place to meet that same night by moonlight.

"Is it you?" Wandith asked on joining Alaron, whose knight supposed him to have retired for the evening.

"Who else would it be?" the squire teased her.

"Oh! Tomorrow night, I hope, it may be *him*—Master Tamba of Caerleon!"

"Tomorrow night? You show little admiration for the virtue of patience, sweet maid."

"But the moon is already waning, and it has been such a long, maddening time on the road, without any chance at all. . . . Oh, good master squire, let us make it soon, before the moon's dark! And by the time she waxes again, the weather may be so cold!"

"Soon we will make it, then, dear mistress. But did you truly have some difficulty knowing me by the light of half a moon?"

"A little," she confessed. "Only a little. . . . There are so many new folk around us here, and who knows where they might all be going, about a manor like this one?"

"How, then, will you be sure of him by even less moonlight tomorrow night, sweetling? He is much of a size with more than one man here—I myself, to name but a single example."

"Oh! I'll know him by my love!"

"Wilt thou, indeed? Well, my shrewd and discerning little maid, let us step for now into one of these bowers, where I can better light my candle for this evening's work." Chuckling inwardly, he let her lead the way to the more westerly of the two bowers—where, there still being limits to her newborn temerity, she waited for him to open the door.

Now, many of you may expect Alaron to make his move right away, while closeted with his intended victim on this, his first fair opportunity. But stop and think: Right now, she knows exactly who she is with. And, lacking—as he supposes—the shame or prudence or whatever you choose to call it of a gently born female, she might be fully capable of accusing him after the act to his master, or even to all the manor, including the dear dame to whom he aspires as platonic courtly lover. Whereas, if he plays the game just a little while longer, he may hope to trick Wandith into thinking that he is Tamba . . . and then, even if she should afterward decide to complain aloud, it will be Joiselette's unwitting page on whom the worst falls.

By now you might be thinking Alaron de Sableblanc rather a monstrous fellow. And yet, considering that he hopes only to deflower a lowborn wench newly freed from serfdom, his own century would see his intended crime as venial and trifling in comparison with his master Sir Harald's mortal villainy of abducting that much-admired and virginal gentlewoman, the Aloof Fair One.

As soon as they were safely inside the bower, Alaron used his flint and steel to light the fine beeswax candlestub he had that afternoon filched from the lord of the manor's office, and by its light showed the marveling maiden what else he had filched: an elderly set of wax writing tablets, and a stylus with one end pointed for scribing the letters and the other end flat for wiping them out again in order to imprint new messages. If she was disappointed that this method would leave her no inscribed mementos at all to scratch and crumble against her breast, she was nevertheless blessed with enough burgeoning practicality to appreciate the new system's other advantages.

She dictated: "Meet me by moonlight, Tomorrow night—No, it'll be tomorrow when he reads this—This very night."

Alaron nodded sagely. "But he will need more direction than that, dear Maid Wandith. And why not meet him here, snug inside this romantic bower itself?"

"Oh, good! Please, good Squire Alaron, put it into courtly words for me this one more time."

He wrote, and "read" it back to her as:

> "Within the bower to the west,
> I'll wait this night. Oh, make me blessed
> To meet thee and fulfill our quest."

What he had really written, instead of the mere nonsense marks he had formerly made on the forest leaves, was a message for someone else entirely, which you will read along with its intended recipient, when the time comes a few pages further along.

"I will certainly see that it reaches the right hands," he assured Wandith meanwhile. "Where will the harvesting take you tomorrow?"

"Into the woods with Father and Mother, for nuts and mushrooms and small game."

"While you are in the woods, both Master Tamba and I are to help gather apples in the orchard. Well, my maid, should I fail to bring thee his response, know that it will have been for simple lack of opportunity, and await thine answer here by moonlight."

"I will, oh! I will! Thank you so much, good, kind Squire Alaron!" Up she jumped, threw her thin little arms briefly around his neck, and then scampered away, to lie excitedly awake for much of what was left of the night.

That artless embrace tweaked Alaron's conscience sufficiently that he was about to consider leaving the innocent child to fortunate disappointment on the following night—when, taking time to investigate the bower's simple, home-carpentered furnishings, he found that they comprised a sort of functional if compact scriptorium: a storage compartment in the slant-topped desk held quills, inks, penknives, and suchlike, while the seat of the chair was a chest or coffer holding sheets of parchment both blank and written upon.

Pulling out several of the inscribed sheets, he scrutinized them by the light of his candlestub. In this shady bower, someone was composing a book of knights—a record, as it appeared, complete with diagrams of their shield devices, of every champion who had ever visited Beaumarches, either in person or in the tales of other travelers. Someday, no doubt, when the unknown scribe-illuminator had amassed enough pages, they would be gathered up into a bound volume; but for now they still lay loose.

Seeing what he held, Alaron commenced to search even more eagerly through these sheets for one in particular that he guessed must be there . . . and, finding it, he whistled a long, low whistle. He had known, of course, from the time they rode up to Beaumarches Manor and he recognized the place by sight, after having mislaid it, by name, amongst all the other places he had visited with his former master. The welcome these people gave them had puzzled him for a time, but now he saw that they were simply courteous— or wary—to a fault.

The absence of even one sheet was likely to be noticed, and the absence of this particular sheet, at this particular time, sooner than that of any other. The bower's regular occupant would immediately suspect that the thief was one of the new arrivals, too. But they were a fairly numerous party, the new arrivals, including a young child—and small boys were famous for their mischief. Moreover, it had by now occurred to Alaron that, lightly though his social world at large might weigh the seduction of a lowborn girl by a highborn youth, his immediate master was as faithfully devoted to this particular family of former serfs as they to him, and therefore liable to take a much bleaker view than society at large of the affair.

All things considered, then, our villain—for so I think we may safely consider Alaron de Sableblanc in this episode—felt temporary possession of the parchment worth the risks involved. True, he had as yet no perfect idea of how he would use it; but for all that, he could still hope to have it back before its loss was discovered, occupied as the scribe-illuminator would surely be on the morrow, along with every other able-bodied Beaumarchian, in the work of harvesting food for the winter.

Next day, while the rest of Garth's family went into the woods with the smith's lad to serve them as guide, little Nubbin, being as yet just a trifle overyoung for hunting nuts and mushrooms, stayed in the apple orchard gleefully riding the Quiller Lion around from tree to tree, gathering windfalls and putting them in two baskets slung saddlelike across the beast's back just below his mane, each basket almost big enough to have held the boy himself.

Joiselette, too, back in her black robe, was helping with the apple harvest, along with Tamba, Alaron, and even Sir Harald, who rather enjoyed the idea that there were times and places when every capable party expecting to eat the food could and should share the effort of bringing it in, regardless of rank. That accounted for the entire group of new arrivals, barring the rest of the animals: Goblin and most of the other horses were grazing in the meadow, Garth and Gytha had taken Mistwraith into the woods with panniers on her back, and Mouser the cat was off somewhere on his own feline explorations.

Also working the orchard were Sir Philibros, Dame Iris, and Maid Procne; but Felicitatus, as steward, stayed at the storehouse to see the apples properly sorted and set aside for cider or buried in hampers for the winter. And, on learning early in the morning that Sir Harald intended to help pick apples, these conspirators had clad the younger daughter in her mother's oldest and shabbiest gown, bound her blonde tresses up beneath a plain brown kerchief, and sent her quietly into the woods, with instructions to seek out and spy upon Garth's family, while Dame Iris put on one of Philomela's kirtles and allowed her own pale hair to trail out loosely beneath her headscarf. Despite the difference in their ages, these two gentlewomen were, as I have said, much of a size and, with the mother's silver hairs barely visible among the gold, they might from a little distance, or from the back, be mistaken one for the other.

Although disappointed, then, Dame Iris was not really surprised when, on going round from one side of her latest apple tree to the other, she discovered a set of the lord of the manor's own wax tablets lying on an exposed root, as if left there on purpose for her to find.

She remembered that Sir Harald's squire had stopped briefly at this same tree before. Seeing her turn from a neighboring tree whose boughs she had plucked of all the fruit within her reach, the squire had smiled, waved as if to tell her that she would find good gathering here, and himself moved respectfully on. Now she looked round in time to catch his face turned toward her. Next instant, he was diligently plucking apples whilst the notes of his whistled tune reached her across the intervening distance.

Beyond the squire, she could see Sir Harald and Joiselette, laughing over some joke as they worked at a tree on the orchard's far side.

Ducking back around the tree so as to screen herself more or less from the squire's scrutiny, Dame Iris opened the tablets and read:

"'I loved thee when I saw thee last.
Since then, full seasons five have passed:
A perfect knot of five has flown,
And love has into worship grown.'"

Holding her basket as though it were filled, she headed
as unobtrusively as possible back to the storehouse, whis-
pering a word as she went to her dark daughter Procne,
who whispered a word to Sir Philibros; and within a few
minutes they were all gathered together with the steward,
discussing this new development, never doubting but that
Dame Iris had indeed been mistaken for her fair daughter,
and that Squire Alaron had delivered the message on his
master's behalf.

"So," mourned the priest, "it is even as we feared."

"And he has swallowed the bait already!" Felicitatus
chuckled. "The one thing is to be regretted, but the other
to be welcomed, as lending us the opportunity to unmask
him and lay our complaint before Sir Kay without further
suspense."

"But what is this about 'full seasons five'?" Maid
Procne puzzled, frowning with something that, in other circumstances, might almost have been mistaken for jealousy.
"This knight has never seen my sister—nor any of us—
before yesterday."

"The great tournament of Tenebroc took place about
five seasons ago," Felicitatus replied, as if that answered
all. "Summer, autumn, winter, spring, and another summer, to bring us to this autumn."

"But none of us attended the great tournament of
Tenebroc," Maid Procne protested.

"No," her mother replied, being wiser in the ways of the
world, "but does he know that? It was a great press of
people, by all that we have been told, and one of man's
oldest romantic ruses is to pretend to previous acquaintance with a maid whom he wishes to seduce."

Sir Philibros added, "Nor can he as yet be aware, my
maid, of thy diligence in keeping record of each and every
knight we meet or hear tell of, so that had we attended at
Tenebroc—"

"She would have gathered far too much material for
her great book-to-be!" Felicitatus cut in with a laugh. "And
hardly had sufficient leisure to copy it all down, even

working every atom of time from that occasion until now. Nay, dear Mistress Procne, I do not mock thy labors. Far from it!—when they have already more than proven their worth, this week alone."

"Well!" Procne replied, still frowning and also, now, biting her lip a little. "What shall we do about it, then?"

"Why," the steward went on, "if you will be so good as to take my counsel, since he has already swallowed the bait, let us play him a bit on the line until we have him well and truly in place for our net. Let us return him an epistle of encouragement and assignation—"

"And then," Dame Iris seized the word almost eagerly, "let me be the one awaiting him there, in place of the maid he expects, and let the rest of you lie hidden nearby, ready to take him in the attempt."

"This is too brave of you, Mother," Procne cried. "Let me be the one!"

"Nay, dearest daughter. I am the one whom he has already mistaken for thy sister. You have not our coloring, and are larger boned, besides. Moreover, I am in any case no longer a maid, and should he wax violent in his passion, and careless of actual identities—"

"Then I am younger and stronger to hold him off or evade him until the rest of you spring forward!" Procne persisted. "Mother, it is not fair nor right that you should take all the risk upon yourself!"

"Nevertheless, it is her prerogative, my maid!" Felicitatus said peremptorily. "And it is wisdom, if only to keep the same bait that has already worked once. We must, of course, name for the assignation a time and a place that will aid in maintaining the masquerade as long as desirable."

"Philomela's bower," Dame Iris suggested. "Tonight, by moonlight."

"But what of his other companions?" asked Sir Philibros. "The squire, we know, is sufficiently implicated to have delivered his message, though conceivably with little cognizance of its contents. I find it difficult, however, if not intolerable, to credit evil of the Lady Joiselette; and Master Tamba, this page by profession, remains an unknown element in the tangle."

Said Felicitatus at last, "I conceive one very simple test

that ought to clarify matters greatly, at least in the latter case."

Thus it was that Procne waited on the far fringe of the orchard until Sir Philibros brought her word that Sir Harald's squire had departed in the direction of those places that everyone, villain and hero alike, must visit from time to time, and nobody, lowborn or lofty, can ever visit on behalf of another. Sir Harald himself was still in the orchard, true; but in the context of this intrigue, pretended though it was on the conspirators' side, to put the lady's reply directly into the knight's hands would have looked suspiciously open, besides failing to serve the present purpose. Instead, Procne brought the tablets to Tamba.

"Good page," she addressed him, "how truly do you serve our new master?"

"Rather less than anyone else hereabout," he answered, "seeing that it is the good Lady Joiselette to whom I owe my own primary and immediate allegiance. But, since she is like a sister to Sir Harald, I think that I serve him none too ill."

"Well!" Procne paused half a moment, as if considering. "Your friend, his own squire, gave my sister these tablets, with a message from him to her. May I entrust them to you for him, with her reply?"

"Madame, you may entrust me with your life itself!"

He did not add in so many words that he would justify her trust, nor did she fail to note his omission, and judge therefrom that he was in the game up to the crown of his curly head.

In fact, as we know, this was Tamba's first inkling that anything culpable might be going on under their noses; and though he accepted the tablets with every secret intention of scrutinizing them himself before passing them on, his motives were of the purest.

So pure were they, that he brought the tablets first to Joiselette, along with the explanation of how he had got them, and begged her to open and read them first . . . although he took care to do all this well out of sight of anyone else.

She read:

> "'If thy love
> Full seasons five hath had to grow,
> Time it is that you should know
> My kiss.

> "'When above
> Tonight's moon shines, then let us feast
> In the bower to the east
> On bliss.'"

If you think you glimpse the steward's touch in this, your theory marches closely with Joiselette's, who remarked after a single reading, "It's very much like the verses Felicitatus sang at the banquet yesterday, only the rhyme scheme is a little different. Maybe he composed this in haste."

"It was Maid Procne who entrusted it to me," Tamba repeated, "as if from her fair sister, saying that it was for Sir Harald."

"Well, then, let's take it to Sir Harald," the Maid of the Wood said. "Though I think it's going to surprise him."

Of course, she was quite right. As we know, for once in his life Sir Harald was completely guiltless of the mischief that had been going on around him; nor was this type of underhanded intrigue his style, even in his most villainous phases. All that he could think to say on reading the rhymed message was, "Are you sure she meant this for *me*?"

Tamba wrinkled his forehead in diligent thought. "Damsel Procne's exact words—let me see. . . . First she asked whether it was not you whom I served, my lord, by name—I would swear with utter confidence that she named you at that point—but then afterward, in handing me these tablets . . . 'your friend his squire,' she said—that would be Master Alaron—'gave my sister this message from him. May I give it back to you for him, with her reply.' No . . . in all that speech, I cannot recollect that she actually repeated your name, my lord, any more than she did that of your squire, so I suppose that the 'he' and 'him' most intimately concerned in all these last communications could conceivably have been our Master Squire Alaron. But that was not the meaning I drew from it. I clearly understood her to mean Your Lordship."

Sir Harald shook his head. "That cannot be. Even if I— What if it is not Maid Procne's sister . . . but Maid Procne herself is party to this intrigue? . . . I cannot even believe it of Maid Philomela, let alone—"

"Sir Harald," Joiselette suggested, "haven't you noticed how similar these verses are to the ones Master Felicitatus sang yesterday? Suppose they are all in it, baiting a trap?"

"For Alaron? God's Blood, if that young villain—No, as an older villain myself, it befits me to go gently. Good Tamba, take these tablets to him, but say nothing of having shown them to us, and let us see whether or not he brings them back to me."

"Bravo, sir!" cried Tamba. "If he keeps them for himself, then the whole intrigue belongs to him."

"And, by . . . by the tails of all the comets in Heaven," our knight laughed, remembering this time to modify his oath, "I should like to be there myself when they spring their trap shut on him!"

"But suppose," mused the page, "suppose that he should bring them to you, sir, with their cryptic message?"

"In that case . . . in that case. . . . We will not talk about that case," Sir Harald decided with a frown. "What purpose could these good people have in trying to spring a trap on me?"

❖ ❖ ❖

By now, Alaron had been back in the orchard long enough to fill one basket with apples and begin filling a second, whilst eagerly awaiting the lady's response to his message. Tamba had been crafty enough, however, to keep the tablets well out of sight while discussing them with Joiselette and Harald; and, if Alaron had glimpsed the three exchanging pleasantries on the far side of the orchard, there could be little in that fact alone to awaken his suspicions, seeing how long they had traveled together before ever he himself joined their company.

Thus, when half an hour later the page approached and furtively showed him the closed tablets lying half buried in Tamba's own basket of apples, Alaron felt no alarm, only a hint of disappointment that his lady should have allowed a go-between into the affair. Still, remembering that Dame

Iris was, after all, a married gentlewoman—and married to the manor's chaplain, at that!—he saw her double need for discretion even in a matter of pure Courtly Love, and said only, "Good master page, do you know what you carry?"

"Apples," Tamba replied, "and a pair of pretty wax writing tablets bound up with green thread, handed me just now by one who intimated with some assurance that you would know better than I what to do with them."

"How curious! And did she give you no other clue by which to guess their contents?"

"My lord, who is a page to sniff out the secrets of a squire well on his way to knighthood?" And the page, who had more than ten years' advantage of age on the squire, gave him a conspiratorial wink.

As soon as Tamba had left him, Alaron buried the tablets beneath his tunic at the belt, carried his full basket of apples to the storehouse, and after delivering them slipped away out of sight behind the building to peruse his lady's reply in private.

Be it recorded in partial mitigation of his guilt, that on his first reading it struck him with a vast and hollow disappointment in the pit of his stomach. He did not at all want from his Ideal Lady of Courtly Love the same thing he wanted from a mere little serfborn tumble-in-the-straw! On rereading and deeper study, however, he began to find in it all sorts of symbols and innocent allegories that would have amazed both its true and its purported authors. Did not the very saints frequently liken the love of God to mere carnal intimacy? Then why should lady and worshipper in the court of Love Ideal not copy the same allegorical style?

Having thus satisfied himself that his Ideal Lady remained ideal and meant "know" and "kiss," "feast" and "bliss" in only the purest of Platonic senses, he pressed the inscribed message fervently to his lips before wiping it smooth and rapturously—in remembrance of the words it had so lately borne—secreting it once again beneath his tunic, close to the sheet of parchment he had borrowed from the west bower, wrapped in his largest linen handkerchief and pressed against a providential scrap of leather to keep it clean and uncreased during its journey, for greatest safety and convenience, about his person. The green thread that She had fondled in re-tying the tablets, he reverently bound round his right arm above the elbow, where it would be hidden by his sleeve from profane glances.

Meanwhile, needing no other pretext than his right as lord of the manor to explore his new holding at will, Sir Harald went in search of the place that the verses had named for tonight's questionable tryst.

He soon found the twin bowers, standing where they did near the shore of the large and placid lake. "In the bower to the east," the verse had said. Entering that pleasant little cell of stone, wattle, and thatchwork, he studied it well. Here were an embroidery frame with a half-finished altar cloth; a stout wooden chest to serve as the needlewoman's chair while she sat at her handiwork, and to hold her fabrics, threads, and precious needles safely during her absences; and a narrow, cushioned bench apparently in case she should wish to rest awhile from her labors. There was also a prieu-dieu, or kneeler, which made the place seem a curious choice indeed for romantic intrigue. More furnishings, the little building could scarcely have contained; and, if he could take the message of the wax tablets at face value—which he began to misdoubt— he thought that the frame and chest, at the very least, would have to be pushed far to one side, along with the prieu-dieu.

After a moment of admiring the fine embroidery work without touching it, he left the eastern bower and started across, in curiosity, to the one on the west. His hand was already on its door handle when a cry of "Sir!" arrested his attention.

He turned. Maid Procne had just come into sight around the edge of the eastern bower.

"My lord Sir Harald!" she repeated, quickly stepping closer. "What do you do here?"

"Acquaint myself with the manor grounds . . . and you, my maid?" He could not help but remember that it had been she who handed Tamba the tablets, but he strove mightily to keep any hint of that knowledge out of his voice.

Nevertheless, she flushed. "Sir, these bowers are . . . are meant for my sister and myself, we two maids, alone. Even Sir Almovitus respected our solitude here."

He stepped back from the west bower at once. "Pardon me, my damsel, I did not know that. If that is the rule of Beaumarches Manor, I, too, will respect it. . . . But which is whose, if I may ask? Or do you use them jointly?"

"Sir," she answered after a short hesitation, "you were about to go into mine. The other falls to my gentle sister. Not even I intrude upon her meditations there, nor she upon mine here."

He sighed. "I must confess that, knowing no better, I have already been inside that bower—no, never fear, she is not there at present. I saw nothing but her embroidery—it is exquisite work, that I could admire without fingering." He saw no invasion of Maid Philomela's privacy in mentioning the altar cloth that she must bring out eventually for all to view.

"As you say, my lord, my sister does extremely fine embroidery. I do not. . . ." Her color rising still higher, Maid Procne went on, "But perhaps you have already been inside my bower as well, to notice what I do there?"

He shook his head. "No. Yet I cannot believe that it is so little worth seeing as your tone suggests, my damsel."

She sighed in her turn. "It is . . . clumsy. At least in part. I flatter myself, my lord, that I am no mean scholar. Good Sir Philibros, who dearly loves Greek and Latin and all things bookly, taught me that much well enough, and also, both he and my good mother, being of gentle birth, have taught me not a little of knights and their devices and the ideals of chivalry. But we have never had anyone here from whom I could learn the secrets of illumination and fine lettering."

"I am sure that your father and mother have been excellent teachers, and you an excellent scholar."

"Thank you, sir, but it is Philomela who will carry on the beauty of our mother's needlework. Strange that I should seem to take after Sir Philibros. . . ." Her voice trailed away so suddenly that I might have used a dash in place of four dots, only a dash would suggest that Sir Harald cut rudely into her speech, which he most certainly did not!

Instead, after waiting long enough to feel sure that she was not about to resume speaking on her own momentum, he turned to a different subject. "Maid Procne . . . was yesterday's feast truly prepared in honor of my coming? Or had it been meant—" drawing a deep breath, he plunged ahead "—for a wedding?"

Her startled gasp suggested that his guess had been correct; but, recovering herself quickly, all she said was: "My lord, what makes you suppose that?"

"A number of things. I could not—and still cannot—see how you could have been so sure of the exact day we would arrive, when we were not sure of it ourselves. And there were the flowers and kerchief you turned over and over in your hands, my maiden, as you stood there with your family and the steward on the chapel step. Then there were the talismans baked into the buns—in the castle of my birth and life until last year, we used such tokens at Yuletide; in the castle where we lay over last winter, they baked them into their New Year's pies; and I am told that at King Arthur's court they chew their pasties and saffron cakes with especial care on every holiday of the year, and at every wedding. Somehow these seemed less suited to the mere welcoming of a new lord—especially with such tokens as candle and candlestick, two matching halves of a broken coin, and the pretty ring I drew myself. I must confess that our good steward's explanations yesterday for that ring and certain other tokens struck me as thin and unsatisfying."

"I am sorry you feel that way, my lord. Do you always fear the worst of silly signs and portents when they point to your own good?"

"My damsel," he went on in as gentle a voice as he could muster, gazing at her as deeply as he dared, "the bridegroom, I take it, was to be Master Felicitatus himself. Were you to have been his bride?"

Maid Procne drew herself up straighter. "And if I was, my lord? Suppose that we had planned a wedding, and suppose that the bride had been myself—what then?"

He drew a long, quavering sigh. "Why . . . what puzzles me most about all this . . . if indeed I surprised you by coming unexpectedly on the edge of a wedding . . . why should you suddenly hide the fact? Why not go on with it as you had planned—give a double meaning to the cele-bration, and allow us to join in wishing you—that is, the happy couple—well?"

She cast him an appraising look. "And perhaps, my lord, in paving the bridegroom's way with *jus primae noctis*?"

He frowned. "I am not the scholar you are, my maiden. It's a phrase I seem to have heard somewhere, but—God's Blood!" he cried as the connection hit him suddenly. "But King Arthur abolished that custom long ago—it is forbidden everywhere in his realm."

"Forbidden, perhaps, but not yet utterly dead and abolished everywhere," Procne replied with some bitterness. "Not as long as the lord can pretend to the outside world that he was guilty of nothing but simple seduction."

Sir Harald put a hand on the bower stones to steady himself, jerked it off again in fear of appearing to make free with her solitude. "God's Blood! Then Sir Almovitus? . . ."

"My father, sir, in all probability, although Sir Philibros kindly pretends otherwise."

"But—if this is so—why did all of you wait so many years before taking your complaint to my lord Sir Kay?"

"I would not wrong my true father," Maid Procne replied. "In most other ways, he was a good lord to us. It was he who arranged for my mother's bridegroom and true love to be ordained at the hands of His Grace the Bishop of Winchester. Only, as I grew toward womanhood, he began less and less to treat me as his daughter, more and more to look at me as if Sir Philibros might have fathered me in truth."

Sir Harald could not help groaning and turning briefly away. When he uncovered his eyes and turned back, Maid Procne was gone.

"I think that he *cannot* be the same one. That discrepancy in the device is all-important," Procne whispered to her mother beneath a secluded tree in the orchard. "I was on the very point of showing him the sheets of my book."

"Thank all the saints that you did not!"

"Mother, you *must* let me take your place tonight in Philomela's bower!"

Dame Iris shook her head. "These knights may have smooth tongues, my daughter, along with an incredible instinct for persuasion and dissimulation—"

"No, Mother, he was sincere in every word. I could swear it on my soul!"

"Thy very young soul, child; and I pray that our Lord God would refuse that oath. Who knows but that Sir Harald has already examined thy book-to-be on his own account?"

"I know that he has not! For I hid out of sight behind my bower until he went away, and he did so almost at once, and never touched the door."

"Have you thought that he might already have been inside thy bower, and but made pretence of being about to enter for the first time when he heard thee coming?"

"But have *you* thought, Mother, if he guesses me to be the bride, why should it be my sister whom he means to seduce?"

"A knight may have other reasons than the right of first night, my child, and Philomela is fair as any minstrel's dream—more fair, I think, than that one of the report we had last summer. Moreover, he is black of hair and brows—as dark as Sir Almovitus himself—and may for that very reason prize fairness all the more in womankind." At her dark daughter's sigh, the mother added, "But thou art equally comely, in thine own way; and a powerful man inclined to evil, denied his first choice, might snap all the harder at his second."

"But if there is no real danger, as you assure me, with Sir Philibros and Master Felicitatus outside awaiting thy call—"

"No, Maid Procne of Beaumarches," Dame Iris replied, emphasizing her decision with three separate signals: her mother's prerogative to interrupt her child's sentence, her use of Procne's full name and title of respect, and her tone of voice. "Though there will be no danger at all, I will not risk either of my sweet daughters to even as much small danger as will never arise!"

On this day, when all hands were so heavily turned to the harvest, no formal meals except supper had been planned. Instead, the tables were left set up in the manor hall, still laden with the broken meats of yesterday's banqueting, for everyone to feed upon today, catch as catch can. Here, closer to the hour of None than Sext, Sir Harald finally ran Alaron to earth, as the squire poured a mug of ale to wash down his thick slice of bread piled high with cold beef and cheese.

"My lord!" the squire exclaimed, quick to lay his own meal aside, as befit him, in order to serve his knight. "What may I fetch for Your Lordship?"

"I hardly know, Alaron. I thought you might have something . . . of a special nature . . . laid up for me already."

"My lord?" Alaron's puzzlement looked genuine.

"Come, lad." Sir Harald made a show of glancing around the hall. Only a few others were there just now, and all of them stood or sat making their meals at the lower table. "We are private enough. Where is it?"

"My lord . . . how could I have prepared it to have ready for you, before even knowing what it is of all this profusion that you might most enjoy on your tongue today?"

Though there were few others in the hall just now, that could change at any moment. And Sir Harald would give his squire every chance . . . or at least spare him public disgrace, if possible. "Prepare me the same nuncheon as you have there for yourself, lad, and bring it to me in my office. I would spend an hour studying what records, documents, and letters—" he laid a special stress on that last word "—my predecessor may have left behind."

He failed to reckon with the fact that he had just handed Alaron a forewarning of sorts, along with a few precious moments to ponder defense and counterattack.

The office of the lord of Beaumarches was excellently provisioned, with no fewer than three sets of wax writing tablets. Sir Harald identified one of them as the set Joiselette and Tamba had shown him that morning. The questionable message had been wiped away, leaving no trace, but here were the gouge he had noticed in the board cover, the scratch in the leather hinge, the nick in the stylus. Clearly, after receiving it back from Tamba—and, presumably, reading it through—Alaron de Sableblanc had polished the message away with as much care as he polished rust from a helmet, and then returned it to its place in his master's office.

After so arranging it on the desktop that his squire could hardly help but notice it, our knight turned his attention to the documents in the strongbox. He had only a moment or two of thumbing them with what show of absorption he could muster, when Alaron arrived with a tray of bread, meat, cheese, ale, and two rosy-cheeked fresh apples.

"My lord Sir Harald," he said, moving the tablets aside—one-handedly and a bit overcasually—in order to clear a place beside the strongbox for the tray.

"Very well, Alaron. We are completely alone. You may relay it to me now."

The squire set the tray down and blinked, in that order. "My lord? I have brought Your Lordship's nuncheon. What else would you have?"

Sir Harald retrieved the tablets and held them up. "These bore a message meant for me, did they not? May I not assume that you committed it to memory before erasing it against prying eyes?"

"My lord! My lord, I had hoped you would never learn of this!"

"So I would wager," the knight remarked coolly.

"Sir Harald, my lord! *What* they intend against you, I cannot tell, but the *why* of it—that, perhaps, I can illuminate. My lord, forgive me—I am but the messenger—and I had hoped never to have the cause to show you this. . . ." Groping beneath his upper garments, he brought forth a flat packet of leather and linen, unwrapped it, and laid a single sheet of parchment on the strongbox.

Sir Harald picked this parchment up and stared at it. The heraldic diagram of a single shield met his eye; it was blazoned with his own coat of arms as it had used to be, the bend entirely black across the ermine-speckled field. Above the diagram a blank space had been left, as if for the knight's name—whenever the scribe should learn it—but beneath were the words:

> *This villainous knight, who favors his left hand and arm, was surprised whilst foully abducting a maiden, to his eternal shame, against her will, when she had been traveling alone, trusting in God and our good King Arthur's Law for her protection. Having thus defied both Heaven's will and that of his earthly monarch, this Knight of the Bend Sinister did further compound his infamy by traitorously and left-handedly striking down the Black Chevron Knight, q.v., after pledging his surrender, and escaping with the poor maiden*

ere her valiant would-be rescuer could sufficiently recover himself to offer effective pursuit. May the name and fame of the Bend Sinister Knight be forever shamed and blackened in all courts of the world.

Sir Harald turned the sheet over. On the other side he found pictured the shield of his late nemesis, the Black Chevron Knight, with a blank space above it waiting for the name, and below it the caption:

This noble champion graced Beaumarches Manor early in the first summer of our liberation from Sir Almovitus (late of Beaumarches), at which time he of the Black Chevron had destroyed two fierce dragons, slain the wicked ogres Tryphon, Hyphon, and Zertuxes, and defeated innumerable other malefactors, of whom one alone, the Knight of the Bend Sinister, q.v., had ever escaped him, by dint of striking him with a foul, left-handed, and treacherous blow after having knelt and pledged his surrender.

"My lord?" the poor squire ventured, already wishing that it were possible to undo what he himself had just done, and also what he had failed to do last summer. "My lord Sir Harald, what could I have said? At the time we stopped here, *he* was my rightful lord! In loyalty, how could I have called my own rightful lord a liar?"

"Alaron," Sir Harald replied in far too quiet a voice, "you may go now."

Alaron went. It was only after he had shut the door behind him that he heard the mug of ale shatter against the wall.

He shuddered, sighed, and took some time to assuage his conscience with various considerations—each one quite true and valid in itself—to the point where he could again look forward with pleasure to the evening ahead of him.

In all, four small parties had set forth to forage the forest for nuts, mushrooms, small game, and what few berries might still remain to be gathered. It was midafternoon before Maid Philomela managed to work her way around through the woodlands with polite pretexts from group to group until at last she found Garth, his two womenfolk, and the smith's lad, who was striving manfully to flirt with young Wandith.

"My maid!" the smith's lad exclaimed on seeing the chaplain's daughter, and the other three, less accustomed in addressing their betters to make the distinction between married women and unmarried—and, besides, today her hair was bound up beneath its kerchief—echoed, "Ladyship!"

Until the coming of Sir Harald's party, the chaplain with his wife and daughters had been the only gentlefolk resident at Beaumarches for more than a year, and before that the only other had been Sir Almovitus himself; so both sisters were happily accustomed to living on amiable terms with serfs and peasants. Even dear Felicitatus was by birth a simple yeoman, difficult though Philomela found it to remember that fact.

Now, after returning their greetings, she looked back as though attempting to catch sight of the group she had most lately left, then returned her smile to Garth's family, held up her small bow with arrow still nocked, and explained, "I appear to have outstripped them in my chase after a cony—which seems to have eluded me anyway."

"Might be the rabbit took fright at us, my lady," Garth apologized.

"No matter! It was running for its life, and I for a mere morsel, as Æsop said."

"Which one is he, my lady?" asked Garth's wife.

Philomela laughed. "My father will tell you, or my sister, out of their great love of books. We have eleven in our library!" It was a large number, as those days counted private libraries. "Much," she went on to the smith's lad, "run back to Orthric's party and tell them I will hunt awhile with Garth and his family."

The smith's boy bobbed his head and disappeared in the direction of her nod.

The first part of her secret mission was accomplished. The second and more difficult part remained. For she liked Garth and his family, so that the fear of finding out something to their discredit fretted at her heart. But Sir Harald had spoken with Felicitatus of appointing Garth, freedman though he was, to the understewardship of Beaumarches; so, if there were anything unsavory to be learned, it had best be learned as quickly as consistent with delicate tact.

Like the Boy Ihesu in the stories Father Chaplain of Quillerstone used to tell them, Nubbin had slipped away when everyone thought somebody else was watching him. Only Ihesu was older when He did it, so many years older that Nubbin couldn't even imagine ever being that old— twelve whole years old!—and Nubbin had the Quiller Lion to protect him, not just a lot of old Templars (which Nubbin thought was another, grander word for temple priests).

They were playing and giggling in the meadow between orchard and woods, feeding the better windfall apples to Goblin and the other horses and tossing the wormiest ones at the cows, when they saw Sir Harald coming. He was carrying his shield and sword, but not wearing his armor, and he was hurrying away from the manor house so fast, without ever looking around to one side or the other, that he was almost on top of them before the lion growled and made him look around and see them.

"Sir Harald, my lord, sir!" Nubbin greeted him solemnly, bowing the way he had been taught.

Sir Harald stopped and looked down at him. "Young Nubbin. Who is guarding thee?"

"The lion is guarding me, my lord, sir. Do you want an apple?" Nubbin held up the best one he had, one without any worms at all, that he had wanted to store in his own stomach.

Sir Harald shook his head and told the lion, "Lion, guard him well."

The lion rumbled a little and nodded.

Nobody else being on hand to hush him, Nubbin went on, "Where are you going, my lord, sir?"

"I am going to . . . to save Beaumarches Manor from a— an ogre, boy. A wicked, evil ogre!"

"Ooh!" Nubbin's eyes opened wide. "Are we all in great danger, sir? Shall I run and warn everybody to hide?"

"No! Nobody else—none of you are in danger, Nubbin. I can see to that! You are to tell no one of this, lad! Do you understand? You are to tell no one at all about seeing me here! Lion, guard him well!" Sir Harald repeated, and then hurried on without waiting to hear Nubbin's answer or see his solemn nod.

Nubbin stood thinking hard until Sir Harald had disappeared into the woods. But surely "no one at all" couldn't mean Joiselette, too, could it? Because there had been tears running down Sir Harald's cheeks, and big, strong knights didn't cry unless they had something very, very bad to cry about. And nobody could make things to cry about go away like Joiselette. When Sir Harald said, "tell no one at all," he couldn't have meant the Lady Joiselette.

The lion thought the same, because when Nubbin asked him about it, he purred and nodded again. So they went to seek her out together.

And now, in these next several pages, you are likely to notice something peculiar about Joiselette's movements. I mention this only to reassure you that I noticed it, too: It is not mere carelessness on my part as chronicler, but something that happens often enough in old hagiographies to have been given a technical Latinate name of its own.

Deep in the woods, Maid Philomela said, "It appears to me, Goodman Garth, that you would make Master Felicitatus a fine understeward."

"I don't think your rare steward needs any helper, my lady. Not when I see how he's run Beaumarches this last year and more, with no knight around at all."

"Why, but he has had all of us to assist him, friend! I feel sure that he would far rather rely upon one understeward alone," said the cunning damsel (who had her own reasons for wanting to see the steward with more time on his hands). "And you really must overcome your shyness of addressing me as 'maid' and 'damsel' until I am married . . . whenever that might be."

"I don't question you about that, my . . . my maid—er, lady. Only you must have someone here already who'd be better for the office than me."

"Had we had a single one such man, friend Garth, he

would be acting as understeward already, and not all of us together."

Gytha said comfortably, "You served Sir Harald very well in place of squire, my husband, all last year until he found my young Lord Alaron. You would serve him very well as understeward to my Lord Felicitatus now."

Wandith, listening with half an ear as she scouted for nuts, said nothing, but only daydreamed about the coming night.

Maid Philomela went on, "Were you in attendance on him every hour, in every knightly adventure, all that time you served him in the place of a squire?"

After a longish pause, Garth replied, "Not quite always, my lady—maid. But most of the time."

"And was his shield always just as it is now," the gentle-maiden went on merrily, "with the bend half black and half red?"

Goodwife Gytha began, "That it was not—"

"Hush!" Garth exclaimed. "Listen!"

All of them listened, turning in the direction Garth's head was cocked. Even stolid little Mistwraith stood still beneath her burden of wild-harvest with both her ears pricked toward the quarter in question.

The sounds of metal striking down on metal came to them—blow on clamoring blow—crashing, clashing, slashing, smashing across the distance.

"Oh, Father!" Wandith cried, clapping her hands. "It must be knights fighting! Can we go and see them?"

"No!" he answered with no pause at all. "That is . . . Maid Philomela, will you allow my wife and daughter to see Your Ladyship safe back to the manor? I must go to spy this out, myself alone."

Wandith began, "But, Father—"

"Husband," Gytha cut in, soberly enough to stop her daughter's protest, "take care."

"Wife, that I will—but one alone can creep through woods more silently than four together, with donkey or without." After giving wife and daughter each in turn a kiss and a few words whispered in one ear, he added, "Go you now, and make sure to keep our lady Maid Philomela safe. And if you meet anyone else, warn them to go back to the manor with you."

Then he turned and disappeared, two or three paces carrying him out of sight among the thick trees and forest foliage that still, even in autumn, could screen so many foraging parties from one another.

What words Garth had whispered to Gytha and Wandith, Maid Philomela was too polite to inquire, even in the present circumstances; but not another word could she draw from either of them regarding Sir Harald's shield, and Goodwife Gytha even pretended that she had begun to talk about something else entirely when her goodman's warning cut her off.

Garth could not know what the noises were but—after some of Maid Philomela's questions—he could guess, and fear. When at length the sounds suddenly stopped, he hastened all the harder toward whence they came. He squashed two fine clusters of choice mushrooms underfoot and never so much as noticed.

At last he came out into a little glade that almost overlooked the lake, and found Joiselette staring at Sir Harald's sword where it stuck upright in the ground.

Above it, wedged tight in the stump of an old, lightning-blasted tree, was what the faithful freedman eventually recognized as Sir Harald's own shield, in sorry condition, all banged and battered, with bits taken out of the borders and one whole corner sheared clean off. The whole device was dirtied as if handfuls of turf had been hurled against it.

And the knight's sword, also nicked somewhat about its edges, had been thrust through a piece of parchment, pinning it to the ground beneath the spoiled shield.

At Joiselette's nod, Garth silently pulled the great sword loose while she knelt and gathered up the parchment. She frowned at it: It showed Sir Harald's shield the way it had used to be, with its big stripe or "bend" all black, from bottom to top.

Joiselette read the words aloud. Hearing them, Garth felt his soul grow grayer and grayer.

"Oh, my lady!" he said at last. "Why here? All those places we've been and they'd never even heard of him before—why here?"

She turned the parchment over, and there was the

Black Chevron Knight's shield drawn plain. "This hardly tells us *why*, but at least it tells us *how*," she commented, and then read him what it had to say about Sir Harald's enemy.

"But, my lady," Garth protested, "I can't believe he would ever do that—make believe to surrender and then strike out treacherously like that!"

"No, Garth, but you were not there to see it with your own eyes. None of us were."

"My lady . . . Master Alaron was the Black Chevron Knight's squire before Sir Harald's, wasn't he?"

She nodded sadly. "Yes, Alaron may have witnessed it. And seen no harm, at the time, in letting his then-master recount it however he wished, to whomever he wished."

"But in that case, my lady, Master Alaron may have been here before, at this same manor."

"And remembered it better, perhaps, than its people— fixed as they were on the knight—remembered the squire's face more than a year afterward. And perhaps they are all courteously keeping quiet as they wait to see how Sir Harald will acquit himself here in person."

"My lady . . ." Garth glanced fearfully at the lake, which could be glimpsed just beyond the trees, with sunlight dancing on its surface.

This time Joiselette shook her head. "No, Garth, if he had intended that, he would have worn his chain mail, to weight himself down. And he was not wearing it. Your son made that point very clear."

"Then where is he now, my lady?"

She held out a finger for one of the little birds hovering around her to hop upon, lifted it closer to her ear, and stood awhile as if listening to its chirps before she answered, nodding toward the other side of the woodland from the lake, "He is wrestling with his angel again. Don't worry, Garth. Go home to the manor, but say nothing about this to anyone. He will be back."

An hour or so after Alaron returned to the orchard, Tamba approached him with a soft and delicate step that whispered of confidences to come.

"Sir," the page murmured conspiratorially, and gave the squire a sidelong wink, "if you will be so good as to follow me, I can lead you to something that may please you well enough."

Curiosity dispelled most of what conscience-pangs Alaron had not yet reasoned away, and he followed Tamba readily back to the manor house. They sought out its southwest wing—which was opposite and therefore as far as possible from the south*east* wing, where the squire had left his knight in the master's office (and, for all Alaron knew, he was weltering there still)—and therein a small room that had obviously been used for little save storing oddments since the time of the old Romans. Here the very last of Alaron's qualms of conscience dissipated as he laid eyes upon a beautiful couch of finely turned and gilded wood, burnished to a rare gleam, replete with a thick and downy cushion covered in tawny velvet, with silk-cased pillows to match.

"Now, am I mistaken," Tamba inquired, "in supposing that Your Squireship might find some impending use for this pretty something?"

"My good Tamba, you have shown excellent taste and judgment, along with admirable discretion! Now, if you would finish your favor in as fine a fashion as you have begun, pray help me bear this exquisite trifle to some secret spot from whence we can more conveniently move it else-where come dusk, with less likelihood of being overseen."

Softly, dusk began gathering the manor folk together to cap their busy day with a communal supper. Alaron de Sableblanc watched with renewed apprehension, but Sir Harald never returned to the great hall. We, of course, know why; but Alaron had spent the afternoon in a diligent effort to avoid his knight, and congratulated himself on his success until now.

Nor was Alaron the only person to glance around with anxiety. Joiselette, back in her borrowed garments of white and yellow, appeared tranquil enough. So did Garth, his wife, and their little Nubbin of a son, but only when they looked at Joiselette in her place at the high table. Otherwise, their anxiety seemed almost to rival Alaron's. Wandith, too, looked fluttery; but, the squire reflected with less pleasure than he had anticipated, Wandith might have looked that way in any case, and he thought her gaze was directed rather at the page who stood behind Joiselette than at the master's empty chair.

The Quiller Lion, at least, must be calm enough. Alaron presumed that he was under the table asleep at Joiselette's feet, hidden by the hall's own hounds and cats, as well as by the festive white tablecloth that still remained from yesterday. The others who sat at the high table—that is, the chaplain; his daughters; and his lovely, gracious lady, whose countenance at once soothed and further agitated our poor squire whenever he stole a glance at her—spoke quietly of neutral matters, as if borrowing their mood from Joiselette.

Once or twice, when he could do it without being observed, Tamba caught Alaron's eye and winked.

Among the other folk, murmured questions began to rise on every side. At length, the cooks having readied some hot courses to enhearten this repast, the steward stepped up to the high table, looked over Sir Harald's chair at Alaron, and asked:

"Good squire, where is our new lord?"

Questioned pointblank, the young man hedged. "Master steward, when last I knew, he was in his office. He may still be there, examining documents."

"He must have a great many of them to examine, then," Joiselette remarked with a smile. "Would you kindly go fetch him, Alaron?"

"Thank you, my lady," Felicitatus seconded her with a respectful nod. "I was about to make the same request, myself."

Alaron went with pounding heart, to find the door wide open and the office in something of a shambles, thanks to the mug of ale and two fresh apples that had been hurled across it and the tray of food that had been dashed upsidedown onto its floor. Of Sir Harald there was no sign. The telltale parchment, too, had disappeared. Alaron set things a little to rights as well and quickly as he could, carefully closed the door behind him, and stood outside it awhile, pondering what was best to say.

Finally he returned, made his bow, and reported: "My ladies and damsels, my lord Sir Philibros, and good master steward, my lord Sir Harald begs you to sup without him. He wishes to work in his office yet awhile."

Joiselette sighed and looked at Alaron in a way that came near causing him to reconsider his decision; but all she said was: "In that case, Alaron, you'd better take him something on a tray. And, Tamba, why don't you go along to light his way?" For already the interior of the house was growing somewhat dark.

So, a very few moments later, Alaron again found himself on the way to the empty and ale-reeking office, this time with another tray in his hands and an unsuspecting, lamp-bearing companion at his side.

"Tamba, my good friend," he confessed as soon as they were well out of earshot of anyone in the hall, "Sir Harald is not in his office."

"Is he not?" Tamba whistled softly, his eyebrows rising in the lamplight. "Where is he, then?"

"I have no idea."

"Then he is missing. Why did you inform the manor otherwise?"

But for holding the laden tray in both his hands, Alaron would have gestured in distress. "He is a knight fully grown, able to guard himself. I thought perhaps, if he has gone somewhere alone, he would prefer these people not to know of it."

"And, moreover, I think you have a blossom carefully cultivated for your own plucking this night. Have you not?" Again the page winked knowingly. "Well, Master Squire Alaron, as you say, our Sir Harald is a knight fully grown and properly dubbed. And he has suffered before from these little freaks, as I know better than you, having been acquainted with him longer. The wisest course might indeed be to wait for him to slip back in his own good time. Meanwhile, has it occurred to you what a fine opportunity this gives us, while everyone is in the hall supping, thinking that we are with your knight, and there is still light enough out of doors to see our way without overmuch stumbling, to carry yonder exquisite couch to wherever it is that you wish it to rest this night?"

"He had me help him carry it into the bower on the *western* side, my lady," Tamba reported to Joiselette when supper was over and the manor folk dispersed for the evening.

"The western bower," Joiselette repeated. "Maid Procne's bower, by what Sir Harald told us this afternoon."

"But were not the words of that message, 'When above, Tonight's moon shines, then let us feast Within the bower to the *east*'?"

"Your memory does not fail you. And the eastern bower would be Maid Philomela's."

Tamba whistled. "Does our ambitious young scapegrace of a squire plan on courting two in the same moonlit hour?"

"And which two?"

"Well, we ought to know soon enough, seeing that Diana all but chases Phoebus from the sky tonight. But, my lady," the page added on a sober note, "despite my words to Alaron, I can hardly help fearing a little for Sir Harald."

"Tamba. Good Tamba, thanks for your concern. But, as I told Garth, our knight will come back."

Meanwhile, in the chaplain's house, the conspirators of Beaumarches were holding their own last council before the night's entertainment.

"I confess," Felicitatus began, broaching the subject on all their minds, "that I was astonished by his discourtesy in refusing to join the rest of us at supper."

"His conscience may already have begun to prickle at him," the priest suggested.

"Why, that seems even more reason for an outward show of courtesy and proper order in all things among us, his new people! This is, after all, but his second night here, and for all he knows or guesses, we prepared for his arrival yesterday as we would have prepared for a visit from King Arthur himself!"

"No," Procne said, with a glance at her mother—who was the only person she had hitherto told of her encounter with Sir Harald, and who had lost no time in giving it an unfavorable gloss. "He has guessed otherwise."

Philomela gasped, "He *has*?"

Felicitatus seconded her by demanding, "What, exactly, has he guessed?"

"That our festival was indeed to have marked a wedding; that you, Master Felicitatus, were indeed to have been the groom; and that I myself was to have been thy bride!"

"And, guessing this, he opted to seduce, not you, but your sister? Well! Perhaps his character is not quite so bad as we had feared."

"Felicitatus!" Philomela exclaimed, giving him a slap on the wrist.

"I meant, my lady, that while our noble King Arthur has expressly forbidden *jus primae noctis*, I have yet to hear of him making any similarly severe law against various simpler forms of seduction."

"From what I witnessed, with my own eyes and ears, of his court," Sir Philibros put in, "too many such laws would leave him with very few knights to populate his Table Round. Our own lord Sir Kay, and possibly the archangelic Sir Gawen—"

"'Possibly'?" cried Procne. "Only 'possibly'? Must I recopy *that* leaf, too? I mean—that is—Oh, now I am sure that the crimson half is all important, and Sir Harald is *not* the Knight of the Black Bend Sinister!"

"No, Sister," said Philomela. "Sir Harald's device was not always as it is now. Goodwife Gytha had begun to tell me, but her husband hushed her before she could reveal more. So his bend may once have been entirely black, though I cannot say for sure."

"Well!" said Dame Iris. "Whoever he is and whatever he guesses, he plans to seduce our dear daughter Philomela, by means of messages borne forth and back by his own squire, and this I cannot and will not abide."

Procne made one more attempt. "Of course not, Mother. None of us can nor will abide it! Only let me be the one to take my sister's place. I am younger than you, to elude him better, and I am darker, to give him the greater surprise."

"Your scheme is not too badly thought, my maid," Felicitatus nodded.

"I agree," said Sir Philibros. "It would mean all the less danger, my own dear love, that in the dim light and shadows he might mistake thee for our fair daughter, whose countenance and coloring are so like thine own."

"Men!" cried Dame Iris. "Mark me, the both of you, and mark me well. I will not allow either of my daughters to take this risk on my account—for it is the mother who protects her children and not the other way around, as Holy Writ itself and all these other books you love so much ought to teach thee, husband! Nor will I leave him the slightest chance of mistaking me for my fair daughter, when once the deception has gone just far enough to expose him utterly, and no farther."

"True," the steward agreed. "We might lose that chance, should he see at once by Maid Procne's coloring that she is not his intended prey." And, as Sir Philibros still looked a little dubious, now that the hour was hard upon them, Felicitatus reassured him, "Fear nothing for thy wife, good chaplain! Will we not all be lying there in wait, with torches ready to kindle at her first call?"

Although not included in the various secret conferences, the blacksmith and his lad had been privately recruited to stand with the conspirators. It would of course have been impermissible and unthinkable for the manor folk to offer violence to their lawful lord under any provocation whatsoever; but the mighty-muscled smith, who had once wrestled a bear, could easily clasp his brawny arms about almost any man to hold him harmless but unharmed, and both steward and chaplain agreed that, in certain circumstances, their good overlord Sir Kay might sanction such restraint being put upon his liege knight.

At first Sir Philibros had not wished either sister to stand watch with the four men; but Procne and Philomela joined in insisting upon their rights and in this much, at least, their mother backed them up. By now the half-moon was rising rapidly into an almost fully darkened sky, so while the rest of the group set out for the bowers, Sir Philibros went to summon the smiths and Procne made her way to the chapel for a lighted candle that they would guard, sheltered in a leathern sheath, until the moment came to kindle their torches and leap forward.

Just inside the door, she paused. There on the floor Joiselette sat facing the altar, the fine hanging lamp from far Constantinople picking out the white and yellow garments she had borrowed from Philomela. She was singing softly:

"Oh, Everywhere, You hit Your mark
Both in the daylight and the dark."

Whatever might have come before, that couplet seemed to end the mysterious maid's Compline hymn, for she quietly looked around, smiled at the newcomer, and rose to her feet.

"Maid Procne, is that you?" she asked with no trace of guile. "I'm so glad to see you! Would you mind if I sat awhile in your bower tonight?"

Procne could think of nothing to say but, "Wh—Why, my Lady Joiselette?"

"Why, what other reason would I need, than to enjoy the night sounds and watch the moonlight playing over the last leaves? You must sit there often."

"Sometimes I sit there awhile by night. Usually by day, or at dawn, sometimes during the evening twilight, now and then at night; but I will not be there tonight . . . though my sister will be in the other. So yes, my lady, feel free to use my bower—it is the one to the *west*—as your own."

Harald de Folgeste sat hunched over with his head buried in both arms and his back to the stump of a fallen forest giant that had swollen too large and rotted at its core. That was all the clearing he had around him, where the old tree had taken some smaller ones down with it in its fall.

His heart was so heavy that its weight, much more than the effort of demolishing his own shield with his own sword, had exhausted him. He thought wearily that he would exchange it for another heart: tear off the last of his knightly garments and run away afoot to some distant land where he could pass himself off as a runaway serf and accept the penalty for that in preference to the penalty he was presently paying for his own true sin as a knight.

The only difficulty with this excellent plan was that it required more energy than he could at present command. He would just sit here awhile longer, while dusk deepened around him into full dark, and then began to lighten again a little as the climbing moon managed to peer between the trees—although he remained scarcely aware of it, since no light at all seemed able to reach his soul. . . .

It may surprise some readers that anyone who has

even once felt the kiss of God's Presence could ever again fall into quite so bleak a mood as this; but the tangible kiss of God may perhaps compare with the manna in the desert, which could not be hoarded up for the distant future.

Something nibbled at the hose above Sir Harald's ankle. He looked, and saw a young cony, who did not take fright at his movement but only glanced up, blinked both round eyes, and returned to its tender, bloodless nibbling.

The small beast sat illuminated by a ragged black hem covered with living glowworms and fireflies. Harald looked higher, and saw Joiselette, cloaked in a cortege of wild woodland nightlife.

"So," he greeted her heavily, "it has come at last. All these months, and it has happened at last . . . of all places, here."

She smiled and sat on the ground beside him.

"They knew," he went on. "All along, they knew. How much longer before they had cast it back on me?"

"At worst, they could only have suspected. You had made that change in your device."

"I would not have wanted to live as their lord under such deception! At least I have done one honest deed, leaving my confession for them to find."

"A rather foolish confession, Harald de Folgeste! It was a good shield. It had served you well."

"I will never have the use for it again."

She laid her fingertips gently on his arm. "Nor was that parchment properly yours to damage."

"God's Blood!" His fists went back to his head. "*She!* Of all of them, it was *she* whose hand had set it down in black and white!"

"Yet she had never breathed a word of it to your face, had she? And when she set it down on her parchment, she had yet to meet you in person."

"My lady . . . Oh, my Lady Joiselette . . . I am fickle! First the Aloof Fair One; and then Maid Deborah, who was worth a dozen of the first one; and now Procne of Beaumarches. Three, all in little more than a single year!"

"As for the Aloof Fair One," said Joiselette, "you never had any right to her at all. You simply imagined her invitation, and then you were too stubborn to back away when she let you know her true feelings. And Deborah was already betrothed. It was noble of you to rest grateful for her friendship alone, and there is no dishonor to either her or you in letting someone else wake your heart up again, however soon."

"And, once again! . . . That she is already another's—I could bear that. Even though that other is my own steward, even though I must see them day by day, year after year— I could bear it. If she were happy with him, I could learn to rejoice in seeing her happiness, from whatever distance I must. And if he were to make her unhappy, then let God help him, for I would—"

What Sir Harald would do in such an event to the hapless Felicitatus can most generously be inferred from the force with which his left fist struck the earth at his side, leaving a deep print.

"But that she should believe me . . . that she should have believed it from the moment she watched us ride in, from the first atom of time that she read my shield—My God!" he exclaimed in a sudden change of tone. "All this time, and I have never given a thought to—but it was *he* who brought me this—and she keeps her parchments in her bower—the *western* bower. *My squire has been prying in Maid Procne's bower!*

"We must get back there at once!" he finished, springing to his feet.

"Here is a complication, Maid Procne!" Felicitatus whispered as she joined the other watchers in the shadow of Philomela's bower. "We have just seen my Lady Joiselette go into thy sanctum of sanctums."

"I know. I encountered her just now in the chapel. She asked my leave, and I gave it."

"Why?" whispered Philomela. "Tonight, of all nights? Oh, Procne, why?"

"Nay, my maid," the steward murmured, "now I see thy sister's wisdom. To have refused—and refused the Lady Joiselette, of all people!—could only have waked suspicion, whereas this way we have one more witness, and one whose word no one will misdoubt."

"But she is his sister!" Philomela still protested. "In fact or in spirit, his own sister. It might break her heart to see him proved so false!"

"It might break her heart?" Procne repeated, and only very alert and sensitive ears might have caught her slight emphasis on the possessive pronoun. "Let it, then!"

"Hush!" warned Sir Philibros. "Someone comes."

They hushed and waited, watching, scarcely breathing. The person who came was small: a small maiden, nearly the same size as Joiselette, but in a simple plain tunic, as plain and brown by moonlight as it must be by day, with a simple wreath of autumn flowers crowning her head.

She looked around from bower to bower, turned her small face moonward for a moment as though concentrating on her directions, and finally went into the bower to the west.

"It is Goodman Garth's young daughter!" whispered the blacksmith's lad.

"By the holy loaves and fishes!" Felicitatus swore softly as Procne's bower door closed behind the girl. "Now, what does *she* do here?"

Wandith went into the western bower and found, not her adored Master Tamba of Caerleon sitting in the light of a flame-tipped wick, but the Maid of the Wood sitting wreathed in fireflies and glowworms. And what she sat on was . . .

Whereas Alaron de Sableblanc had never seen the Quiller Lion as a couch, Wandith and her family had, along with all the rest of Quillerstone's people, every year on the birthday of their absent lord Sir Godfrey, when Sir Harald had used to honor the old custom of bringing it out—not, in his case, to sit on—but rather to show everyone what they must never, never sit on nor meddle with.

"My Lady Joiselette? . . . But that is. . . . But he is a couch again!"

Smiling, Joiselette slid over to one end of the couch and patted the other end with her hand.

"Oh, no, my lady! I don't dare—I'd never dare sit on it! Not even beside you, my Lady Joiselette!"

"But didn't you come here tonight hoping to do something every bit as dangerous?"

"Oh, dear! My lady . . . my lady, Master Tamba will be here very soon, and I don't think he's ever seen it like this. . . ."

Joiselette shook her head sadly. "No, Wandith, it isn't my page who plans to meet you here tonight. Tamba never knew anything of all this until today, and then he found out quite by chance."

"You mean—Oh, my lady!" Wandith's hand went to her mouth as understanding dawned. "Oh, how could he? My lady, what shall we do?"

"Just one thing." Joiselette stood up and began shedding her beautiful white and yellow garments. "We are much the same size, you and I. . . ."

"He comes!" whispered the smith's lad.

"Odd." Felicitatus squinted, but while half a moon makes far more difference than many a modern city dweller might imagine to an unelectrified countryside by night, its illumination still remains limited and somewhat deceptive. "I measured our new lord for a larger man than that."

"Sir Harald is much larger!" Procne whispered on a note of hope. "Taller, and broader of shoulder—and this one's hair is far too smooth and fair!"

"All of which," Sir Philibros murmured, "might be a mere trick of moonlight and starshine."

The blacksmith said nothing, but flexed his great muscles.

So soft they kept their communications, that the newcomer noticed nothing, but vanished unsuspectingly into the eastern bower. Procne readied the candle flame to kindle their torches, and the blacksmith was flexing his muscles once again, when Felicitatus whispered, "Hush!" and pointed to the western bower.

"It is the Lady Joiselette again!" whispered Sir Philibros. "As is plainly manifest by the glowworms, the fireflies, and the moths about those old white and yellow garments of thine, my Philomela."

"Leaving Garth's daughter alone in my bower?" Procne wondered.

"Yet they do not sufficiently illumine her face," mused the priest. "Nor do they seem so merry as usual."

"Pilate's left eyebrow!" Felicitatus swore softly. "Does *she*—can *she*—be playing procuress?"

At this, shock and amazement held them gripped so fast that as they stared after the departing female, they momentarily half forgot the bower in whose shadow they themselves stood.

Let us catch our breath, now, and consider things.

Dame Iris believes that Sir Harald is coming to seduce her fair daughter Philomela, and that she will surprise, baffle, and foil him by revealing herself as the mother of his intended mark. For this purpose, their clever friend and soon-to-be son-in-law Felicitatus has devised a poem promising greater amorous favors than any of them mean the seducer to enjoy. And, in order that the trap should not be sprung too quickly, Dame Iris has been waiting in the dark, with neither candle nor lamp, only traces and shadows of moonlight seeping into the bower.

Alaron de Sableblanc, on the other hand, has never for an instant mistaken the mother for the daughter. He knows exactly whom he expects to find in the bower to the east; but he has read into her pretended invitation only the most courtly and idealized of intentions.

"My lady!" he cries—though softly, not wanting to be overheard in the bower to the west, where he has other fish to fry later—and throws himself on both knees before her shadowy form. "Ah, my most beautiful and beloved sweet lady!" And he gropes for her hem, with intent to bestow upon it the most devout and chaste of adoring kisses.

"Sir?" Dame Iris replies. Remember, she has not been acquainted with either of them for very long. While Alaron saw and loved her last year from a distance, she, along with the rest of the manor, was really paying more attention to his master of the Black Chevron; and, though last night she dined at Sir Harald's left hand, today she has not seen the knight at all since morning. "Thy voice sounds so young!" she ventures at last. "Has love alone so greatly rejuvenated thee?"

"Good my lady!" he answers, making his voice as low and husky as he can. "Though my love be as young as the fledglings, it is at one and the same time as old as the hills. For has not Love been the greatest power in all the world ever since the Golden Age of the Ancients?"

"The greatest power indeed, my lord—and the greatest joy!"

"Joy? Ah, yes, my own fairest lady, the greatest joy in all this world it is to pledge and offer you my truest devotion, and the great power it will lend my arm when I am made true knight!"

"When thou'rt made? . . ." she falters. "M—Master Alaron?"

"Ah, fairest Dame Iris, whom I have adored with all my heart ever since my first sweet glimpse of thee these five long seasons past. . . . Grant me but thy favor to bear always next my heart, allow me but to seal my vow with one kiss on thy gracious hand, and you make me the happiest of mortal men!"

Poor lady! This is hardly how Sir Almovitus had handled her all those years ago, nor her dear husband either— good spouse and true though he is, but strict in his dedication to the priestly principle that all Courtly Love, so called, is at best mischievous and at worst mortal sin. So flattered does she feel now at the thought that a handsome young squire twenty years her junior should knowingly beg to make her his liege lady, that she gives him her kerchief, lets him kiss her hand, and never raises the alarm at all.

Having already been ensconced in Philomela's bower when her fellow conspirators began to witness the various comings and goings, Dame Iris knows nothing of the maiden in her dark daughter's retreat. She knows only that Alaron's intentions toward herself are both complimentary and innocent, and that, after all, neither of her dear daughters is in any immediate danger from Sir Harald.

And now, things are going to happen very fast. Please bear with my poor, harried pen.

When Alaron issued from the eastern bower, he gave his lady's kerchief the most reverent of chaste kisses, tucked it devoutly beneath his shirt, and heaved a long sigh of pure ecstasy. Then, coming down abruptly from the heights, he squared his shoulders and set off merrily for the western bower, ready after his near-religious experience to enjoy the release of earthier refreshments.

Even as the door of Procne's bower closed behind him, the conspirators were tumbling into Philomela's, anxious both for the mother's safety and her explanations.

They were not yet all inside when the roar of the Quiller Lion split the night, and they all commenced tumbling out again. Procne, who, being at the back, was still outside, turned and touched her candle to her pitch-smeared torch just in time for its flare partially to illuminate Alaron's fall from grace as, thrusting wide the western bower's door, he rushed out wild-eyed, stumbled, and rolled upon the ground.

From behind the western bower, Garth, Gytha, and Tamba were half falling over one another in their haste to reach the front; and also the maid in Philomela's old white and yellow surcoat and kirtle was rushing back to the scene—though now the torchlight showed her to be Garth's daughter Wandith.

Meanwhile, Sir Harald and Joiselette had reached the spot. He stood on the edge of the woods and stared at Joiselette—for once illuminated only by the light of moon, torch, and stars—standing in the doorway of Procne's bower, laughing, wearing Wandith's brown gown and wreath of flowers, one hand resting lightly on the lion's head. The knight whirled round—he thought he caught one glimpse of Joiselette still at his side, but it might have been only the moths and fireflies and other night creatures scattering from where she had stood a heartbeat ago, to join the rush of their fellows from a temporary hovering place round young Wandith to the one and only spot where the Maid of the Wood stood now.

She looked across at him, grinned, and winked.

No one else seemed to have noticed. The blacksmith had strolled over and thrown both brawny arms around the squire, at once hauling him to his feet and holding him fast (as you knew he must do to somebody by the end of this scene, as soon as I told you he was going to be watching with the conspirators).

But Maid Procne, finally catching sight of Sir Harald, stepped over to him, bowed her head briefly, looked back up, and said, "Sir Harald, my lord! I am so very glad that it was not you!"

Heartened by Maid Procne's greeting, Sir Harald shepherded them all back to the manor, where he ate for the first time since that morning, bade everyone seek their beds so as to be fresh for the morrow, and then himself disobeyed the spirit of his own command by sitting wakeful more than half the night, pondering and worrying.

As his liege lord, Sir Kay, had remarked in granting him Beaumarches, for six years he had indeed judged all the petty crimes, disputes, and misdemeanors of Quillerstone Castle—but always as Godfrey's deputy, and always among folk both the brothers had known all their lives; and, in that time, no matter of major importance had ever arisen until Sir Harald's own great misdeed. Now, already on only his second day as resident lord of Beaumarches, he must pass judgment in a fairly serious matter upon his own squire; yet, he sensed, in a larger measure it would be himself, the judge, who was on trial, liable to be petitioned away from here like their last lord.

In the dark before dawn he dozed a little, and dreamed; but soon got up again and dressed. About daybreak Garth found him in his office, nodding off by candlelight. Seeing his lord in serious danger of slipping out of his chair, the faithful servant softly woke him with the news:

"Sir, I hope it may please you, I have fetched your shield and sword from the place where you left them, and laid them up safe for you in my own new cottage."

Sir Harald sighed. "Thank you, good friend. It pleases me far better than the condition in which I remember leaving them where you found them. You see, Garth, this is why I want to name you understeward! What of . . . the parchment?"

"It lies, sir!"

"Ah. You know what it says, then?"

"Joiselette, sir. She read it to me. It is that Black Chevron Knight's foul lies. You would not have struck him down and run away, after surrendering!"

"No. He . . . let us say, he somewhat embellished that part, to enhance his own reputation. As to his other glorious deeds, we know nothing."

"Master Squire Alaron does, I doubt not!" Garth muttered.

"But as to my kidnapping of the Aloof Fair One, of course it is perfectly true and factual, as you well know, seeing how you yourself tried to argue me away from that crime. Would I had listened to your excellent advice!" Sir

Harald held out his left hand. "Where is it, Garth? Where is the parchment?"

"Too much of it is still lies, sir. It deserves to be burned!"

"But you have not burned it yet?"

After a moment, Garth shook his head sullenly. "Not yet, sir. I meant to do it . . ."

"Garth, good and trusty friend, thy understewardship is slipping a little away! That parchment is neither thine to burn, nor mine to have wounded. And it may, perhaps, be needed today." Sir Harald wriggled his fingers.

With another sigh, Garth dug the parchment out from beneath his tunic—unconsciously echoing Alaron's action of less than twenty-four hours earlier—and put it into Sir Harald's hand.

The rising sun had not yet quite parted company with the horizon, but was still laying its sparkles across the lake in a wide orange-gold swathe, when Sir Harald approached Maid Procne's bower, the parchment heavy in his hand. He knocked at her door and, neither expecting nor receiving an answer, opened it softly, meaning to lay the sheet just inside the threshold and leave again at once.

She stood at her writing table, her back to the door, flipping through her sheaf of parchments with desperate singleness of purpose.

He lost no time alerting her to his presence. "Maid Procne!"

She turned, flushing. "Sir Harald, my lord!"

"My maid, I knocked. Did you not hear my knocking?"

"I . . . must have mistaken it for another sound, my lord. A woodpecker, or a squirrel knocking a nut against a stone, or an otter on the lake. . . ."

"My maid . . . I think that this, perhaps, is what you search for." Still without stepping into the bower, he extended his hand with the piece of parchment.

She took it, glanced at it, and flushed more deeply.

"My maid, I did not take it. I have never set foot inside your bower, nor so much as seen its interior, until this moment."

"My lord, it must have been your squire. He would have been inside, here, planning . . . what he planned, toward that unfortunate little maiden."

"It was I who damaged it, however. I will make good the expense of it."

"Pray you, think nothing of this small injury," she answered, thrusting one delicate fingernail through the slit his sword had left in the parchment. "I can easily sew it up," she went on, "and it will serve to remind me. . . . I think that all this writing must be rubbed out, in any case, and revised completely."

"No, not completely. But . . . Maid Procne, my mother was serfborn, my father's leman, and I do not know—have never known—how far, at least in the outset, she had been willing to accept that life. I do not call the report of the Black Chevron Knight unjustified, but my misdeed was . . . a misguided attempt to win a bride of my own, one whom I had at first thought willing. I would never attempt to force myself between another man and his bride!"

Abruptly, as if fearing to say more, he turned and took his departure whilst she was still floundering for a reply.

The case was tried that midmorning, after Mass and a hasty breakfast. Again Master Felicitatus inquired whether Sir Harald might not prefer to pass judgment from the thronelike seat of Sir Almovitus.

Sir Harald shook his head. "This chair will do. It has some little experience, being the same one in which you yourself sat to judge such cases as cropped up throughout this past year."

"All of them," Felicitatus replied, waving his hand, "fortunately slight and easily disposed of."

"But, Master Steward, you are yourself not above judgment in this present matter."

Acknowledging the truth of Sir Harald's last words with a grave nod, Felicitatus stepped down from the dais into the front row of the assembled manor folk. Strange though it may sound, he appeared neither ill pleased nor ill at ease.

Not so poor Alaron de Sableblanc, who stepped bravely forward, alone, to accept his judgment, looking as if he had slept reasonably well, but eaten almost no breakfast—which was, indeed, the observed case.

"No, Master Alaron," said Sir Harald, "step back yet a minute or two more, and await thy turn."

Keeping his face a careful blank, the squire obeyed.

Thankful that his surcoat, at least, had escaped yesterday's fit of destruction, Sir Harald gazed around the great
hall. All the Beaumarchians—save only the shepherd, who,
as on many estates in those times, led an existence more
isolated than that of most contemporary hermits—stood
silent and attentive; but their lord, still almost a stranger
to them, sat completely alone in his place on the dais, feeling more isolated than his lonely shepherd. This time, even
Joiselette and the Quiller Lion waited among the manor
folk; the great beast had taken advantage of his prerogative as an animal to lie down, but Joiselette—once again
wearing Godfrey's black, cast-off palmer's robe—stood, the
fingertips of one hand brushing the lion's mane between
his ears. They, too, had been involved, however noble their
motives, in the intrigues and deceptions of yesterday; but
all the dogs and cats of the manor hall clustered near her
as well, leaving not one old hound nor graying feline to
share the dais with Sir Harald.

The kindly chaplain of Quillerstone had used to be fond
of quoting a Gospel passage in which Ihesu promised the
blessed Apostles that they would sit on twelve thrones
judging their own twelve tribes. More than ever before, Sir
Harald wondered if He had not in fact been threatening
them with the most dire of punishments for their own sins.

Yes—one cat, after all. Garth and Gytha's Mouser, who
had shared the journey from Quillerstone, suddenly took it
into his head to prowl forward in full feline regality and
leap on the dais to curl at Sir Harald's feet. The knight
guessed that Joiselette had given this particular cat a little
nudge, as yestereve she had somehow directed the night
creatures' movements.

Sir Harald cleared his throat and made a beginning.
"First: It has come to my attention that there has been
some talk, some wondering and argument on both sides of
the question, as to whether I am or am not a certain Bend
Sinister Knight of whom you had news a year ago this past
summer.

"Let me say at once that I am indeed that same knight,
and that in taking prisoner a damsel who traveled alone, I
did indeed commit a crime for which my name deserves
perpetual blackening everywhere. What the Knight of the
Black Chevron, who brought you this report, could not

know, was that I sought this maiden for my unsullied bride, and that she finally married my brother as untouched as on the day I had accosted her.

"Of the various assorted heroic deeds of the Black Chevron Knight, I can tell you nothing. I will say only that, in the matter of my own battle with him, my account would differ somewhat from his. Besides him and myself, there were only three witnesses to that encounter. One of them is my brother's wife at distant Quillerstone—and she still bears me, I fear, a bitter grudge. The second one, the Black Chevron Knight's other squire, is I know not where. As for the third, last year he bore witness, by silence if nothing else, to the truth of his then master's account; so if he should change his witness now that I am his master, you will have equal justification in believing either version.

"For the crime I have confessed, I have already been judged, punished, and—I trust—pardoned, by those who know me best, if not by the rest of the world." Without taking time to describe how informal had been his trial, or how much of the punishment had been of his own devising, he went on: "For the part that my squire played in yesterday's deceptions, it is of course my duty to discipline him—as it is my duty to discipline myself for the hours yesterday when I left you, thinking to spare you the trouble of petitioning for my removal. Now, if you intend to send that petition at your earliest opportunity, begging our good Sir Kay to remove me as he removed Sir Almovitus, and find you yet another lord—say so here and now, openly to my face, so that we may drop this matter at once and return to the work of hunt and harvest."

"Bravo, Sir Harald!" Joiselette murmured . . . though how it was that he heard her, he could not have said.

Felicitatus took one step forward and replied, "As one who stands in some small danger of judgment over yesterday's fooleries, I say that Sir Kay appears to have chosen well enough for us this time, and that it behooves us to accept his decision."

"So say I, also," Sir Philibros seconded him.

"So say we all!" grunted the blacksmith, and, to show their agreement, the rest of the assembly sent up a cheer that made the lion first lay back his ears and then add an agreeable roar of his own.

Mouser lifted his head, looked around, yawned, stretched, and settled down again at Sir Harald's feet.

The knight drew a deep breath, exhaled it as softly as possible, swallowed, and resumed: "Well and good. Now, as for the essentials of yesterday's 'fooleries,' as our steward styles them, here is my understanding of them. Let whoever knows better correct me."

The principal reason he recapped the events was that even in those days, even on a smallish and self-contained manor, gossip could distort and confuse facts. Since we already know the facts, I need not record Sir Harald's account of them.

Reaching the end of his summary, and finding that his understanding was accurate and nobody had any corrections to offer, Sir Harald repeated, "Well!" and added, after another deep breath, "Stand forth—no, not you, Alaron, not yet—Goodman Garth, Goodwife Gytha, John the Smith, and Much the smith's lad."

The four named stepped into the clear space before the dais. Wandith, clad again in the white and yellow, kept bravely to her place in the front row; but innocent little Nubbin, on the other side of the lion, hesitated a few atoms of time and then ran after his mother, to stand holding her hand.

"You four," Sir Harald pronounced, "had no other involvement in any of this than to wait and watch in order to lend a hand at need. Garth and Gytha acted in loving duty as parents, the smith and his lad in loyalty to their steward. I find more in your actions to commend than to condemn. Master Garth I sentence to the understewardship of Beaumarches Manor for a year and a day, and after that, should he acquit himself as well in that post as I suspect he will, for perpetuity. That is all: You four I dismiss with thanks and gratitude."

They bowed and melted back into the front row, Garth looking somewhat proud in spite of himself, and Gytha leading Nubbin—who, as soon as he was back in his former place, dropped her hand and resumed fondling the lion's maned head.

Sir Harald tasted some of the promised joys of judgmanship, and this heartened him for the next round. "Dame Iris, Maid Procne, Maid Philomela, and Sir Philibros," he resumed, taking secret satisfaction in the steadiness of his voice.

They came forward holding hands in a chain. Only Maid Philomela betrayed any sign of uneasiness, while Maid Procne gazed up at Harald with emotions he dared not, for the minute, attempt to fathom.

Looking instead at Sir Philibros, he pronounced, "You four would appear to bear somewhat greater guilt in these fooleries. Yet against this I must weigh certain fears you entertained of myself—false fears, yet not without some foundation in report and even in fact. Thus you, too, acted as you believed for the best, with laudable and noble motives. I pardon you fully. You also may step back."

They did so, Procne still staring at Harald with the same expression; he stole another glance at her even as he uttered Tamba's name.

The page stepped forward jauntily, his lips pursed as if whistling too low for anyone to hear.

"Master Tamba," Sir Harald repeated sadly. "Confess truly, now: Were you ever aware, or did you ever so much as suspect, the depth of Maid Wandith's devotion to you?"

Tamba shook his curly head. "Of course I could see that she liked me very well as a traveling companion, and listened more attentively than some of the rest of you to my least little quip and tale. But that she entertained any such flattering romantic aspirations toward my not entirely deserving self—no, my lord, that I never knew, guessed, nor suspected."

"Accepting your word on this point, I must acknowledge that, for the rest, if I were to condemn you, I must needs condemn those whom I have already pardoned, and also myself . . . for I, too," he reminded the assembly, "having learned something of these matters at about the same time as my lady's page, and through his instrumentation, played some small part in bringing about the fooleries of yesterday evening. Therefore, Tamba, thou too art pardoned and dismissed, with thanks for thy loyal service."

"Which thanks, my lord, I gladly render back to you in my turn." Grinning, the page returned to his place with a graceful bow.

So much for all the easier judgments. Guarding another great sigh, Sir Harald said, softening the blow he must give by repeating the title he applied to her on next to no social authority: "Maid Wandith!"

She came forward very meekly, lifting her face just often enough to make sure that she positioned herself properly before the dais. She could not know that Sir Harald had already privately consulted with her parents as to the judgment he would pass on her, and knowing might have made little difference. Her borrowed kirtle and surcoat, finer though they were than any garments she had ever before worn in her life, could lend her little comfort now, might even seem a badge of shame. She looked as if she had enjoyed far less and far worse sleep than Sir Harald himself, and her eyes were red and puffy besides from weeping. It broke his heart to study her, but he frowned and said what he must.

"Wandith, Wandith, my poor young maid! You have been playing with fire." (And who should know better about that than Harald de Folgeste, even though each and every one of his own amorous ambitions, guilty or honest, had so far fallen as empty as Wandith's own.)

She hung her head still lower.

"Surely, Maid Wandith, you knew better?"

"Yes . . . sir . . . but . . ." She could say no more. Her shoulders shook a little. Garth and Gytha, Sir Harald saw, were bearing up with almost as much difficulty as their daughter.

He ended it as quickly as he could. "Thy guilt in what happened yesterday was as great, as knowing, and as intentional as that of any other person here present—save only one—and therefore I cannot dismiss thee as simply as those others. But far too many of thy elders, wisers, and so-called betters have set thee very poor examples to follow, and thou hast been severely punished already, both in the disappointment thine own deceiver and would-be betrayer caused thee, and in standing here bravely before me. I lay on thee no further punishment than this—and all the rest of you people of Beaumarches must help and assist her: In addition to the obedience thou naturally owest thy good parents until thy marriage and even after, for a year and a day thou must never once allow thyself to remain alone in the company of any one man above the age of seven years, saving only thy father, and during that time thou must attend every catechism lesson our learned chaplain gives, missing none of them for any reason other than grave illness." Sir Harald had ascertained on his first afternoon, without dreaming he would need the information so soon, that Sir Philibros freely shared his religious learning with all of the manor folk who could and cared to come, each Wednesday, Friday, and Saturday afternoon, when neither pressing work nor high holiday intervened. "Now, my maid, you are forgiven and dismissed."

She managed to say, "Thank you, sir," lift her head, and smile at him through her tears before stumbling back to her mother's side.

Sir Harald drew his deepest breath and said: "My Lady Joiselette."

She came forward and stood watching him respectfully, though he heard her humming the melody to whatever hymn she had thus far managed to refrain from singing aloud.

"My lady, my lady!" he asked, staring at her in wonder. "How can I judge thee? What power would I or any of us have to pass sentence on you?"

"You would have no power at all over me," she answered, mischievously quoting the Passion Play at him, "if it were not given to you from above. Therefore, you must judge me exactly as you would anybody else."

"In that case, I must judge you as guiltless as any of the first nine I called forth, and perhaps even more praiseworthy. For, though you seem to have taken it upon your own authority to arrange the outcome of what happened last night in the western bower, I think we owe you a great debt of gratitude that it came out no worse than it did."

Spontaneously, the gathering broke into applause—even, somewhat nervously—Alaron de Sableblanc. The lion gave another roar, and Mouser, as if on signal, chose the opportunity to yawn and stretch again. Through it all, Harald and Joiselette continued gazing at each other. Once, he half opened his mouth, but she shook her head very slightly, and he left his question unvoiced as to how she could have come to him deep in the woods whilst still at the same time maneuvering matters at the bower.

She smiled and went back to her place, humming again, quite softly.

And now, at last, Sir Harald said firmly, "Alaron de Sableblanc."

Having waited so long, and made so many false starts forward, this time Alaron hesitated until Sir Harald repeated his name. Then, stepping before the dais, he said: "First, my lord, before you pass your sentence, pray allow me to tell the truth about your enemy, the Knight of the Black Chevron."

"Squire, would you bribe me or even let it appear that you had tried to buy my leniency?"

"No, sir. But whatever sentence you pass will almost certainly be less than my guilt deserves, and so, if I bear my witness afterward, it may appear mere gratitude for your leniency. As you yourself have remarked, it can at best be the testimony of the Bend Sinister Knight's squire against that of the squire of the Black Chevron Knight. I would give the Bend Sinister Knight's squire his best chance of being believed."

"But the Bend Sinister Knight's present behavior is more at stake here than his past behavior, Master Alaron, and so you must hear your own sentence first."

"My lord, may I not even confess at once to Maid Procne that—"

"No!" Sir Harald cut in hastily, his heart pounding hard. "Alaron de Sableblanc, in all this business, thine has been the greatest guile and guilt of anyone here present, from the day you first made up your mind to play an innocent little maid false and perhaps even let the blame fall on one who knew and suspected nothing about it.

"I will not cast thee off," Sir Harald went on after snatching a breath. "God knows how greatly we all of us stand in need of mercy—both His and one another's—and, if I have never sinned in these matters quite as thou hast sinned, my own record is hardly such that I can cast the first stone, nor even the second or third. So I will pardon thee, even invite thee to stay on as my squire until such time as thou art dubbed knight, whether by my own hand or that of a better man. Yet your guilt cannot be simply dismissed unpunished.

"If you choose to stay with us, it must be upon these conditions: For a year and a day, you are to serve Maid Wandith as your liege lady, to the exclusion of any other, in all matters innocent and lawful. When not in service to me, you are to hold yourself at her beck and call for any harmless errand whatever—save that you are never to be alone in her company, nor in the company of any other woman, maid or lady, highborn or lowly. You are also to take upon yourself any additional penances—extra days of fasting and suchlike—as Sir Philibros will know better than I how to assign."

"My lord," said Alaron, "I have already begged to serve another as my lady, and, I think, been accepted."

"Then you must beg her—in the presence of a third party, of course—to be excused from her service, at least for a year and a day."

The squire did not look overjoyed, but he bowed and said, "My lord, painful though all this seems to me, especially as concerning my . . . *former* liege lady—not that my Maid Wandith deserves less of me, but that the other, whom now I must desert, deserves more—it is still less than my offense merits. I fear it will rob my testimony concerning the Black Chevron Knight of its worth. But may I offer it anyway, now that you have passed your sentence on me?"

At Sir Harald's nod, Alaron turned to face the folk of the manor and went on:

"The 'two fierce dragons' that my former master destroyed were in fact tiny, harmless lizards he skewered for target practice. The 'ogres Tryphon, Hyphon, and Zertuxes' were ragtag outlaws, somewhat dangerous indeed to small children or lone and unarmed peasants, but hardly a fair match for a mounted knight in full arms and armor, even had they attacked him all three together, which they did not—he surprised and cut them down one by one. As for the 'innumerable other malefactors' he boasted of defeating, I know not who or what they may have been, for certainly I never saw any of them during my time with him.

"But as for his dealings with my present master, so far from surrendering and then striking him down treacherously, the Bend Sinister Knight defeated him soundly, if somewhat ridiculously, and then it was the Knight of the Black Chevron who turned tail and fled like a coward. As for the Aloof Fair One, at that time I could not have said which of those two knights was protecting her from the other, but now I call her very fortunate indeed that the Knight of the Bend Sinister saved her from the Knight of the Black Chevron's notion of rescue. They met again a second time, only this year, when he of the Black Chevron, mounted and in full armor, rode with his lance at Sir Harald—who was afoot, unarmored, and bearing no other weapons save his shield alone—and Sir Harald nevertheless managed to unhorse him. In that fall he took his death and I, fully disgusted with his pufferies, bullyings, and assorted treacheries, gave my service and loyalty to the better knight.

"Now you must believe whichever you will—the silence with which I appeared last year to approve my former master's account of himself, when I merely, in loyalty, bit my tongue to guard against contradicting him; or the words I volunteer now, of the knight who has just penanced me— more leniently than I deserve, but still none too lightly, as all of you can bear witness.

"And, Mistress Procne, my maid," the squire added, almost as an afterthought, "the matter my lord prevented me from confessing to you before now: It was I who pilfered that parchment from your bower and then passed it on to Sir Harald."

"I had already guessed as much," she answered, with a nod . . . and perhaps a hint of mischief in the glance she tossed Sir Harald as she went on, "Thy truthfulness in this last confession, Squire Alaron, argues well for that of the rest of the testimony you offer us today."

Alaron bowed again and walked with a determined swagger, not back to his former place in the line, but to a new position just to the left of the dais. By that rule, Sir Harald mused, Joiselette ought to have sat down on the step at his feet; but, keeping this thought to himself, he gripped the arms of the chair and said:

"Master Felicitatus, steward of Beaumarches."

Felicitatus strolled forward, almost casual in his respect, rested his hands politely behind his back, and waited.

"Master Steward, I think that yesterday's fooleries— excepting only that part of them arranged by my Lady Joiselette to foil Squire Alaron—were all of your device and engineering, were they not?"

"They were, good my lord. In the plots involving Sir Philibros and his family, I was the chief and foremost conspirator."

"Thy tone and smile are trying to tell me that thy motives in all this were as noble as theirs, but I am not to be hoodwinked. As you yourself confess, yours was—if not the guiltiest blame—nevertheless the greatest guile in spinning the web in which you thought to catch me, your own lord. Therefore, on thee, Master Felicitatus of Beaumarches, I pass this sentence: Thou art to continue, at once, this very afternoon, the marriage you were about to celebrate two days ago, when you were so foolish as to let my arrival stop you.

"If you still harbor any misgivings," Sir Harald added, as they all stood as though stricken speechless, "I will take care never to be out of sight of some, at least, of the rest of you until tomorrow morning."

"Your pardon, my lord," Felicitatus assured him. "We hesitated, no longer in suspicion of you, but in surprise at our good fortune." So saying, he turned and held out both his arms.

Maid Philomela rushed joyously into them.

"Maid Philomela?" Sir Harald was surprised into exclaiming. "Master Felicitatus, is this thy bride?"

Pushing her way forward again, Maid Procne knelt before the dais. "Now it is my turn to beg for mercy, my lord. Two days ago, still misled by the lying report of that false knight, your enemy, I did indeed snatch the wreath and veil from my sister, thinking to misdirect you if necessary. I should have confessed the truth before now, but . . . in punishment, my lord, pray sentence me to be one of those continually in thy presence until my sister's marriage is safely consummated."

"That sounds like a fair offer, Sir Harald!" Joiselette called to him. "I'd take her up on it, if I were you."

It was no simple matter, after that, to dismiss his first manor court with any great modicum of dignity.

At Yuletide, Maid Procne married the lord of the manor, and her mother was forced to admit that a dark man might sometimes prefer a dark mate.

As her wedding gift, Bride Procne presented Sir Harald

with a new shield, forged and crafted by the manor's own artisans, and which she herself had carefully painted with the device that had confused her on his arrival and that she had since come to love dearly.

Felicitatus sang:

> "Joy besprinkles us today
> As Love, made formal with a vow
> To last forever from this now:
> As long as blossoms blow in May,
> As long as children laugh and play,
> So long will loyal Love endow
> Us joy!
>
> "Though grief may follow, grim and gray,
> Though sorrows make us bend and bow,
> Yet Love can weave that then with now,
> And lead us finally to the Day
> Of Joy!"

Joiselette sang:

> "Oh, Everywhere, You consecrate
> Twin souls into a single fate,
> A living symbol of the Love
> That, pressing from below, above,
> From every side, around, about,
> And from within as from without,
> Melds all together in one whole,
> Each helping each to one great goal
> Of Everywhere into each soul!"

Maid Wandith sang nothing, but bade Master Squire Alaron crack and shell a great pile of nuts for her and her little brother, while Much the blacksmith's lad looked watchfully on.

PART THE FIFTH:

The Passing of Joiselette

"Oh, Everywhere, Whose turning wheel
Contains all lands, all starry skies,
Who in unfolding lives reveals
Thy mighty power to harm and heal,
Instructing every soul to feel
The force of Thy divine replies
To questions whispered, shouted, asked
In battlefield or calm debate—
While ending every phase of fate
You pave the way for what comes next."

Harald hardly knew how he heard Joiselette's last hymn, but hear it he did. It first entered his dream—a pleasant dream even at the outset, in which multitudes of cheerful people whiled their leisure harmlessly away in a vast meadow filled with flowers and birdsong as they waited to enter a great walled city of clear and shining gold, it became a glorious vision upon the arrival of Joiselette's song. Then, bit by gradual bit, he awoke and was lying at ease in his bed; but the song, along with the feeling of peace, flowed seamlessly through from dream into waking.

Another Pentecost had come and gone, the second since the tournament of Tenebroc. Sir Harald had served his annual month of duty at King Arthur's court (which was something like his rent to Sir Kay for the manor he held), and, this time, Joiselette had left Tamba there, telling him it was high time he reached a steadier arrangement with that certain damsel of Dame Guenevere's retinue, while she herself replaced him with an orphaned lad of eleven, called Clarance, whom she brought back to Beaumarches as page to all its gentlewomen. Gentle as they were in our modern sense of the word, as well as in the old sense of "highborn," it was less labor than education, and Clarance counted himself among the most fortunate people in the world.

All the rest of Sir Harald's original party were still at Beaumarches, and still very well. Alaron's enforced year of special service to Wandith being almost over, he might in a month rededicate himself to Dame Iris, or choose to hold his devotion free for whatever damsel or dame waited somewhere for him to meet during the knight-errantry he intended to pursue a few years hence; in most ways, however, he had proven himself steady, loyal, and probably deserving of knighthood . . . another twelvemonth or two, and they must begin planning the ceremony . . . and, meanwhile, Much the blacksmith's lad continued in his honest attentions to the understeward's daughter.

Garth was doing and faring very well in his new position, and would surely be glad to continue. Nor had Master Felicitatus shown anything but satisfaction in having a capable assistant who, by helping shoulder the burdens of stewardship, gave him extra hours for the delightful duties of bridegroom.

The first flush had not worn off Sir Harald's own marriage, would never quite wear off. Dame Procne had accompanied him to King Arthur's court, and been accorded a welcome due more to her true worth than to the justly renowned courtesy of even that famous company. Sirs Gawen and Ywen unfortunately happened to be absent on adventures, but Sirs Letron and Labigodés exhausted themselves searching for the best phrases in which to sing her praises, and even Sir Kay grunted once, in mellower mood than usual, "Well, vassal, so you managed to justify my judgment and pull a plum out for yourself into the bargain."

But, for all that, even reporting that the ladies had treated her as graciously as the men, even planning to return with her husband every year in due course, she had been as grateful as he to come home again.

She lay beside him now, still slumbering pleasantly in the starlight that sifted softly into their chamber. Joiselette's song had not awakened her; how it reached Sir Harald's ears remained a mystery, for the Maid of the Wood had always until now refrained from singing where and when she might wake anyone who slept.

Very softly, so as not to disturb his dearest, who, pregnant as she was, treasured her sleep when it came, he rose and went to the window. It was glazed, for they still had glass in King Arthur's glorious days, as we have it again after an intervening Dark Age; only their window glass was not quite so smooth as ours. Through its bumps and ripples he glimpsed, not precisely a figure, but a wavery mass of glow-worms and fireflies that glided, wraithlike, through the darkness, with the hint of a large, feline shadow at its side.

Pulling on tunic and bliaud, he made his way outdoors in time to catch sight of them just as they disappeared into the fringe of forest separating field from lake. He followed and, midway across the field, stubbed his toe on something hard—the handle of a sickle.

He could not know that, many years hence, this same sickle would give him his death wound in a foolish hay-making accident. Having lived in a sense by the blade, as a knight of those days was fairly well bound to do, Sir Harald would indeed die by the blade—but also, at the same time, in his bed, ministered to by Sir Clarance (who would by then have become chaplain to Beaumarches in the place of old Sir Philibros), surrounded by his people, beloved and regretted by all who knew him . . . even, a little, by the Aloof Fair One, when eventually she would come to hear of it. All that, however, still lay many decades in the future, when he would have become an honored grandfather. For now, all he could know was that a fine new farming tool had been carelessly left out in the field. Hanging it on a low branch to keep it a little safer from the dew, he continued along the path he felt sure they had taken.

When he emerged from beneath the trees, he saw them waiting before the tranquil water, watching the moon rise. The sky that night was cloudless; the moon, full, huge, and golden. Already halfway above the horizon, it appeared to fill almost an eighth part of the heavens, while Joiselette and the Quiller Lion stood quietly in light-limned outline against its soft radiance.

At Harald's approach, they turned. Lowering his head, the lion butted it on the knight's leg with a playful purr. As for Joiselette, she smiled, held out her hand, and said, "Walk with me a little way."

The moon was laying a broad, bright highway of light across the barely rippling lake. Joiselette stepped matter-of-factly onto this path, and did not sink.

Thinking at first that it was an illusion—for, of course, the water was barely a single knuckle's length deep this close to shore—Harald followed, and felt with the sole of his own bare foot that it was no illusion.

One of Joiselette's hands in Harald's and the other on the lion's mane, they strolled for several yards along the path of moonlight. At length, however, she turned to the lion and said, "Now it is time for you to find yourself another friend. Sir Ywen took a great fancy to you back there in the land of Wisten."

The lion nodded, and then retraced his steps to shore.

"Must I go back now, too?" Harald asked.

"Not for a little while yet," she answered with a squeeze to his hand, and they walked on across the water.

"How will I explain to the rest of the manor that you have gone?"

"Oh, don't worry about that. I've already said goodbye to everyone else. Clarance and Sir Philibros and a few others in person, the rest in pleasant dreams."

"And me last of all?"

"And the only human to walk on moonlight with me, sir, so count thy blessings without complaint!"

"I was not complaining. . . . That evening of the great fooleries, then . . . you truly were in two places at one and the same time, were you not?"

"'Bilocation,' Sir Philibros would call it, if you ever told him about it. But, of course, I might simply have been a figment of your own half-dreaming mind, when you thought I came to you in the woods."

"How, then, could I have found my own way back so unerringly, if you were not truly at my side?"

"Why, the sooner you learn your way through your own new homeland, the better."

They walked on a few paces further in companionable silence, until finally she stopped and murmured, "Now, Sir Harald, my dear good friend, it is time for you to go back."

"Will I ever see you again?"

"Of course you will—eventually. Meanwhile, between now and eventually . . . from time to time, perhaps, as clearly as you do now. And, in a sense, I will be with you always."

Reaching her hands to his shoulders, she pushed him

into the water up to his knees, thus enabling herself to bend over and kiss him on the forehead. As she walked on toward the moon, which by now had climbed wholly above the horizon and was shrinking to its proper size, he smoothly bobbed to the surface once more. Finding his feet and lower legs still completely dry, he sighed and, not quite willing to turn back just yet, began by simply looking around at the shore.

Dame Procne was standing, smiling, both hands atop her swelling middle, midway between Sir Harald and the water's edge.

He hurried back to her. "My lady! You must not still be standing here on the water when this miracle ends!"

"That will not be for a few moments yet. My lord, our babe has quickened. Here—feel him kick!"

After he had felt, and wondered, and lifted his face again to hers, she first kissed him on the lips, then smiled beyond him and waved. He, too, turned back to see Joiselette, a distant figure now, giving them both one final wave of farewell.

He returned it. Then, when Joiselette lowered her arm, Procne caught her husband's hand and said, "Now, my lord, we will have time enough provided we waste none of it."

They had time enough, but maybe none to spare. For, although as soon as their feet touched dry land they turned around at once, hoping for one more glimpse of her, the Maid of the Wood was gone completely from their sight.

AUTHOR'S AFTERWORD

Take care what you write when young.

While still in college, I began writing stories about a curious creature called (among other things) Joiselette and a left-handed knight named Harald de Folgeste. A few of these stories enjoyed limited publication before I classified the whole series as "juvenilia" and spent about a quarter of a century trying to forget I'd ever done it.

Then in 1987, Mike Ashley, one of my favorite editors, conceived the idea of a series of short novels inspired by and set in the Arthurian world of Chrétien de Troyes; and Harald and Joiselette came back to me. Let me caution any reader who has or finds any part of the original cycle, to accept nothing contained therein until and unless it reappears in the new version. For example, both the boyhood episode involving turtles and the outline of Sir Harald's eventual death are drawn from 1960s stories. His family history, however, has been totally revised from what appeared in a small-publication semiprozine; and while owners of my 1967 self-publication *Bar Sinister* may scent symbolic echoes in the wolf that flees from the polite knights' party to the Maid of the Wood, and in Sir Harald's quick protest against stripping knighthood dishonorably away from Tobias, these remain mere echoes—inside jokes.

The first time around, Sir Harald eventually sat at the Round Table of Arthur's successor (according to Malory),

Constantine son of Cador of Cornwall; but he never found a bride. Nor am I any longer satisfied with my old explanation for Joiselette: I now consider her an entity of considerably wider and more mystical significance than I did back in the 1960s. Aside from certain well-known and long-established Arthurian figures, the only members of the original supporting cast to make it into the new are Harald's horse Goblin and—in a far happier role than he originally played—Clarance. The only way the two versions could ever be reconciled would be through appeal to the theory of alternate universes, one more or less Malorian, the other Chrétienesque.

In casting about for analogues to the kind of popular material Chrétien de Troyes must have drawn upon in inventing the Arthurian romance, I settled on Sir Walter Scott's *Ivanhoe* as surely the most popular and notable knightly romance, apart from the Arthurian saga itself, to have come out of the English-speaking tradition within the last two centuries. The two episodes mined from this vein were first conceived as the entire novel. When, sadly, Mike Ashley's dream of a series of Chrétien-inspired Arthurians failed to materialize and my agents informed me that there would be no hope at all of peddling so short a novel stateside, I decided to expand my inspirational range. After all, if Beaumarchais was good enough for Mozart . . . While, to those readers who recognize the Warrior Woman of Part the Second, I can only apologize for failing to show her in action.

—Barnes, Wisconsin
October 1999

PHYLLIS ANN KARR is the author of many recent works of fiction, including *My Lady Quixote, Lady Susan, Frostflower and Thorn, Meadowsong, Perola, The Elopement, Wildraith's Last Battle, Frostflower and Windbourne*, and *At Amberleaf Fair*. Readers of *The Follies of Sir Harald* will find two of her works of special interest: her Arthurian murder mystery, *Idylls of the Queen*, and her reference work, *The Arthurian Companion*, re-released earlier this year by Green Knight in a revised edition. A freelance writer, the author was born in a Navy hospital in Oakland, California, and was raised in the northwest tip of Indiana. She currently resides with her husband, Clifton Alfred Hoyt, in Bayfield County, Wisconsin, a long county without a single traffic light.

Pronunciation Guide

Joiselette (from French *joi* [joy] + *oiseau* [bird] + *–ette* [suffix indicating "little, small"]): DZWA–ze–LET or JAW–se–LET (three syllables, accented about equally on the first and third).

Folgeste (from French *fou, folle* [mad] + *geste* [deed]): FOAL–JEST (two syllables, equally accented).

Gawen (usually spelled *Gawaine*): I so strongly favor accenting this name on the *first* syllable that I have finally gone to an alternate spelling. This pronunciation can be found in every dictionary I have thus far checked. I beg my readers to accent the first syllable at least when reading my fiction.

Ihesu: YEA–zoo. This can be spelled *Jesu*, but at risk of being mistaken for a typographical error for the modern version of the name.

More PENDRAGON™ Books from
GREEN KNIGHT PUBLISHING

<u>AVAILABLE NOW</u>

The Arthurian Companion
Second Edition
by Phyllis Ann Karr

Written in a warm and entertaining style, *The Arthurian Companion* contains over one thousand entries, cross-referenced, annotated, and carefully revised for the second edition. It is an alphabetical guide to the "who's who" of Arthurian legend, a "what's what" of famous Arthurian weapons and artifacts, and a "where's where" of geographical locations appearing in Arthurian literature. An extensive chronology of Arthur's reign is included. Revised and corrected, this new edition of *The Arthurian Companion* is a valuable reference for fantasy fans, researchers, and lovers of medieval romance.

PRAISE FOR *THE ARTHURIAN COMPANION*:

"THE ARTHURIAN COMPANION IS ONE OF THOSE RARELY FOUND REFERENCE BOOKS THAT ONE WANTS TO READ FROM COVER TO COVER."
—*American Reference Books Annual*

"RANKS AS AN INDISPENSABLE REFERENCE WORK FOR ANY FANTASY LOVER'S SHELF."
—*Realms of Fantasy*

GK6208. ISBN 1-928999-13-1. 592 pages.
$17.95 US; $26.95 CAN; £11.99 UK

Exiled from Camelot
by Cherith Baldry

The court of Camelot is unsettled by the arrival of Loholt, King Arthur's illegitimate son. Driven by the need for an heir, the king embraces the stranger, though not everyone in Camelot so readily accepts the mysterious young man. Arthur's seneschal and foster brother, the redoubtable Sir Kay, is especially wary of Loholt's motives. And when Loholt is killed, Kay finds himself under suspicion of murder.

Stripped of his knighthood, Kay forges an unwilling alliance with the renegade Briant and his lover, the enchantress Brisane, who seek to bring down the men closest to the king. If Sir Kay cannot redirect their plot or win back the court's trust, nothing will save Camelot from the twin threats of war and evil sorcery.

PRAISE FOR <u>*EXILED FROM CAMELOT*</u>:

"AN ORIGINAL NOVEL OF CONSIDERABLE MERIT."
—*Science Fiction Chronicle*

"A REMARKABLE STORY."
—*Realms of Fantasy*

"ONE OF THE HALF-DOZEN BEST ARTHURIAN NOVELS I HAVE YET READ."
—Phyllis Ann Karr,
author of *The Arthurian Companion*

GK6207. ISBN 1-928999-16-6. 320 pages.
$14.95 US; $21.95 CAN; £10.99 UK

More PENDRAGON™ Books from
GREEN KNIGHT PUBLISHING

<u>AVAILABLE NOW</u>

The Merriest Knight
The Collected Arthurian Tales of Theodore Goodridge Roberts
edited by Mike Ashley

Noted Canadian author and poet Theodore Goodridge Roberts was fascinated with Sir Dinadan, perhaps the most practical of the Knights of the Round Table. Roberts expressed his affection for the character Malory dubbed "the merriest knight" through a cycle of bright and witty tales published throughout the 1950s in the popular magazine *Blue Book*. Toward the end of his life, Roberts created a final Dinadan adventure and set about collecting the stories into a single volume, but he died before that book saw publication

Under the guidance of editor Mike Ashley, *The Merriest Knight* gathers for the first time all of Roberts' tales of Sir Dinadan—including the previously unpublished "Quest's End"—and several other long-lost Arthurian works by this master of the stylish adventure yarn and the historical romance.

GK6210. ISBN 1-928999-18-2. 528 pages.
$17.95 US; $26.95 CAN; £11.99 UK